AGENTS OF CHAOS

AGENTS OF CHAOS

FEDERAL AGENTS OF MAGIC™ BOOK FOUR

TR CAMERON   MARTHA CARR   MICHAEL ANDERLE

DISRUPTIVE IMAGINATION

Copyright © 2019 TR Cameron, Martha Carr and Michael Anderle
Cover Art by Jake @ J Caleb Design
http://jcalebdesign.com / jcalebdesign@gmail.com
Cover copyright © LMBPN Publishing
A Michael Anderle Production

LMBPN Publishing
PMB 196, 2540 South Maryland Pkwy
Las Vegas, NV 89109

First US edition, June 2019
Version 1.01, July 2019
Print ISBN: 978-1-64202-336-7

AGENTS OF CHAOS TEAM

Thanks to the JIT Readers

Dave Hicks
Diane L. Smith
John Ashmore
Micky Cocker
Misty Roa
Jeff Goode
Dorothy Lloyd
Larry Omans

If we've missed anyone, please let us know!

Editor
The Skyhunter Editing Team

CHAPTER ONE

Moonlight glittered on the water of the river to his left as Rath patrolled the rooftops and moved steadily toward the part of town where the security agency was located. Below, headlights and taillights colored the streets as the late evening traffic crawled through the city. As long as no one looked up, they would have a nice, normal drive home.

If they happened to tilt their heads skyward and see the three-foot-tall troll who ran along the perimeter of a building, they would no doubt find it unusual. If they happened to watch when he found the edge and leapt confidently into space, they would probably find it alarming. If they saw his carbon fiber wings spread out to catch the air and allow him to glide smoothly forward, they would undoubtedly wind up in an accident.

It's not every day you see a flying troll. Rath laughed out loud, even though Gwen was the only entity there to hear it. The AI spoke in his ear. "Safe landing ahead. Wing drop in three, two, one...." The double triangles on each side retracted with a whir into the large rectangular container on his back. He landed cleanly and jogged to a halt to survey the next building, which was too high to glide to.

After his first several nights on patrol, he had determined that he needed better equipment. Kayleigh, who had tasked a drone to follow him, watched the recordings and agreed. They had created the flight suit without mentioning it to Diana in advance. He had demonstrated it for her with a leap from the roof of the security agency as she departed one evening, which resulted in a call to the blonde technician within seconds of his landing.

Their exchange had been loud. It had also involved several words he'd been cautioned not to use around strangers. The tech's side of the conversation was audible as well, a notable fact since the phone's speaker wasn't that powerful. In the end, Diana had apologized to him and Kayleigh but insisted he needed a backup plan. *She'd probably been thinking of a parachute.* He laughed again.

While the back of the body-harness he wore was devoted entirely to the wings, the front was a different matter. The chest straps bore holders for miniature grenades, currently filled with a sonic, a pair of flashbangs, and a pepper. Diana still didn't want him using fragmentation or incendiary grenades since he had a habit of fighting close up. She probably wasn't wrong. His utility belt held a healing potion, the comm repeater that allowed his AI to function, and loops for the baton holsters strapped to each leg. It also carried a device that captured and compressed air, released it when triggered, and automatically refilled in moments.

At the center of his chest lay the equipment Kayleigh

had provided as a safety net. It was a motorized winch with a super-thin, ultra-strong cable attached to it—military technology the tech had bartered for with a counterpart in the Army's R&D division. The line was connected to a launcher mounted on the inside of his right wrist. This also had a narrow flexible tube running down to his belt and held a grapnel that looked like a small arrow. He raised the arm, and Gwen gave a soft chime when he had it lined up properly. He fired and a burst of compressed air launched the projectile to the top of the next building. The wire snapped taut, the tines deployed, and it latched onto the edge. The winch automatically engaged, yanked him from his feet, and pulled him quickly up to the other roof.

And this sight would cause even more crashes. Spider-troll. Heh.

He clambered over the side and disengaged the device, pressed the button to snap it closed, and slotted it back into place. He loved the toys, but most of all, he loved being out and about in the city he had chosen as his own. It felt like home now, and he had a responsibility to protect those who lived in it as best he could. That was why he was out this evening like he often was. During the daytime hours, he traveled with Max, who also had a few new toys of his own. Rath didn't engage in too many night patrols, maybe a couple each week, but tonight was different.

On a reconnaissance day, he'd overheard Professor Charlotte Stanley mention something that had stuck with him. She was part of a group—they called themselves a vigilante team but laughed uproariously when they did so —that did good in the city and told another member she'd noticed an increased number of questionable people around certain liquor stores in the downtown area. Rath had been waiting for something like that, so he suited up and took to the rooftops. Below, the man he'd followed from the first alcohol store continued to amble along the street and acted as if he was purely an innocent pedestrian. However, the way he flinched and tapped his phone when any police presence was detected nearby suggested he was out for more than simply an evening stroll.

The troll thought he might have seen the man before but couldn't be sure. If he had, though, he was sure about when and where—at the warehouse the night the stupid pirate-looking person had been whisked away by his henchmen. Rath was still angry that he hadn't been able to stop the car, and maybe, just maybe, the man on the street below was the one who'd shot at him and forced him to abandon his pursuit. If he was, it only made him all the more rewarding to track.

He wanted to descend a little closer, but he'd given his promise to Diana—surveillance only and no mixing it up unless absolutely necessary. While his definition of necessary didn't always align with hers, Rath tried to think about such things from her point of view. *Teammates have to be able to trust one another.* So he stayed high, tracked the man, and made sure the drone followed as well. Hopefully, the bad guy would lead him to bigger, badder criminals. And, eventually, to the pirate whose hat the troll had sworn would soon be his own.

His quarry turned onto another road, and Rath readied himself for a jump and a glide across the car-filled street below. It would be the most dangerous of his maneuvers, a flight followed by a mid-air grapnel. Gwen's suggestions made it easier, but it remained risky. Naturally, the idea brought a huge smile to his face. He walked to the edge to familiarize himself with what was needed, then stalked as far away on the roof as he could. He'd need as much momentum as possible when he launched himself over the gap.

Rath started to run but a sound brought him up short and he slid to a stop a foot from the edge. His smile had been banished by a fierce scowl. He listened carefully and heard it again. What sounded like muffled screams and scuffling rose from the lane that ran between this building and the next. He raced to that side and peered down to where five men in hoodies surrounded a well-dressed man and woman. One thug guarded the alley entrance while the other four struggled with the victims. Three of them wrestled with the man, and one held the woman's arm twisted behind her back and her face pressed to the wall.

"Gwen, have drone follow first bad guy."

"Affirmative. I'll do my best, but we may lose him."

Rath shrugged. "Can find again. Call police to come to the alley. And ambulance."

It was about eight stories down, depending on whether you counted the oversized floors of the building across the way or the normal ones of the building he was on. He retrieved the two flashbangs from his bandolier and palmed one in each hand, then walked to the edge. The alley's narrow width meant he'd need to swoop along it, then turn and glide back to expend a little of his velocity. *The timing should work.* "Ready to fly, Gwen?"

"Affirmative."

He primed the grenades and tossed them to land near

the group surrounding the man. A running leap took him from the roof, and the wings snapped out as he leaned to curve to the left. The steering functioned by adjusting the trim slightly as he shifted his balance, all coordinated by the AI in ways he didn't understand. All he cared about was that it worked, and now he could fly. He spiraled toward the front of the alley and aimed for the man who held the woman in place and who had begun to react to the clattering a few feet away from him.

The troll closed his eyes an instant before the grenades detonated and his headphones protected him from the sound. He reopened them as Gwen chimed and retracted the wings to release him gently in a perfect descent toward the man who already stumbled from the nearby concussion. His feet caught the thug in the shoulder and he lurched forward to crash onto his side. The noise when his skull struck the concrete echoed off the walls, only barely audible above the shouts of alarm from both the victims and the perpetrators. *One down, four to go.*

The AI's voice sounded satisfied. "Two minutes to police and ambulance." Kayleigh had told them the systems might become more personalized and if this was the form it took, Rath was all for it. He drew his batons and flicked to extend them fully, then charged at the nearest enemy, who still reeled from the grenades' detonation. A pair of quick strikes at his knees toppled him effectively and he howled in pain. The troll moved on to the next target. He leapt and stabbed the batons into the man's back. The snapping discharge of the built-in stunners was deeply satisfying and the ruffian arched his spine and collapsed. Rath landed on top of him—maybe a little harder than needed—and gave him a modest kick to the temple to keep him down. The troll had neither sympathy nor patience to spare for those who attacked innocents.

Especially those who gang up on them. He rose and faced the remaining pair, who had gathered at least some of their senses. The troll smiled at them, and they scowled in response. The one on the right had a long dirty beard and pulled something that looked like a short leather club from a pocket. His companion was clean shaven and bald and drew a knife from behind his back. It was smaller than the ones the ARES members carried but still a respectable weapon. Rath nodded at the choice, and the enemy frowned uncertainly.

The one on the left spoke. "Big mistake, messing with us, little bastard."

He shook his head. "Mistake is yours. Every action causes an equal and opposing reaction." Of course, he growled the last statement to imitate the movie character in the Guy Fawkes mask.

The one on the right laughed. "And what'll that reaction be? Us beating you down, that's what."

The sobbing man with the damaged knees choked out, "Hit him once in the face for me."

The man with the knife twitched the weapon in invitation. Rath grinned. *This would be much more fun if Max was here.* He barreled at his adversary and jumped to block the knife strike with his left baton. The man's eyes widened as the troll's feet struck his chest less powerfully than he probably expected, but Rath had never intended the kick to do any real damage. It was the other man who was his target.

He pushed off, launched himself at the thug with the tiny club, and aimed a right hook at his face with all his momentum and strength behind it. Cartilage crunched as the man's nose broke, and the troll delivered another one-two punch as they fell. He flung himself aside before his adversary made impact and landed on his feet beside the one he'd wounded in the legs. He stabbed him nonchalantly with the stun batons and the man stiffened before he passed out.

Rath's weapons vibrated to indicated that he'd drained them by half and they were now drawing from the supply in his vest to charge. He frowned. *Need better batteries. Must have more hits.* Kayleigh had increased the power, which he loved, but at a cost. He twitched one of them at the remaining opponent, who turned and bolted out of the alley. Rath sighed. *Boring.* He raised the barrel of the grapnel and fired it with a press of the stud on his glove. The arrow struck the man in the back of the head and shoved him onto his face before he reached the street. The line retracted, and he reloaded the device as sirens sounded.

By the time the police officers arrived, the troll had already made his hasty retreat to the rooftops and scanned for the quarry he'd originally been following. "Gwen, the drone?"

"Lost him in a tunnel. It's headed back to base for recharge."

He shrugged. "We'll get him next time. For now, must finish patrol." The troll smiled again as he leapt from the building in a long glide to resume protecting the city.

CHAPTER TWO

Diana's days now started earlier than ever after the whirlwind house purchase. Even though the actual closing was still several weeks in the future, they'd moved in on a rental basis immediately since hotel living wasn't all that comfortable with a troll and a dog in tow. All three were excited about their new home. So was their newly added roommate, who had claimed the finished basement as her own.

Kayleigh was far too awake for six in the morning. The tech virtually glowed as she led a still waking up Diana on a walk around the perimeter of the property and pointed out the positions she'd chosen. She gestured toward tall trees near the front corners of the yard. "Camera locations there and there, high up, wireless, and solar powered."

Diana took a sip of her coffee and burned her tongue. "Bloody damn. Ow." She waved at the sky. "You're aware we're in Pittsburgh, right? It's the third cloudiest city in the country behind Buffalo and Seattle."

Kayleigh frowned and shook her head. "Don't be a

Luddite. There's enough sun to power the cameras. And the sensor grid."

Her next sip went down better, and she sighed appreciatively. "The what now?"

The blonde grinned. *Wench. It's not fair for her to look so put together this early. She even has makeup on, for...goodness' sake.* Diana was working on censoring her language, as Rath was all too interested in picking up new words and using them at inappropriate times. Kayleigh gestured again and drew imaginary lines around the property. "Motion, thermal, and sound sensors on every side. Wireless again."

"What about jamming?"

"If someone jams them, we'll know to be worried, won't we?"

Diana held in her exasperated sigh. *Overly perky people need a good slap from time to time to keep them centered, don't they? I think I read that somewhere once. It'd be for her own benefit.* "Excellent point. Are you sure a line of marching sentry robots around the perimeter wouldn't be a better choice?"

Kayleigh flipped her off, and Diana laughed. The tech pointed again, this time toward the end of the street that led to the main road. The other direction stopped abruptly as the hill they were on ended in a sheer drop. "Cameras at the intersections. There's a version of Alfred running in the house, and he can easily track which cars should be here and which don't belong."

Diana pushed her hair behind an ear as the wind tried to deposit it in her coffee mug. "You have Tony Stark envy."

"Please. I'm way smarter. And I could do so much more if my boss would free up the cash."

She shook her head. "The mobile armory is the first priority. If we don't get that figured out, Cara will kick both our asses."

"I'll hide behind you."

"I'll dodge. Then where will you be?"

Kayleigh gave a theatrical sigh. "Why did I agree to stay in Pittsburgh again?"

"You love us. Don't deny it."

"Oh, I'm denying it."

Their discussion was interrupted by a faint buzzing. They both snapped their heads up to search the sky, and Diana moved the mug from her right hand to her left in case a blast of force was called for. The sound intensified before an Andercarr delivery drone swooped around the house across the street and moved toward its drop zone. The quad propellers lowered it to ground level, and the clamps released to deposit one of the three boxes it carried gently on the sidewalk, about halfway to the front door. They watched together as it rose, reoriented, and flew off swiftly.

Diana shook her head. "It would be a perfect way to deliver explosives."

The tech shrugged. "Drones are here to stay. Andercarr's security is solid, and we have a line into their transponders and flight information. Alfred would have alerted us if it wasn't an authorized delivery. We should get more sensors into the neighborhood so we have more warning."

She nodded. "No argument there."

"And we need deterrents that Alfred can operate."

"We've talked about that."

"Yes, and you're wrong, so we'll keep talking about it until you realize that."

Diana looked at the roof of the two-story yellow brick house where Kayleigh wanted to mount a disguised turret atop the chimney. "I'm not giving your pet AI access to a rocket launcher. That's a hard no."

The tech turned in a circle with her arms extended. "Look around you, boss. There are so many angles of attack here in suburbia. If your hope is secrecy, well, that's maybe not entirely rational given recent events."

Ouch. Way to throw my last house getting burned down in my face. Too early for such cruelty. Not cool, blondie. "No on the rocket launcher."

"Rail gun."

"Are you insane?"

The tech laughed. "More than one boyfriend has suggested that might be the case. How about a focused EMP?"

"That's a real thing?"

"Well, perhaps focused is the wrong word. Directional. It would probably mess up the houses along the path but not in a permanent way. We'd rely on the fall to kill an inbound attacker, rather than the actual pulse."

Diana frowned. "Could the AI manage not to drop it into a house?"

"Of course. And his name is Alfred. You should get used to it. Say it with me. Al-fred."

"Oh, my God, why did I agree to let you move in with us?"

Kayleigh's laugh was one of the best things about her, guileless and enthusiastic. "Because it's your fault I had to come here. So, guilt. Plus the fact that you know life will be more fun with me around."

She shook her head with a chuckle. "You call this fun, do you?"

Her response was preempted by the appearance of a gleeful dog and bouncy troll. Max started his day the same way he had every one since they'd moved in—he dashed across the entire property and barked at any birds, squirrels, or errant twigs or leaves that dared trespass in his domain. Rath rode on his back, his purple hair bobbing, and the tinkling sound of his laughter filled the gaps between the Borzoi's outbursts.

The tech laughed again. "Everyone except you seems to be having a great time, boss. There might be a lesson in that to consider."

She's not wrong. "Fine. EMP sounds agreeable."

"And gas grenade launcher."

Diana sighed. She didn't have a good argument against that one, other than the shattering of her dreams of a normal home life. *Normal. Hah. Rath and Max killed that long ago.* "FFS, yes, a gas grenade launcher." She crossed to the Andercarr box, which was shrink-wrapped against any unexpected weather. Still a little cautious, she peeled the film back and opened it to find a small black jewelry container covered in cheap felt.

Kayleigh stepped beside her and looked over her shoulder. "Engagement ring? Do you have something to tell us?"

She barked a single laugh. "I need to have time to date to become engaged unless it's a psycho stalker of some kind."

The tech chuckled. "So, Bryant then."

Diana groaned. "Maybe you'd better get those defenses up sooner rather than later." She opened the box. It was a cheap-looking necklace with half a heart pendant at the bottom. A small note read "Congrats on the new place. Miss you. Also, my landlord's a jerk." It was signed with a stylized L. She pulled the chain out and held it up to dangle in the light. The letters "Be" and "Fri" were etched to the left of the jagged break in the half-heart.

"Good advice. Be Fri. It's like a sign from above that we should be able to fry any enemies. Let's put a lightning gun up there."

Diana slipped the necklace over her head. "Somehow, I don't think that's what it means. And you're merely upset that no one sends you Best Friend jewelry."

"Yeah, not since grade school, anyway."

She shook her head sadly. "Jealousy is not a good look on you, Kayleigh."

The tech laughed as she turned to wander back into the house. "Everything is a good look on me, boss, especially in comparison to some people who shall not be named but who should really think about dealing with their bedhead before making an appearance in public in the morning."

Max arrived and jumped on Diana before she could come up with a fittingly scathing reply, and she knelt to pet him. Rath took the opportunity to run up to her shoulder when the Borzoi rolled over on his back for belly rubs. "Did you sleep well, Rath?"

"Yep, did."

"Anything exciting on patrol?" She'd mostly given up on worrying about the troll since he'd proven time and again that he was fully capable of taking care of himself. *Mostly.*

She laughed to herself. *He's probably safer than I am at any given moment.*

He nodded. "Stupid pirate henchman. Followed but lost him."

"Even the drone?"

"Tunnel."

"Drat." He grinned in reply. "We need some sort of invisible launchable tracer. Maybe you should suggest that to Kayleigh."

"Will. Flying is awesome."

She laughed. Rath knew she'd been against the wings at first and still worried about them in unguarded moments. *He's getting better at working me. Now he only needs to add a little more subtlety, and he'll be able to fool me. Mental note: keep him away from Sloan.* "I'm glad. And the grapnel works fine?"

An oddly satisfied expression slid onto his face before he responded. "Is excellent."

"Good." Her phone buzzed, and she pulled it out. A sigh followed, accompanied by a frown. "Hey, look, just when I thought I might have some time to work on the house, Nylotte has decided it's a training day."

Rath grinned. "Fighting mode. Must train. I could help."

She laughed at the idea of the Drow contending with a wound-up troll. "The timing is probably not right for that quite yet, my friend. I need to make sure I can defend you if she decides to be a b...witch about it."

His fangy grin showed that he'd caught the unfinished word. *Dammit. I mean, darn it.* Diana threw up her hands in defeat and headed back into the house, patting the pendant where it lay beneath her t-shirt. *At least I'm able to safely portal down there now. That's a plus, anyway.* As she walked through the door, the tech's mocking voice sounded from the basement. "Hey, keep it down up there, you sound like an elephant. Did you gain weight out in the yard or something?"

Even though ninety-nine percent of her wanted to throw a force bolt down the stairs to gently adjust Kayleigh's attitude, she headed for the coffeepot instead. *We did agree that we were equals at home, so I can't nail her for insubordination. Besides, I'll need every ounce of magic power I have to deal with my caring and supportive mentor.* She grinned, already thinking about her revenge. *You got lucky this time, blondie. But of course, you realize this means war.*

CHAPTER THREE

Nylotte had warned Diana against attempting to portal into her shop at any time other than when the Drow expected her, so she waited impatiently for seven-thirty to arrive. She'd spent the previous hour plus getting ready, fueling with coffee, and avoiding food. She tried not to eat before her practice sessions for fear of the ways her teacher might attack her body and mind. Throwing up in the training space was doubtless frowned upon. *To say the least.*

As their lessons had progressed, Diana's wardrobe had changed in self-defense. Gone were the more comfortable clothes she'd started with, replaced by black tactical boots and pants and a close-fitting leather jacket that would help absorb the scrapes when the woman's magic blasted her to the hard basement floor. Her only nod to fashion was the concert t-shirts she always wore underneath. Today, it was the Cure, from the Disintegration tour. *Maybe that's not the best choice, actually. It might give her ideas if she saw it.*

But the time to change had passed. The clock ticked over, and she harnessed her will and sent it into her hands, then circled them to create the outline of the portal she wanted to bring into being. It wavered into reality, and she probed it carefully to ensure the correct barriers were in place. A trip to the World in Between was not on her agenda. The Drow hadn't warned her that others could mess with her portals, but she also hadn't told her they couldn't. Paranoia was rapidly becoming Diana's default state.

She stepped through and the sense of dislocation that always accompanied portal travel unsettled her. Thankfully, she managed not to stumble and turned in a slow circle, looking for her teacher. The basement appeared to be empty. She frowned, then smiled as her metal bracelet grew cold on her wrist to signal the presence of illusion. On instinct, she summoned a force shield as the first ice blast materialized from a corner of the room. It struck her defense and wound around where it met the floor as the Drow tried and failed to knock her feet from beneath her. *It may take a while, but I learn.*

She hadn't made ice magic her own yet and had managed little more than a snowball when she attempted it. Instead, she reached for lightning, which she had shown some improvement with. Nylotte had described it as strengthening the paths—a useful way to think about the different magics as power flowing down different channels. She spread her fingers wide and discharged a low-powered wave that radiated out in a flat arc. It revealed a body-sized oval slightly offset from the source of the ice blast, and she summoned and hurled a ball of force at it with a quick snap of her arm.

Her teacher wavered into visibility and intercepted the sphere with one of ice, then flicked her fingers to send frozen darts hurtling at Diana's face. She summoned her shield again and envisioned it as a curved buckler instead of a wall. The magic rebounded as it struck and bounced the shards back toward the Drow. Nylotte stepped aside contemptuously, smiled, and fired cones of confined lightning at the trainee's head and feet.

She had time to swear before the blast at her legs slammed into her and knocked her down. The wicked energy licked at her body, put holes in her trousers, and scarred the leather of her boots and jacket. She growled and rolled back to vertical, relegated the pain to the background of her brain, and gathered the remaining lightning that sparked around her. Quickly, she added her own and returned the blow with attacks aimed at her teacher's feet, stomach, and head.

The Drow summoned a curved shield, and Diana marshaled her will and kept the magic flowing toward her. She increased the energy feeding the top stream, and the barrage forced Nylotte to one knee as she battled the power that pushed into her. Hope grew, and she pushed more of her energy into the attack. The Dark Elf dove to the side and sent a low wall of force at Diana. She leapt over it, but as soon as she left the security of the floor, her teacher created tentacles to capture her.

The shadowy limbs stopped her momentum as they slid around her body and trapped her arms. She struggled, but they only grasped harder, and she had a flash of fear at what would happen if these were the barbed versions she'd faced from the enemy leader they'd captured. Not for the first time, she wished she was allowed to wear anti-magic gear while training with the Drow.

That would show her. Oomph. The tentacles tightened. She choked out a protest. "You've... made...your...point..." They didn't release her and the inability to draw breath began to take a toll, judging by the blackness that crept in at the edges of her vision.

Fine. Be that way. It wouldn't be the first time she'd passed out during their training sessions. She gathered the breath that remained to shout a curse at her teacher. Instead, however, she held it as the woman's gaze met hers and she spoke in a fierce whisper. "You can do this. Find your fire."

Diana's mind plunged inward to the lava pool at her core. When she reached the cavern that sheltered it, she saw the mostly illuminated paths that barely managed to reach the molten flame were blocked by small walls of stone on either side. She twitched her telekinesis to adjust her trajectory and delivered a blast of force at the farthest one an instant before she careened into the closest.

Both barriers evaporated, and fire traveled up the paths. Energy surged through her, more rejuvenating than breath could ever be, and she vaulted upward. She ascended at the pace of the rushing flame and opened her eyes on the external world as a burst of incandescence erupted from her suspended form. The shadow tendrils disintegrated, and she had the satisfaction of hearing Nylotte shout in alarm before her mentor huddled under a hasty shield. Diana fell from three feet up and landed on her side with a groan.

She rolled over to face her teacher and cackled in a mixture of disbelief and relief. "Your teaching style sucks, woman."

The Drow let the protective barrier fall and rose smoothly. Her all-black all-leather outfit was none the worse for wear, unlike Diana's jacket, which was scarred and her trousers, which were mostly in shreds from the lightning, fire, and tentacle attacks. The Dark Elf smiled. "Were you not such a resistant learner, I wouldn't have to go to such extremes."

Diana rested her face on the cool stone of the floor. "You'd do it anyway."

Nylotte's laugh, as always, communicated unexpected joy. "Yes. True. Now get off your ass, lazybones. We have much more work to do to teach you to control the flames."

Hours later, when her energy had run out and she'd used her allotted healing potion for the session—*why the hell won't she give me a damn energy potion too*—Diana knelt on a cushion in the training space and drank the special tea that would lower her barriers to allow Nylotte to see inside her. When she'd asked whether they might switch it around to let her into the Drow's head, the woman had laughed darkly and replied, "Not while I live, Diana Sheen."

They materialized beside where her recumbent form lay on a large stone table. The paths and chakras were more visible now than they had been on her previous visit, and she could see the newly illuminated path of her fire magic, a crystalline orange that crossed the path of her pure white force magic. Where they met, the colors influenced each other, each branch extending away from the intersection shaded by the other color for a time. "Does this mean I can draw upon the same pool of power for force and for fire?"

The Drow's snowy white hair seemed lighter in this place with a little extra bounce as she nodded. "That is indeed what it means. To some degree, it will happen without direction. You should find both powers increased in strength. As you develop more control, you should be able to manipulate it with intention." She sounded nervous for some reason.

"What are you not telling me?"

She sighed. "It is a dangerous line you walk, Diana. You wield great magical strength but do not have a deep pool of power with which to fuel it—a result of the human part of your heritage. If you aren't careful, you might do irreparable damage to yourself."

"To my magic, you mean?"

A shake of the head. "Your magic is not separate from you. If you go beyond your physical limits, you will pull on your magic. When you go beyond your magical limits, your physical self will be used as fuel. I'm sure you felt the weakness after your fire blast earlier."

She had. A thrill of fear shivered through her as she shook her head in denial. "Wait, you're saying that I'll kill myself with magic?"

The woman turned from regarding Diana's illuminated representation to face her. "No. If you expend it wisely, if you focus on maintaining your resources, you can use it safely. However, your past exploits do not suggest that such wisdom is your natural state."

"Did anyone ever tell you that you're not all that nice?"

The Dark Elf grinned widely. "All the time. I consider it a compliment."

"You would."

Nylotte nodded and didn't speak, merely gestured to wave away the imaginary world and return their consciousnesses to the basement of her shop. Once Diana had regained her bearings, her mentor asked, "So, do you feel stronger or weaker than you did when you arrived today?"

She frowned and tried to get a sense of her power level. It was a slippery thing. "Weaker."

Another nod. "Logically. Using magic you are unfamiliar with is also more draining." She produced a transparent plastic vial with a screw top. The liquid inside glowed sapphire. "This is an energy potion, as you are well aware. For most sensible folk, it's no more dangerous than a healing potion as long as it is rarely used. For the unwise…" She stared at Diana with a raised eyebrow. "It can make one feel stronger than they actually are and lead them to consume more energy than the potion supplies."

"Your faith in my discipline is truly heartwarming."

"Quite the contrary. I have great faith in your discipline. It is your commitment that worries me. Self-protection seems a secondary concern when it should be your primary focus. You cannot continue to fight if you are dead due to poor decision making." She paused for a moment to let that sink in. "And it's not my job to warm your heart. It's my job to drive some sense into that impenetrable object you keep inside your skull."

Diana sighed and took the potion from her teacher's outstretched hand. "So what you're saying is that despite the fact that I feel like dirt, I shouldn't swallow this simply because I want to."

The Drow rolled her eyes. "Congratulations, you have understood and taken to heart literally the smallest part of my warning. Well done."

She smiled. "You're so easy to annoy." When Nylotte huffed in reply, she laughed. "Okay, my most amazing mentor and teacher, thank you for this day's instruction and for the potion. May your worthless student ask one last question?"

The Dark Elf tilted her chin upward, and Diana didn't need to be telepathic to know she was thinking, "If you must."

"Is there a counter to Rhazdon's Defense, or are we well and truly fucked?"

Nylotte laughed once at the coarse phrasing but sobered quickly. "A little from column A, and a little from column B." She leaned forward on her cushion and held a palm up. Above it, the image of a long sword and a pair of matching daggers appeared. "Legends refer to these complementary pieces to Rhazdon's Defense, known collectively as Rhazdon's Vengeance." They rotated gently, and the image was sufficient for Diana to see the quality of the workmanship and to note the multifaceted purple gem that lay in the pommel of each.

Her teacher flicked her middle finger gently, and the sword grew in size and detail. "The main blade is reputedly named *Fury*. The magic it supplies is unclear, but words passed through the years suggest that the sword imparts power to its wielder that is triggered by anger."

Diana groaned. "Is nothing simple?"

Her mentor laughed darkly. "Of course not. If it were, would you be here?"

"A very valid point. However, I am coming to simply adore your company."

A snort. "Sure, Diana, sure." She twitched her fingers again, and the daggers grew. "One is Angel, the other Demon. Again, there are many rumors but not much in the way of actual historical fact. The one persistent truth seems to be that they must be used together. There are no records of mixing one dagger with the sword, nor of using one on its own, only of both."

"And they are effective against Rhazdon's Defense somehow?"

Nylotte shook her head with a frown. "Not as such. They are simply tools that may possess a similar power level and may be willing to work in proximity. When artifacts are hostile to one another, even when used by different people, they tend to add chaos and discord where none is required."

The Drow looked speculatively at the blades that hovered over her hand, then gestured them away. Diana watched them waver and vanish before she rose tiredly to her feet. "Is there any chance of a ride home?"

That grin appeared again, the one that seemed condescending but somehow warm in a hidden, sarcastic, probably-making-fun-of-you sort of way. "But of course, protege. Mind you, watch out for the tentacles."

Diana put a fake smile on her face. *If I didn't need your help to portal out of here, I'd have some choice words for you.* She listed them in her head until the moment she stepped through the portal, made it three feet, and collapsed onto her living room couch, already asleep.

CHAPTER FOUR

Cara lowered the rear gate of the SUV and pushed it closed with a soft click. They were several blocks away from the target, but it never hurt to be careful. She whispered, *"Procidat,"* to activate her illusion necklace. There was no indication that anything happened, but the nod Anik gave her confirmed that her disguise was in place. She led her two teammates to the staging area, and they all crouched in the shadows, their dark uniforms and gear blending in seamlessly.

She whispered again, this time to the AI contained in the metal collar that rested flat against her neck. She'd been third in line after Diana and Rath, and tonight was her first action with the device. "Quinn, objective status."

The AI's female voice, warm with an edge of sarcastic sass, replied "No change. Traffic in and out as expected. No evidence that target has left the building."

"At least he's a predictable scumbag." They'd identified the level-three bounty through one of Kayleigh's scanning algorithms, made possible by their new access to the city's entire surveillance grid—a small fact the local PD would probably have a problem with if they knew. The man they sought usually worked as part of a gang and displayed no obvious magic when with them. He freelanced every so often, though, and indulged in the wanton destruction of property through the liberal application of arcane fire.

Fortunately, when people were present in the structure he'd marked for demolition, he provided a warning in the form of a magical shout and potential victims had obligingly fled. Without exception, by the time the authorities arrived, he had vanished. They'd only identified him when they located camera coverage of the lookout point from which he admired his handiwork on his last job, which had destroyed a newly constructed apartment building.

Tony suggested there could be an ulterior motive at work, that rather than being a simple firebug, the man might be a freelance property assassin of some kind. Anik countered that he might be reading too many novels, but privately, Cara could see it as a possibility. Corporate espionage had always been an element of the business, and to imagine such activities on the forefront of the magic-human interface and a small step over the line of legality wasn't much of a stretch.

The asshole is lucky no one's died as result of his games, or this would go down very differently. His mundane gang limited itself to those in the game and had thus far avoided killing anyone. They'd also popped up on the radar of the group Sloan had infiltrated as a hindrance to their advance in yet another organization. Tonight's action was, in part, to clear the path so their undercover face could get deeper.

There are too many levels. I liked it better when we simply kicked ass and didn't worry about the rest. Even as she thought it, Cara knew it wasn't true. The intelligence and strategic sides of things appealed to her almost as much as the tactical, which fit her role as second in command extremely well.

"Quinn, let's hear them." A soft chime signaled the AI's acknowledgment of the order, and after a short pause, it activated the directional microphone on the drone. The bar the gang used as a clubhouse had only a few windows, and those high and small, but the equipment was sensitive enough to pick up vibrations as sound waves reached them.

At first, a cacophony of music and gabble fed into their earpieces, but Quinn quickly applied algorithms to eliminate the unnecessary noise. The AI focused on conversations in sequence and switched to a new set of voices after several seconds until Tony said, "That one," over the comm. Cara relayed the command to the AI. A few moments of imperfect resolution followed as the system tested various sound filters. Finally, the sounds of three men resolved into enough clarity that the BAM agents might have been sitting at the next table.

The first spoke quickly and with a heavy Pittsburgh accent. "Boss, we're in this to make money, not to wait around for some wicked witch to decide it's time for us to do something. The crew is all here. Let's go break some stuff and take some stuff."

Another voice offered a grunt of either acknowledgment or approval, she couldn't tell which. The third, when it spoke, was cultured, accent-free, and with a low, even cadence. "We need to wait and see what happens. We knew that joining up with Marcus and his group would mean giving up some choices."

When the grunter replied, he was almost an average of the other two and placed between them in speed, accent, pitch, and timbre. "Well, it was one thing when Marcus was in charge, right? Even after, when that Vincent dude called the shots, it was okay. But the witch, man...she's crazy."

"Vincente," the third voice corrected. The team exchanged nods to confirm their agreement that the speaker was the target. "And yeah, she's nuts. But hopefully, we'll have Marcus back soon—at least, that's the word on the street."

Cara ordered, "Quinn, send that whole conversation to Kayleigh for analysis and flag it for the boss's attention. I don't like the sound of that. Also, keep the recording going until we get inside. Once we do, move the drone to watch the area around the bar."

The AI replied, "Gotcha. Consider it done." Cara shook her head. *Kayleigh's really outdone herself with these personalities.* She waved, and the team advanced. The building stood on the end of a cramped neighborhood block, and they approached it from the rear.

She found cover in the shadows of the structure. "Anik, do your thing." He moved ahead in a crouch without answering and put his spine to the wall beside the facility's rear exit. The position of the hinges had revealed the door swung outward, so they'd chosen an old school method of blocking it. The demolitions expert extended the sections of a collapsible pole, locked them in place with a series of sharp twists, then wedged it between the handle and the ground. A forceful enough attack might dislodge it, but it would at least provide a delay. He nodded when it was set.

Cara hurried them down the alley that ran along the side of the building not bounded by the street. A dim light filtered from above, but ample shadow provided concealment as they moved forward. They had eliminated the high windows on this surface as a concern since the angles were all wrong for someone to look out of them unless they had a ladder. She stuck her head out of the alley entrance for a quick glance and confirmed that no one was present at the front door. "Is everyone ready?"

Tony's grin was almost audible. "I've been ready for about seventeen hours now. Are you ever going to kick this thing off?"

"Quiet, you, or I'll show you how well I kick things off, starting with your head."

Anik chuckled as he added, "Ready."

Cara gripped her stun rifle tightly and wished she could lead with the AR-15 strapped to her chest instead. She would be the third to move but the first to cross the threshold into the building. They'd received a video of the interior earlier, which showed a generally featureless rectangle with a long bar on the left, tables down the middle, and booths on the right. The place didn't have a kitchen, apparently, and any storage was probably down below.

"Quinn, red lights." A confirmation chime sounded as the AI blocked entry to the area at the nearest streetlights. It wouldn't last for long and wouldn't stop purely local traffic, but they had the access and keeping the number of bystanders down was always valuable. She paused a moment to run through the op in her mind to be sure she hadn't missed anything.

All the boxes held check marks. "Go."

Tony bolted from the alley, ran to the front door, and yanked it wide. Anik was a step behind him and flashed past the opening without breaking stride to throw a pair of flashbang grenades into the large open space. Cara ducked in a second later as those within reacted to the clatter of the canisters. They emitted their warning pulse, and her earpieces and goggles shifted into protective mode as she crouched to the left behind the curve of the bar.

Cries and screams followed the sensory barrage, and she rose to take advantage of the enemy's disorientation. A trio at the bar looked like what she'd pictured from the overheard conversation and she fired at the nearest man. Another goon crashed into her at that instant and the shot went wide and struck the bartender instead. He fell back with a comical look of shock and dismay to disappear behind the bar.

She impacted against the wall, and the man rebounded slightly to give her enough room to free her leg. Using the wall as leverage, she delivered a sidekick into his ribs and felt them give, then shot him with the stun gun as he fell to make sure he stayed down. The three targets abandoned their high barstools and raced toward the back. Their flight brought a smile at the thought of the surprise that awaited them. She fired at enemies who presented themselves and heard the whines of Tony's and Anik's weapons as they did the same. *Easy Peasy.*

A shouted curse revealed that the fleeing hoodlums had found the blocked door. The agents chuckled as they made their way toward the rear and cleared the room as they moved forward. Tony's voice sounded as calm as if he sat at the office. "Maybe we'll get bounties on all these dudes since they're in the company of a level-three."

Anik's humor-tinged reply followed immediately. "And rightfully so. We have a business to run. Dealing with criminals is expensive work."

Cara fired at the last person standing upright in the main room and dashed into the back. An explosion emanated from the small hallway that led to the exit, and smoke billowed out of it. "Damn. It looks like our target found a way through our clever blockade."

The demolitions expert laughed. "If you had let me rig it with explosives, they wouldn't have done so."

"These are not dead or alive bounties. And who knows what bystanders could wind up finding your toys? Not every problem can be solved with explosives."

Tony joined them at the mouth of the hallway. "Actually, every problem can but not every problem should. Arguably."

"Aren't you supposed to believe in the rule of law and stuff?"

The former detective laughed. "Yeah, but I'm also anti-running. And now we have to run."

Anik led the way down the corridor, one careful step at a time. "Maybe you need to exercise more."

She saw Tony's frown out of the corner of her eye as they advanced. "Maybe we need to find more people for the Agency so we have backup when they run." A window opened in their glasses to display the feed from the drone which revealed that the three runners had split up. The leader went straight and the other two headed left and right.

Tony sighed. "I have the one on the right."

Anik said, "Left," and turned immediately when he dashed out the door.

"I'm on the leader." *Heh. Rath would be all over that quote.* The comms remained silent except for breathing as they sprinted after their targets. "Quinn, show me feeds from Tony and Anik." A pair of windows opened to display the cameras mounted in the center of the other agents' glasses frames. The demolitions expert closed on his target in the bouncy view. The man was thin with long hair that trailed his running form. Cara estimated that Anik would have him in another minute, but the camera tilted down as he skidded to a stop. She saw it all from his perspective as he snatched a flat piece of metal from the ground—about twice the size of a license plate—and whipped it like a frisbee at his foe.

The missile flew true and connected with the man's calves to bring him down in a hard stumble and fall. Anik's view bounced again as he closed on the rising man to deliver a perfect jab-jab-uppercut to put him on the pavement for good. Cara grinned and focused on her own quarry, now about ten seconds ahead of her. He wove and shifted his speed intermittently enough that she couldn't be sure of a stun gun shot and didn't want to pull her pistol for fear of a fatal wound. She kept a wary eye on him as she pounded along his trail in case he decided to bring his magic into play.

Quinn closed the window as Anik zip-tied his target and the team leader spared some attention for Tony's feed. His opponent had made it halfway up the ladder to a fire escape when a shot from the stun gun pounded into his back. The man fell at the former detective's feet and his collapsed form wavered in the head-shaking view. Tony panted into his mic. "Idiot. You can't out-climb energy blasts. Hopefully, the fall did his IQ some good."

That window closed as well and left her to focus on the man in front of her. A fence lay a short distance ahead and separated their alley from the street beyond. Suddenly, a blast of flame jetted from his lowered hands to propel him up and over the barrier. Cara growled and angled toward a dumpster, vaulted upward and onto it, then pushed against it to leap off and clear the barricade.

Only a frantic tumble saved her from the blast of fire that set the wooden slats behind her ablaze. Her foe stood before her, his arms raised to show his neutral intentions. His voice was deep and recognizable from the recordings. "We don't have to do this. You can walk away. I take pride in not hurting people."

She rose to her feet. "You call burning down people's property not hurting?"

He shrugged, an elegant move, and his leather jacket rippled in a way that displayed its quality when it fell back into perfect lines. *Diana would be jealous.* "There's hurting, and there's hurting. At worst, I'm inconveniencing individuals and making life difficult for insurance companies."

"Being magical doesn't give you the right to ignore our agreed-upon rules for living. You know, like laws?"

The man laughed. He had perfect teeth in his handsome face. *Okay, maybe it's pretty-boy Sloan who would be jealous.*

"Please. Spare me." He raised his hands slightly. "This is your last chance."

She'd shifted her weight subtly while they talked, inch by unnoticed inch, and arrived at the fulcrum point between preparation and action. Without warning, she hurled the stun gun at him, broke into a sprint, and angled to the right. He blasted the weapon instinctively, and when the fire met the battery, the heat caused it to explode and hurl shrapnel in all directions.

Her foe shouted and summoned a flame shield, while she threw up an arm to shield her face and hoped for the best. A burning line tracked the path of one piece of hot debris as it scraped along her hasty defense, but she ignored it as she curved back toward him. She grinned when she noticed that his cover wasn't wraparound but only protected his front.

By the time he realized her intent, she was close enough to lunge into the attack. Cara's form was perfect as she launched a flying side-kick at his ribcage. He managed to interpose part of his shield, but her boots and tactical pants easily withstood the weak flames. She heard the satisfying crunch as his bones broke, and he fell with a cry. He landed a foot away, and he overcame the pain to extend his arms and deliver a flurry of fire at her face.

She sidestepped, rolled in his direction, and finished the move with a fist that pounded into his shattered ribs. He screamed and writhed in new agony. Truthfully, he wasn't offensive enough for her to revel in the victory—*just another moron*—so she tapped him on the temples with her shock gloves to send him into dreamland. She brushed her clothes off, which hadn't fared all that well against the muck of the neighborhood sidewalk, and looked up when her comrades appeared from around separate corners.

"You're a little late, boys. You gotta work on your timing."

Anik looked at the fallen man and the single remaining piece of the stun rifle that was larger than a fist. "Stunning him was what, too easy?"

Cara shrugged. "The ones who go easy get stunned. When they're disrespectful enough to make me work for it, I'll kick their asses on general principles." The men laughed, and she shook her head. "Why do they always have to run?"

Tony sighed. "The solution is easy. More people. Rath maybe."

"We gotta keep the little guy under wraps better than we have been. But more people is a good idea. You're the principal of this Agency. Go find some." He groaned, and she grinned. "Speaking of which, I'm headed home. Since you are both official with Two Worlds Security Consulting, you can handle the business end." She walked off to the sound of sirens, transport for the criminals summoned automatically by the AI at the start of the fight. She smiled and thumbed her comm. "Quinn?"

"Yes?"

"Playlist one, please."

No acknowledgment came other than the opening chords of The Pretty Reckless's *Going to Hell* filled her ears. As she turned the corner out of sight of the others, she bounced along to the song. *This is the life. I wonder how Diana would feel about us listening to music during missions?*

CHAPTER FIVE

T ony sat behind the wheel of the borrowed unmarked cruiser and tried to ignore Anik, who reclined comfortably in the passenger seat and sang some odd song under his breath. Every so often, the demolitions expert leaned forward to extend a hand toward the controls for the lights and siren or for the computer that jutted out from the dash, which required him to intervene. *Everyone de-stresses in different ways, I guess.* He did it again, and Tony sighed. "No touchy."

The taillights of the police transports glimmered ahead. The large black vans that carried the prisoners from the night's events toward the station for processing were only visible when they passed under a street lamp. The wizard had earned additional shackles, ones that would shock him if they sensed arcane power gathering. It was potentially transformative technology innovated from anti-magic emitters by the head tech in DC. Unlike their bracelets, which were attuned to a specific kind of magic, the cuffs simply measured the quantity of the stuff and reacted when an increase reached a particular threshold. They weren't flawless and were still in the prototyping phase, but everyone agreed that an extra shock to a criminal wouldn't be the worst thing they'd ever done, which made it well worth the risk.

Tony sighed at the pleasant thought of magic users getting shocked. He'd become more and more convinced that arcane power bent its user toward corruption much more easily and often than it did toward charity. *ARES folks hopefully excluded, of course.* "It's always nice to head to the station on the heels of success, rather than with an outstretched hand."

Anik gave a short laugh. "Well, we do expect payment, so there is an outstretched hand."

"But not one seeking a handout, as it were." The other man groaned at the wordplay, which drew a grin. "Anyway, it's rewarding to have a mark in the win column."

"You were right, though. If we had positioned someone in the back, they would've never led us on such a chase. I don't know about you, but running after morons makes me tired."

Tony swung the wheel to take a corner. "Yeah, true, but it takes forever to vet potential agents through our process. Appropriately so."

"Perhaps there is another option."

"Do tell."

The demolitions expert sounded like he'd thought about the topic for a while. "Well, maybe we could bring on independents and keep them at arm's length. They don't need to know about the other side of the house. Hell, they don't even need to know about the back part of the agency. We simply need a pool of people we can call upon at need."

"Basically freelancers."

He expert nodded. "Exactly. There are bound to be people inspired to start their own bounty hunting careers as the city's system gets more robust, which it can't help but do with us in town."

Tony grunted in agreement and followed the vans into the underground parking lot that served the downtown police station. They pulled in at a safe distance and climbed out to stand casually beside their closed doors. The agents continued talking over the car roof while they kept a wary eye on the transfer of prisoners out of the van and into the building proper. "So, how do you think we go about finding these people?"

The tiny scars on the side of Anik's face rearranged themselves as he grinned. "I'm merely an idea guy. Execution is someone else's job."

Tony smoothed his mustache and gestured forward. They joined the procession after the guards behind the prisoners who were manacled to one another with wide leather belts. The magic user was in the center, attached to ordinary scumbags in front and behind him. "Craigslist? Soldier of Fortune Magazine?"

Anik snorted. "Perhaps starting with Bounty Hunter license applications would be a better way to go."

The detective pointed at him. "See, you are an implementation guy. Make that happen."

"Cara told you to do it."

"I'm delegating. Congrats on the new task."

They trudged up two long flights of stairs to reach the

main floor of the jail. Its architecture harkened back to medieval castles, and Tony had more than once marveled at the stone curtain wall that encircled its courtyard and the high towers that overlooked it, both of which could've been taken straight out of a fantasy movie. The booking area was a large open room with intake stations on each of the four walls and benches in the center, and the police processed the newcomers with quick efficiency.

Tony and Anik followed as the mage was escorted to a special holding cell and watched through a thick transparent sheet as a guard secured him to an uncomfortable-looking metal chair attached to the floor. The prisoner sat calmly and the manacles around his feet allowed enough length for him to cross his legs, although he winced slightly as he did so. He looked like a man waiting for a business appointment rather than someone facing jail time. The officer shut and locked the door as he exited. Tony asked, "Can we have a chat with him?"

The prison worker ran his hand over the bald stripe down the middle of his head as he shook it. "Nope. Lawyered up."

He nodded. "I'm not surprised but it was worth asking."

The blue-uniformed man shrugged and walked away without any further conversation. Tony led Anik toward the stairs and headed to the next floor up. "Let's get our just desserts."

"Now you're talking."

The second level held a variety of offices along the walls and rows of paired desks in the center. One room was marked *Bounty*, and they crossed to it and stepped inside the open door. The uniformed woman behind the desk had to be near retirement age and wore thick glasses above a tired scowl. Tony took one of the seats in front of her and waved Anik toward the other. "Hello, Phyllis. How are you this fine night?"

She rolled her eyes. "Mr. Ryan, always lovely to see you." Her tone suggested the opposite. She pushed several sheets of paper across the desk. "One page for the magical, one page for all the non-magicals."

Anik spoke in surprise. "We actually get paid for non-magicals as well? I thought you were screwing around and trying to sound important."

Tony nodded as he filled out the business' information on the sheets and initialed where he was supposed to. "When they're proven to be affiliated with a bountied magic user and are apprehended while in pursuit of said bountied magic user, yes. It's not a ton of money, but every dollar matters, right?"

The demolitions expert's usually cheerful face shifted into a frown. "Doesn't that seem like blurring the edges?"

The woman at the desk shrugged. She sounded tired and a little bored. "The way the government sees it, it's a case of guilt by association. It's similar to a situation where if we were doing a traffic stop and one of the people in the car had a warrant out on them, we would execute the warrant."

Anik scratched his chin. "I can see that, I guess."

Tony flipped the sheet over and signed with a flourish. "The bottom line is that as long as we follow proper procedure, we're within the bounty mandate."

"Is this a new law or something?"

The woman shrugged again. "Old law, new interpretation. It brings clarity to exactly the sort of situation you were in tonight. Also, it doesn't allow for any extra short-cuts if there's not a magical bounty clearly involved. The courts have upheld it that way a couple of times."

The investigator stood to end the conversation and Anik rose beside him, although he still looked uncomfortable. Tony gestured with his chin toward the stairwell, and they turned to go. Halfway there, they were intercepted by two uniformed officers. The man had the build of an athlete with dark hair that pushed regulation length and was handsome and clean-shaven. His female partner had long blonde locks captured in a professional bun and looked like she was no stranger to the gym either.

"I'm James Maxis." The man held a hand out. "I wanted to take the chance to introduce myself. You're something of a legend around here." Tony laughed and released his grip, and the officer shook with Anik.

The woman introduced herself to the demolitions expert first. "Vicki Greene." She repeated the process with Tony. Before he could say anything useful in reply, an amused voice from across the room said, "Don't pay any mind to Starsky and Hutch over there. That pair is nothing but trouble."

In perfect synchronization, the two officers raised their right hands with middle fingers extended, and laughter bubbled through the wide space. It was playful ribbing, one of the things Tony missed about being in uniform. *Although we give and get pretty good in BAM, too.*

The man lowered his hand as he leaned in. "My partner and I heard about your takedown tonight. It sounds amazing."

The investigator's smile was professional. "Thanks, I guess. Is there something we can do for either of you?"

The woman spoke. "Both of us, actually. Jimmy and I met on the first day of boot camp, deployed together, and joined the academy together. We're looking to get into bounty hunting and thought we might be able to learn some important things from you all."

Anik frowned. "You're a couple?"

The man laughed. "Nope. We agreed way back that dating would be a terrible mistake. We can both do better."

The woman grinned and nodded in agreement, and the joke generated a chuckle from Tony. "It seems like SWAT would be your next logical route."

Vicki replied "We are on the list, but it's a long list. Plus, that won't give us experience with magicals."

Tony considered them for a second. *Young, fit, ambitious, all good things. I wonder how they handle rejection.* "Sorry, you two, we're not hiring right now." He ignored the look Anik shot him and extended his hand as the officers nodded.

The man shook it. "If that changes, keep us in mind."

"We'll be here for the foreseeable future," The woman added. "It'd be a great opportunity for Jimmy and I, and a whole lot more interesting than putting in overtime directing theater traffic."

That inspired a real laugh from Tony, and he waved goodbye. As the staircase door closed behind them, Anik asked, "Are they not exactly what we're looking for?"

He nodded and passed through the doorway that led into the hallway connecting to the garage. "They are. We'll have Kayleigh perform some due diligence and see what comes up."

"Ah, that was a psychological move."

"Yep."

"You're smarter than you look, Tony."

"Bite me."

The demolition expert was still laughing as they pulled out to make the short trip to check in at the Cube. The warden received them after the usual security gauntlet, and they settled at a table with steaming coffees in hand. Tony asked, "How are your newcomers fitting in?"

She chuckled darkly and looked thinner than she had before—the stress of the job, perhaps, which kept her from eating properly. Her voice and demeanor continued to communicate strength, though, from the sharp blue eyes to the wiry grey hair. "Well, the Kilomea is still an asshole."

Both men laughed in response, and Tony said, "That's a given."

She went on, "The one-armed bandit made friends with him, and the new guy you brought in after the train fiasco did too. A real coffee clutch of scumbags."

Anik asked, "Have you heard anything interesting?"

The warden shook her head. "No, but we'll watch them more carefully when we put them together."

Tony nodded. "Good plan. Where are they now?"

"Levels two, three, and four. The wizard is on the lowest."

"That makes sense." He took a long sip of his coffee. "What do you need from us?"

She shrugged. "Keep the flow of information going both ways. Share what you hear. Any threats to the facility— even guesses—and I want to know as soon as humanly possible."

Anik chuckled. "Or non-humanly possible, as the case may be."

There was a moment of silence as they all considered those words and she nodded. "Indeed. Whatever the source. Soonest."

Tony stood and extended a hand, eager to end the late night and get to bed. "You got it, Warden."

CHAPTER SIX

Sarah paced slowly in front of the tall windows in her former superior's office. The blinds allowed only the smallest view of what went on below. Each group had gathered on opposite sides of the warehouse from the other, as usual. The magical beings—her people—were enthusiastic to the point of raucousness as they admired some of the many items that had been stolen on the night of her ascension.

Members of the other group, the human mundanes, were quiet and huddled together as if for safety against a predator they did not comprehend. *Which is not far from the truth. Understand me? They never could. Fear me? Rightfully so. They are lucky that events require their continued participation. For now.* Her time in the World in Between had changed her, stripped away the weakest parts, and left only a core of will and focus. A soft *Yessssssss* sounded in her mind as the snake artifact embedded in her arm applauded the transformation.

The witch absently flipped the ornate token she had received the day after the events on the train. She had locked herself in this office, utterly spent, and collapsed into unconsciousness for hours. When she awoke, there had been a formal parchment rolled up on the desk and sealed with a wax disc bearing a stylized "D." She had unrolled it and found the code to the safe, the coin, and a date and time. The clock in her head told her that the indicated moment was nearly at hand.

She took one more look out onto the floor below. The humans were pawns, her people knights, rooks, and bishops. She was the queen, of course, and while Vincente may have been the king, he was ever a stand-in for the real power. The one who should summon her...now. She caught the coin out of the air and it grew warm in her hand.

Sarah crossed to the desk and sat in the chair. The small statuette was already waiting, and she slipped the coin into the depression in the base and turned it into proper alignment. She had examined the artifacts thoroughly and found nothing worrisome about them—nor had her artifact warned her, so she deemed them safe to use. Her efforts at spying on her former leader had shown her the procedure. *He always thought he was so clever and never understood that some magics are subtle enough that his ham-fisted attempts at detection missed them completely. Fool.*

As the image began to coalesce, she took a deep breath and straightened in her chair. A little nervous, she brushed a lock of black hair into place behind her ear. Finally, the figure resolved into a hooded being who transmitted a sense of power simply by his stance. His voice was resonant with it as he spoke.

"Sarah Renkin, thank you for responding so quickly to my request."

Hardly a request. I am not fooled. "Of course." She paused and a frown settled over her features. "I'm sorry, I am unaware of how to properly address you."

The hood hid the upper part of his face, but she saw perfect teeth as he grinned, clearly aware she had poked him deliberately. His reply dripped with condescension. "Master will do, for now."

She suppressed a growl, and her artifact sent dark images into her mind. The reaction must have appeared in her expression because the figure laughed. "Alternately, you may refer to me as Dreven, or sir." A certainty settled over her that he had tested the compulsion placed on her artifact. Between them, she and the magical item identified that spell's efforts and countered them with ease.

"Very well, Dreven, thank you." She nodded regally. "What can the unimprisoned members of our group do for you?" *It's never bad to remind a superior of a former leader's failure.*

The figure raised his hands to the side. "The natural question would be for me to ask you the same—what can you do with your leader imprisoned?"

Oh, touché, dick. "I assure you that anything Vincente could be relied upon to handle, I can accomplish, and probably more effectively. After all, it was my people and I who captured Rhazdon's Defense for you, was it not?"

His teeth went back into hiding as he frowned. "It's interesting that you bring that up. I cannot seem to obtain a clear answer on how the final events of that particular operation occurred. Perhaps you can illuminate me?" The smugness in his voice colored the request and demonstrated that there was more to it than simply seeking information.

He suspects. Fine. No one knows for sure except me, Vincente, and the would-be heroes who tried to stop us. She shrugged. "We were headed for the portal. He was injured, defeated, and I pulled him along with me when the enemy made their final attack. I sent the artifacts through and tried to draw him in with me—to rescue him—when they latched onto him. Some sort of force rope."

Oh yes, she'd noticed the woman use it against her alleged superior and imagined he might have heard about it. "He was yanked away as I struggled against my adversary, but another of them—a troll—attacked and knocked me into the portal. I barely closed it before they pursued me to reclaim the prize." She carefully didn't mention the true happenings and definitely did not reveal the artifact's constant whispered demands to dispose of Vincente and claim his power and authority for herself.

She wished she could see his eyes during the long pause that followed. Finally, the robe's shoulders shrugged. "No matter. Soon, we will retrieve him, and he shall lead again. In the meantime, you must gather your people together and whip them into the best fighting force they can be in the shortest amount of time available. In the very near future, we will act on many fronts, and you will be called upon."

She lowered her gaze demurely. "Yes, Dreven, sir. We'll be ready. You have my word."

He raised his head, and she finally saw his eyes—intense, burning through her own. "Your word had best be good, Sarah, or you will discover what happens to those who fail...or to those who betray." His final words accompanied a release of magic, and the figure ghosted away to nothingness.

Sarah fell back in her chair with a sigh and closed her eyes. The artifact's whisper was intense, almost joyful. *He acknowledges our power. We shall now not relinquish it for anything or anyone. You have done well.* A wash of pleasure flowed through her to ease the constant pain she felt since the return to this world. The artifact was the only thing that could grant her surcease, and it did so only when her actions aligned with its purpose. Fortunately, they were of one mind on the future direction they should take.

She stood, lifted the statuette and returned it to the safe, closed the door, and spun the dial to lock it again. The coin she slipped into a round pendant that nestled hidden between her breasts under the tight black dress she wore. The metal would grow warm if the coin did, allowing her to sense any summons.

Another survey of the office led her to decide then and there that once the Vincente issue was permanently settled, she would have the space redecorated. Expensive wood instead of cheap metal. A place to enjoy rather than a place to avoid. *When I am in charge, that's only the smallest thing I'll change. These people will know what it is to be led. Especially the humans. In fact, perhaps it's best if I give them a reminder right now.*

As she stalked down the stairs, every person who saw her suddenly found a need to look away from her harsh smile and glow of anticipation. *Perfect. Yes, fear will remind you to obey me.* Her wand felt warm in her hand as if it, too, was filled with anticipation for the examples she would make and the service she would require.

In the back of her mind, the artifact whispered, an ever-present partner now. *Yesssssssss. Show them your power.*

CHAPTER SEVEN

Dreven arrived in the ruined courtyard simultaneously with the other council members. He had postponed this gathering as long as reasonably possible following their last round of attacks. His purpose had been to pin down their future plans before he invested the time and effort to bring them together again.

Mostly, he was simply tired of all of them, other than the beautiful and deadly witch who sashayed down the path across from him. He tilted his head in acknowledgment, and she licked her lips. *Once she confirms that I don't possess the artifact, her desire will dwindle significantly, I am sure.* He felt no end of frustration over the matter, despite his knowledge from the start that the armor was not to be his. *Yet. Perhaps someday, though.*

The broken stones witnessed the descent of the others, the dwarf to his left, the Kilomea opposite, the underground gnome, and the witch who completed the circle. Once they were in place, he waved his wand and summoned the protective shield that would obscure them from prying eyes and conceal the sounds of their conversation from detection.

In a breach of etiquette, Iressa spoke first. "What news? Is it all that we expected?" Her voice held a moan of anticipation only partly concealed. Her passion for power was her defining characteristic, the thing that was both the most frightening and most dependable about her.

He raised his hands to forestall other questions. "I have answers for all that you might wish to know. Please allow me a moment to share them before we move on to other matters." The Kilomea, no fan of the witch, twitched her lips at the potential put-down, but Dreven knew that Iressa, his secret partner on the council, would not interpret it as anything more than a friendly tease.

"We achieved each of our objectives on the night in question. More than a dozen teams in various cities stole items seemingly at random to cover the theft of the few things we truly wanted. Along the way, we managed to damage the group which opposes us—this ARES—and more importantly, gathered vital information about it. And, to answer Iressa, yes, we succeeded in retrieving the ultimate prize, Rhazdon's Defense, which is now in the hands of one who ranks above us all."

A mixture of expressions appeared on the faces of his co-conspirators. The dwarf looked satisfied, the Kilomea energized, the gnome frustrated, and Iressa... Well, the look on her face portended both risk and reward for whoever she currently targeted. *Likely someone above, if she can figure out who they are. I must ensure she cannot.* The single exclusive power he held as the leader among equals was the connection to those more powerful than the members of the council, an access he valued as equal to his very life and guarded with fierce jealousy. He would not hesitate to kill any being that threatened it. *Even Iressa, although it would be a crime against beauty to do so.* Dreven knew he walked a risky path in his alliance with the witch, one that could see him lost, but he couldn't resist the game.

The dwarf, Jarkko, spoke into the pause that followed Dreven's words. "It is, unfortunately, the nature of the world that the best prizes flow to those at the top. What is left for us as a reward for our hard work?"

The Kilomea scoffed. "Hard work? What have you done besides talk? My people have been in the thick of things on multiple occasions and have suffered for their efforts. Many are still suffering. If there are rewards to be had, they must come first to us. To them."

The gnome was thoughtful as he spoke. "Now, now, Pesharn, you know that we have all performed our part. Some gathering information, some leveling the path ahead, some working on plans yet to grow to fruition. Just because your participation has been more direct does not entitle you to special treatment."

The giant female looked ready to respond with violence instead of words but Iressa took her turn to speak. "Friends, colleagues, remember that we are still at the start, here. We've struck a mighty blow, one that resonates with our enemies above and below the ground." She turned to face him and raised a crimson nail to touch her lip. "Dreven, what lies ahead?"

He shuddered inwardly, but whether from fear or desire he couldn't say and had no ambition to find out. He mastered himself, locked his arms behind his back, and straightened his spine. "With the addition of the individual artifacts, we make our followers stronger and thus draw closer to our endgame, where we will assert our dominance over the humans as well as those less capable in magic than we are. As it should be. As it must be."

Unknown to the members of the council was the fear that bound those above, shared with him only once by his patron, of something more powerful in the Universe than either Earth or Oriceran, and the need to be ready for it. *If that readiness also comes with power, authority, and subservient beings to do our wills, well, that's simply a bonus.* He looked around the circle and considered the members. Of them all, Iressa was the only one he would take pains to protect when the pivotal moment came. The others were useful tools, at best. *And, perhaps, she might be grateful.*

He shook his head to pull his thoughts back to the present. "Risks and rewards abound, as always, of course." The comment drew a laugh as he'd intended. "It is fair to say that our last effort was the riskiest to date and that the ones to follow will exceed it, one and all. In order to ameliorate that danger, however, there is an opportunity that we cannot pass up."

The dwarf asked, "Will we receive direct support from those above?"

"We'll have their good wishes, as always."

Pehsarn laughed. "So, we have given them one of the most powerful artifacts known to all Oriceran, and their reply is good wishes?" She snorted. "It almost makes all the sacrifice and effort seem worthwhile."

He chucked in response. "Their regard is no small thing, but it is perhaps less...material than we might like."

Ushev only scowled when his turn to speak arrived, and Iressa offered the next query. "So, tell us, Dreven, what is it that you want from us?" The emphasis on the word want was enough that it killed the seductive effect entirely. *Mostly. Okay, somewhat.*

He cleared his throat. "We've identified three names, principals in the enemy organization. We will prepare for our next major strike by acting against them personally."

The dwarf rubbed his hands together in approval. "Oh, yes, exactly what we should be doing. Who are they, and how can I assist?"

Pesharn shook her head. "We have been down this road. It did not end well."

The underground gnome cackled. "Just because you and your people are incompetent does not mean the idea is unsound." The Kilomea growled and shifted her weight toward the smaller creature, who seemed determined to provoke her. Again, the witch intervened. "I will happily join you and Jarkko in taking the lead on this. Three of them and three of us."

He smiled, the outcome exactly what he'd expected it would be. "For Pesharn and Ushev, then, another challenge. We must find a way to break the security around the prison that holds my subordinate and Pesharn's warrior. We'll show them—decisively—that their efforts to contain us are inadequate and always will be." They nodded. "Now, Jarkko, Iressa, and I should converse alone about our operation." He dismissed the shield, and the duo strode away in opposite directions.

Once he had reestablished the barrier to sight and sound, both the dwarf and the witch dissolved into laughter. The stocky male managed to get words out first. "Those two. Working together. Did you see the looks on their faces?" His head tilted back as he fell into gales of mirth. Iressa's laugh was the most appealing thing about her, and again, he had to remind himself of the danger she presented, both in general and to him personally.

She wiped her eyes and shook her head. "They will not enjoy the task you've set for them, Dreven. But now, what of our objective? Who are the targets?"

He smiled. "We've gathered information from all around the northeast portion of their country. Conveniently, they are geographically separated at the moment, so we must plan our strikes quickly to ensure they cannot support each other." The others nodded. He turned to the dwarf. "Your target will be one named Carson Taggart in their capital city. He leads the organization there and overall."

Jarkko clapped twice. "Excellent. I have people there already."

"I know, which is why you are perfect for this man. Iressa, you have his immediate subordinate, the human known as Bryant Bates, who is currently in their city to the far northeast." She purred in reply, and he decided he would not trade places with the man even if a fortune was in the offing. He would not want the witch to attack him with damage on her mind.

"And you?" she asked, her voice breathy and enticing.

"My target is the most appealing of all. One Diana Sheen, who captured my subordinate and will very, very soon learn that opposing us comes at a cost." As he thought of the various punishments and tortures he could deliver to the woman, the darkest part of his mind chuckled contentedly. *A great cost indeed.*

CHAPTER EIGHT

The day was warm and sunny, perfect for a ballgame. They'd decided to park at the office and walk to the North Shore where the city's stadiums stood side-by-side, connected by parking and businesses that served the sports crowds. Bryant and Diana wore dark Pirates home jerseys, and Rath bounced alongside in a white road jersey, the golden numbers and letters gleaming in the bright light from above. All three had identical black baseball caps with the team logo on them.

Diana felt more relaxed than she had in a while. "I'm glad you finally made it down for a game."

Bryant laughed. "Busy busy, you know how it is."

She snorted. "Get real. You could portal down here whenever you wanted."

"Magic leaves traces. Skilled trackers like the Kilomea have the ability to ferret them out. It's always best to stay under the radar when possible."

"Rath is the only troll in town outside the kemana, as

far as I know. I'm not sure under the radar is an option for me."

"Well, then, perhaps you should be the one opening a portal for me."

Diana thought back to Nylotte's warning about expending magical energy and grimaced. "Yeah, maybe not." She changed the subject quickly. "Rath, have you watched baseball on TV to get ready for the game?"

The troll grinned. "Many games. Max enjoys them. Barks when players try to steal a base."

All three of them laughed. Diana quipped "Well, he is a law and order kind of canine, nowadays."

Rath nodded. "Truth."

They arrived at the statue of Roberto Clemente that marked the nearest entrance and reached out to touch it as they passed by. Bryant paused a moment to stare at the memorial. "Sport has always been one of the things that's broken boundaries down between people." He met Diana's eyes with a grin. "Maybe we should have an Oriceran sports league."

She laughed. "We go from world champions to two worlds' champions?"

He nodded. "It's not the worst idea."

"I can see it now. All-Kilomea football and hockey teams."

"Okay, clearly there would be a need to have some rules put in place."

Diana chuckled. "Keep dreaming, BC." She handed their tickets to a uniformed worker, and with three soft beeps from the laser scanner, they were admitted to the park. The team's mascot was nearby, and Rath offered a fist to the giant parrot. The bird tapped it with his own and waved, then stepped behind Bryant and stuck his huge floppy beak over the man's head and covered it completely. Diana and Rath giggled at the sight, and she barely had time to get a picture of it before he shrugged the costumed character away with a laugh.

He turned immediately to Diana. "That stays between us."

"No chance. I already sent it to the team. And Taggart." *I should start an ARES newsletter. That can be the cover of the first issue.* She laughed inwardly at the idea.

"You suck."

"So some have said." They ascended the staircase to the main level, and once at the top, moved out of the flow of traffic to gaze down the long stretch before them. The left side featured small buildings holding food, drink, and merchandise stands, and the right held carts selling more of the same interspersed between stairs down toward the field. Diana clapped decisively. "I need a hot dog—no, two hot dogs, and a pretzel."

Rath piped up "Pizza. Pizza, pizza. Pizza, pizza, pizza."

With a laugh, Bryant added, "Kielbasa and sauerkraut is something this town is known for. It would be an absolute crime not to have it at the ballpark." They wandered on in search of the right stands, and she took note of the many smiles thrown at Rath, interspersed with one or two scowls. All in all, Pittsburgh had proven to be a welcoming town for the troll. Most residents who encountered him took the small alien in stride. *Heh. If they met his eight-foot form, they might have a different reaction.*

They found the pizza, then Bryant's sausage and kraut,

and finally, her pretzel and dogs, along with local beers for the humans and a tropical fruit smoothie for the shortest member of the group. They made their way toward their seats, a couple of rows back from first base. Bryant sat closest to home plate, Diana second, and Rath third in an unspoken agreement to put the humans in the path of any errant baseball before it could reach the troll. *The truth is, he'd probably have a better chance of avoiding injury from a foul ball that we would.*

She thought, not for the first time, about the fact that her relationship with Rath existed somewhere between parent and friend. She had to remain constantly vigilant to avoid being overprotective, which she knew the troll wouldn't welcome and which was unnecessary, anyway. *But the right amount of protectiveness, that's a different story.* Bryant pointed toward the outfield. "I love the view of the city from here. The architects were definitely on the ball." She followed his gesture and agreed with a nod and a groan for the baseball pun.

The PA system warned of the impending start of the game by announcing the starting lineups. Rath was well occupied and took in all the sights the stadium had to offer and stared at the birds that flew overhead. She leaned over to Bryant. "It was an odd choice to put the Cube so close to the regular part of the city. It's what? About four blocks from here?"

He nodded. "They had hoped for secrecy and disguise, don't forget."

"That worked out well."

"Not every plan is a winner. But it's still far enough

away that innocents aren't directly in harm's way in any large number. No more than anywhere else in the city, anyway."

"What was the point of putting it downtown rather than out in the sticks like the Ultramax?"

Bryant shrugged. "They didn't consult me on the decision, given that I was as far down the totem pole then as you are now." She stuck her tongue out at him, and he continued with a chuckle. "But really, I think it was about secrecy and proximity to your base of operations. When they built it, no one knew for sure where in the city the ARES headquarters would be, so they decided on someplace close to the center but not right in it."

"You mean ARES couldn't simply buy any building it wanted?"

"Not even if we were on the books and had full governmental resources to draw upon. Downtown real estate is brutal."

And, of course, the office had to be in the city to provide easy access to the kemana. I get it. She let the conversation drop as the players trotted out onto the field and the game began. Bryant spent some time explaining to Rath how to use the scorecard, and she fondly remembered her father doing the same thing for her many years before. The sights and sounds of the game washed over her in a pleasant haze as the early afternoon flew by. Between innings, while Rath was captivated by the t-shirt cannon and the mascot wielding it, Bryant slipped in some more business talk. "It seems like the bounty hunter agency is doing well."

Diana nodded. "Tony's turned it into a real security

consulting firm, too. We have several clients in the area, and he's done a good job of helping them improve their defenses against both mundane and magical threats. If it were possible to get anti-magic emitters, we'd have more work than we could handle."

He adjusted his ball cap to shade his eyes against the afternoon sun. "That won't happen anytime soon. Those things are beyond expensive to build, and it's a significant challenge to set up the enduring connection to dump the power they absorb into Oriceran."

"You should simply put those purple gems on them and let the emitters charge 'em up. Then, we can carry them around like little magical batteries."

He snickered. "That's so incorrect a description of how the crystals work that I don't even know where to begin to make fun of you."

She laughed. "Bring it, big boy."

He shook his head. "Are there any problems with the co-working space?"

Ouch. Flirting attempt avoided. I must be losing my touch. She looked at him closely and noticed the lines of strain around his eyes. *He's hiding it well, but he's worried about something. Dammit.* "I think we have that under adequate control. Kayleigh checks them regularly, and Alfred watches constantly."

"Alfred?"

Diana sighed. "That's the name blondie has given to the AI that runs the building. And our house."

Bryant raised an eyebrow. "I hadn't realized things had become so sophisticated."

"The only way to keep her in town with us is to let her

chart her own course—within reason. Apparently, working on AI implementation made her happy, so that's what she's come up with. I did deny the computer-controlled rocket launcher mount on the house roof, though."

He choked on his beer and wiped the froth from his face. "Good choice."

She grinned. "Alfred is also fully tapped into the city's surveillance grid now. There are no secrets left since we threw the respect-other-services rulebook out after the incident on the train." She was interrupted by a peal of amusement from the right. They turned to find Rath tossing a baseball with a small girl nearby. She would throw it up in the air as high as possible, and the troll would do a leaping flip to catch it, then land on his seat before he folded to underhand the ball gently back to her. Each time, the girl's laughter grew louder.

Diana smiled fondly and turned to Bryant. "Now, everyone wants a mobile armory."

He shook his head decisively. "It makes you a target. Stick with the chopper for now. Besides, with downtown traffic and street patterns, a big vehicle would be problematic."

She put a whine in her voice. "Yeah, but we want it." He laughed and shook his head again.

A loud cheer went up, and they turned their attention to the field in time to see a home run replayed on the scoreboard, one that not only made it out of the playing field but out of the park and into the river beyond. The Pirates' player ran around the bases with his arms held high in victory, and the crowd gave him the adoration he deserved. Near the end of the game, the part Diana had secretly waited for arrived.

The announcer shouted out the names, and people in giant pierogi costumes appeared on the grass. She pointed them out to the others. "Cara told me about this. They'll race around the field. Pick your favorite. She went with Jalapeño Hanna, Bryant chose Sauerkraut Saul, and Rath picked Cheese Chester. The delicious delights raced and the lead changed several times as the crowd cheered their favorites on. Chester finally eked out a win ahead of Potato Pete. There was much celebration from both the troll and the little girl he'd played with.

The rest of the game passed in a happy blur and the home team scored the winning run in the bottom of the ninth to inspire a short round of fireworks over the river. The three friends joined the flow of foot traffic headed toward downtown and stopped halfway across the bridge that spanned the water dividing the two shores. A multitude of padlocks was fastened to the grate that made up the pedestrian fence—some combination lock, some key lock, and all of them painted or marked up in some way.

They spent several moments reading them in the late afternoon sun, seeing the celebrations people had locked in place for their relationships, the remembrances of those lost and missed, and the wishes, hopes, and dreams for the future. She didn't need to say anything out loud because she was sure they all thought the same thing. *This right here is why we do what we do. So good people can live without undue fear and have the right to chart their own course in the world.* She looked at Rath. "Next time, we'll bring one or two of our own to put on here. Does that sound like a plan?"

He replied with a nod and a smile but seemed less gleeful than he had been while they were in the park. Diana slapped him on the shoulder and said, "Tag, you're it," before she pounded away. The troll's startled laughter sounded behind her, along with Bryant's shouted, "Hey," and she grinned as she heard them start in pursuit. *Tension breaker. It had to be done.*

CHAPTER NINE

W arden Evelyn Murphy stood behind the guards manning the post on level three with her arms folded. They were of a piece—tall, thin, and black-uniformed. The room was not much bigger than the five of them with only a foot of space between where she stood in the center and the diagonals each guard's stool was situated upon. The nearest repositioned cameras and microphones to ensure they would have proper coverage when the prisoners of interest got together. When all was in readiness, the guard gave her a nod and his deep voice intoned, "Good to go."

She nodded and raised the comm on her wrist. "Bring him up." She turned to another of the officers and ordered, "Show me." Three of the cardinal compass points held a large monitor, and one of them lit up with a split-screen feed from cameras on level four.

A team of guards walked into view. Two held manacles and two carried stun rifles. The first pressed the button to activate the microphone and speakers on the second cell on the right, and his voice was reproduced in perfect clarity. "Stand and turn your back to the door." A moment later, the lock released with a loud click and they swung the heavy metal slab open. The front two guards entered while the others aimed their weapons into the space. At the slightest sign of resistance, they would stun the prisoner, and given the close confines, most likely the other guards as well. *It's not optimal, but they knew what they were getting into when they signed up to work the lower levels.*

Moments later, the first pair walked backward from the room with Vincente in tow. He wore manacles on his wrists and ankles with chains connected between them. His restraints slowed the procession's advance as they led him to the elevators. The guard switched to each camera in turn and alternated so they could watch the group walk out of one and into the other. This allowed the warden to keep a careful eye on their progress. The elevator climbed slowly and no words were exchanged.

The guards and prisoner emerged on the third floor, and surveillance lenses watched them every step of the way as they traveled the long path to the common room. When they reached it, the guard put up a pair of cameras on each monitor, and the room's speakers carried the sounds of multiple conversations in the busy space. The convicts wore identical jumpsuits with their personal identification number stenciled in large letters on the back. One of the lenses was computer-locked on Vincente and tracked his movements as he crossed the basketball area toward the tables set on the far side of the area.

His escort halted him and removed the cuffs around his wrists but left those that secured his ankles and the chain that connected them as they withdrew. The action she'd anticipated took only moments to occur, and the warden nodded as the one-armed prisoner made a beeline to join his former employer.

———

Marcus sat across from him and looked furtively around them as if afraid to be noticed. "Boss, it's good to see you. How are they treating you? I wondered when our paths would cross again."

Vincente gave his underling the once-over. The man actually looked healthier than he had before his imprisonment, despite the missing arm. His orange jumpsuit was tight enough to reveal the loss of the minimal flab he'd carried and the gain of muscles in the weeks since his capture.

"It's good to see you too, Marcus. I have no problems other than being stuck in this incredibly boring place. Are they taking care of you?" With a tilt of his head, he indicated camera positions, and his subordinate made a small nod of confirmation.

"I can't complain. Although it's expensive to stay here. They already took the arm, so I expect the leg is next." He chuckled at his own joke and it seemed like he'd told it quite a few times previously.

The wizard rolled his eyes with a slight smile and reached within for his magic in an attempt to use a minor spell to muffle their voices and blur their lips. It failed, as expected, and the power drained away before it could manifest the reality he desired. Marcus shook his head and his boss shrugged. "I had to try, right?"

The man nodded. "All the magicals do. I haven't seen one succeed yet. Now you are all simply losers like the rest of us." He smiled to show he meant no offense.

Vincente raised a hand to gesture at the surrounding area. "Well, it is a prison. Some minor challenges are to be expected."

His subordinate laughed, and it was encouraging that he still possessed the same spirit he had before he'd been captured and lost his arm. Vincente gazed pointedly at the stump that ended below the other man's shoulder. "When we get out, we have the hookup. We'll make you even better than you were before."

Marcus leaned forward, a look of restrained hope on his face. "You're not simply talking? Something's up?"

Vincente nodded. "I met with my lawyer. She told me that plans are in motion outside these walls. Plans that will lead to good results for you and I."

The other man chuckled darkly. "Is that witch Sarah's doing?" The emphasis on the title was more judgment than description. "I'm fairly sure she'd be happy to leave us both in this hole forever, given a choice in the matter."

He shook his head. "No. Word's come down from above on this one, according to the lawyer. It's always possible she's a plant from our captors, but she seemed authentic to me."

Marcus leaned back in his chair and folded his hands together on the table. "So, the higher-ups are loyal to their underlings? That's a rare thing—not including you, of course, boss."

"Not necessarily. More likely, they want to make a statement with the prison and we merely happen to be here. But we should nonetheless have a plan to seize any opportunity that might arise." He looked up and identified the camera positions one more time, then shifted slightly and gestured for his subordinate to lean forward. He flicked his fingers to ensure Marcus noticed the way he kept them out of sight of the cameras and blocked by their bodies.

Vincente lowered his voice but knew the guards would probably still be able to pick them up on the microphones. Fortunately, he and his top people had developed a kind of sign language to use when under surveillance. An open hand held in a particular way meant the statement was false. A closed hand held the same way indicated truth. He made sure his was open. "We're on our own. They won't send anyone in specifically to help us if they do act at all." He saw hope spark in Marcus's eyes at the lie.

The other man nodded. "Damn. I haven't been able to put together any real support in here. No one wants to work as a team." His hand, right at the edge of Vincente's line of sight, was open.

Vincente suppressed a grin and placed an appropriately unhappy look on his face. "I'm disappointed in you, Marcus." He left his hand open for a moment, then shifted it to closed. "Timing is uncertain." He opened his hand again. "But it's probably at least a month away. There's a lot of preparation to do, I guess." He made the symbol for half —his index and middle fingers spread wide apart—then curled and extended them again.

Marcus nodded to acknowledge receipt of the message.

Half, and half again. Not in a month, but probably in a week. He replied, "Damn it all. That's a long time to wait for a rescue that may or may not come."

The wizard nodded, his eyes closed. A week was a long wait in this place. Feeling his magic so close yet unable to do anything with it was one of the most frustrating things he'd ever experienced. Not that he was about to let that show. He closed his fist. "We won't see any help from those at my level, I imagine. The bastards have been good at wrapping us up and storing us away." He opened his palm again. "I guess we're on our own."

The man nodded. He gave the sign for true and asked, "Is it worth talking to some people in here?"

Vincente surveyed the room, half of which was made up of witches and wizards. The remainder was comprised of small clusters of other types of beings—Kilomea, in the main, with a couple of dwarves and Dark Elves as well. "We should talk to the humanoids when possible, but not the creatures. They are not dependable." His fist was clenched. He would be willing to use the others for cannon fodder if entirely necessary but would rely only on those most like him.

Marcus nodded enthusiastically. His superior made a gesture to indicate the end of their secret conversation, and the other man leaned back and raised his voice to normal levels. "Do you get to interact much with others wherever you are? You're not usually out here during play-time." He packed a lot of derision into the word.

The wizard shook his head. "We have an area like this, but when I have time in it, I'm always alone. I presume they keep us separate, although the cell is so silent that I probably wouldn't know if there was a parade going on outside."

"That would suck. I've managed to make an acquaintance or two during my time here." He put his fingers to his mouth and gave a soft whistle, and a man who had stood nearby ambled over. He was bookish-looking but had an edge to him that communicated the chip on his shoulder and a predilection to exercise it by causing harm to others. "Let me introduce you to Warren. He says he's fairly decent with fire. He ran with the gang that knocked over liquor stores we partnered with before."

Vincente laughed. "So, a deckhand?" The Prince of Plunder was a long-standing joke among his group, but a good-hearted one. He had power and had put together a loyal crew, and both those things were worthy of respect. The man scowled. "More a boatswain, really. The boss doesn't do too much without running it by me first."

Vincente grinned. "Well, then. Are more of your people in here?"

"A few."

His grin widened and he extended a hand. "Let's talk about the potential for mayhem and plunder, shall we?"

His new acquaintance shook it and sat in the table's third chair with a smile of his own. "Indeed. Let's."

CHAPTER TEN

The battered pickup truck pulled into a gravel lot outside a large warehouse. Sloan rode in the middle of the bench seat with Mur on his left and Teddy on his right. Two more sedans with gang members swung in behind them, and they all emerged in a mass. Mur had primped for the occasion, his bald head freshly shaved and oiled, and what were probably his nicest black work pants and gray button-down completed the look.

Teddy was his normal sloppy self—jeans and a dirty t-shirt under an equally dirty unbuttoned short-sleeved dress shirt. Sloan had chosen clothes in which to be ignored—dark jeans and a charcoal hoodie half-unzipped over a heavy metal concert t-shirt. His nerves shouted at him, and he took a surreptitious deep breath to calm himself. *You've been in this situation before. It's nothing new. Remember who you're supposed to be—Tommy Ketchum.*

Mur turned in a circle and called, "Inside," in a voice loud enough to carry to the rest of his crew. There were a dozen or so other cars in the parking lot, most of them old but less battered than their own vehicle. Given this, it was not a huge surprise when they entered the warehouse and discovered a crowd of people already there.

To the right was a group of wizards and witches, judging by the wands they held or fondled and the general fancy fashion sense that seemed to accompany the criminal magic users he'd encountered so far. They shot dirty looks at the other occupants scattered throughout the large warehouse floor—groups of five to fifteen each in their own little area. The non-magicals looked almost as nervous as he felt. Hoodies were the uniform of the day, apparently. *Comfortable. Easy to hide weapons in. Logical.* There were men, women, and every skin color he'd ever seen before—short, tall, thin, and fat. A wide variety of individuals, united in their common uneasiness.

The warehouse itself was large and several stories high with dim rows of fluorescent lights hanging down to drive away the early evening darkness. Pallets of presumably stolen goods were stacked in the space at random, grouped together in ways he couldn't begin to understand. Other areas were piled almost floor to ceiling with boxes of mismatched items. It looked more like a garage sale than an actual business.

When a metallic thump echoed from above, every head turned. At the top of a steel staircase stood a hard-looking woman in a tight black dress that left little to the imagination. He immediately identified her as the witch Diana had described and wondered where she'd hidden her wand before he noted the slight bulge under her right sleeve as she began to walk down the stairs. Her high ebony boots looked heavy and somehow threatening and shined when the light caught them. She descended slowly and studied the scene below her, making a show of shifting her gaze from one group to the next. He examined her without trying to hide it, knowing that everyone else in the place would do the same. It was, no doubt, the purpose of her dramatic entry.

Her energy was obvious. It crackled in her gaze as it darted around the room, was visible in the way she clenched and unclenched her left hand, and was evident in the curling of her right fingers as if they could barely be restrained from summoning the wand beneath her sleeve. As she reached the midway point, he experienced the momentary flash of insight that was always so unexpected and so elusive.

It took all his discipline not to stagger at the chaos that roiled beneath her stoic expression. Each element was brutally intense on its own—the pure lust for power, the contempt for almost everyone in the room, the triumphant pride in the knowledge that they were all there for her, and the strange feeling of a deeper presence. He'd only ever experienced something similar to this last sensation when he'd shared minds with a schizophrenic. In combination, the potent elements that defined her were virtually over-whelming.

A hand gripped his arm and squeezed it tightly, and Sloan tore his gaze away from the woman to meet Mur's concerned expression. "Steady on, Ketch. I get that she's gorgeous, but you look like you're ready to lose it there."

Teddy's nervous giggle followed. "Yeah, man, maybe you need to, you know, see a professional and release some tension."

The gang members nearby laughed halfheartedly at the bawdy joke, and Sloan echoed them. Meanwhile, a frightened part of his mind charted escape routes and wondered if he could liberate a weapon, shoot the witch, and disappear in the ensuing chaos. She stopped when she reached three-quarters of the way down the stairs, turned, and swept her energetic gaze across them all again. *This is what insanity looks like.*

The voice that emerged from the sharp face was one part lust, one part contempt, and one part fanaticism. "Welcome, all. Thank you for coming. Many of you know me already, but those who formerly followed Marcus might not. I am Sarah, and with Vincente unavailable for the foreseeable future, I lead this group." She paused as if awaiting a challenge. None came. *They're all probably as freaked out by her as I am.* His hand itched—actually itched—with the desire for a weapon.

She raised a hand and swept it across the assembled people. "All of you have taken part one way or another in our previous adventures." The last word was stretched out, making it a taunt toward someone, he had no idea who. "But now, it is necessary for you all to work together, rather than apart. In order to accomplish this, I will appoint two lieutenants, one to coordinate the activities of the empowered among us"—she gestured at the circle of witches and wizards—"and one to oversee the rest of you." Her disdain was obvious to Sloan, but it appeared not to register with any of the other presumably non-magical individuals in the room.

Sarah pointed first at one of the witches. "Wysse, you will coordinate the arcane." The woman nodded as if accepting a heavy responsibility. She turned and looked over the others, then shrugged as if it didn't really matter. She extended a finger toward Sloan, and his stomach clenched. "You. You, in the gray dress shirt, what's your name again?"

Beside him, Mur stammered "Murray Lensport, ma'am."

She waved dismissively. "You may refer to me as Sarah. Anything else is an insult unless you would prefer to call me Master or Mistress." Mur nodded and wiped away the sweat that had broken out on his forehead. "You will lead these groups. Failure would be..." She paused for a moment, then gave a smile filled with the promise of pain. "It would be a poor choice on your part, one with terrible ramifications for all of you."

Several of the gang members seemed to bristle at the threat, and she hastened to add, "But success will bring rewards beyond what you have been promised before and even beyond what you can imagine. Make no mistake, we are in the big leagues now, people."

From the far side of the warehouse, the chosen chief of the magicals shouted, "Mistress." The head witch turned toward her, an eyebrow raised in a question. The other woman stepped forward. She was dressed the same as her leader, but the cut of the black sheath differed and revealed more than Sarah chose to. Wysse raised her chin and spoke in a voice that echoed through the room. "There is one among us who does not belong."

Sarah's eyes went half-lidded, and the smile that had remained frozen on her face turned into a frown. There was no anger there, merely the regard of the predator about to capture its prey. She raised a palm to the woman. "Do tell."

The witch wandered around the warehouse floor and seemed to sniff the air near each non-arcane person she passed. "As you know, Mistress, one of my abilities is empathy. In this room, there is someone who does not wish us well, one who is in fact right now planning to work against us."

Sloan froze. Again, he forced himself to remain outwardly calm while he made plans inwardly should things go wrong. The other half of his gift—the part that kept him shielded from others' talents—had never failed him before. The witch wandered in their direction and finally stopped behind Teddy and on the opposite side of Mur from where Sloan stood. She raised an arm and pointed at a male trying to disappear into his hoodie halfway across the room. "Him. It is him. He is an informant for the police."

With an unearthly shriek that made almost everyone present cringe, dark shadowy tentacles surged from Sarah's outstretched left hand and snaked to the man in an instant to lift him from the floor. He struggled but couldn't break free of the initial ones, much less the half-dozen that followed. The witch in charge shifted her gaze in their direction. "Murray, your first official act in your new role is to eliminate this interloper."

Mur gulped and looked ill as he shuffled toward the struggling captive. One of the cookie-cutter gang members produced a pistol and set it in his hand as the bald man moved past him. He reached the informant, who redoubled his efforts to escape, his shouts of outrage or apology muffled by the tentacle over his mouth. Mur gazed at Sarah, who nodded regally. He aimed and fired in an instant, and the man's head snapped back, a perfect hole drilled above his left eyebrow. The tentacles unwound, actually seemed disappointed now that their task was complete, and dropped him carelessly. The new human leader handed the weapon to the person who had loaned it to him as he returned to his former position.

Sarah had a cruel smile on her face. "Very good. Lieutenants, come and discuss future plans with me immediately. The rest of you, wait a while and do not agitate one another. Transgressions will be dealt with harshly and instantly." As Mur and Wysse walked toward her, she made a final pronouncement. "Once we have formed our separate divisions into a unit and determined who is best at what, we will embark upon an operation that shall make any other you've been involved with seem like child's play. Organize your affairs to be ready to leave town at a moment's notice." She turned and led her new team leaders up the stairs.

Sloan returned Teddy's confused look in kind. *I don't know what that crazy witch is up to, but I am one hundred percent certain it'll be bad for everyone involved, but especially so for whoever is her target.*

CHAPTER ELEVEN

Diana entered the building through the garage tunnel as usual, and the tiny version of the troll who had adopted her sat on her shoulder. The additional cars outside were a pleasing sight, a visible sign of their growth. *We're seven now, including Rath, but could still use one or two more. A fighter and a specialist tech, maybe.*

They turned to the core and joined the rest of the agents already gathered for the morning status briefing. Cara handed her a mug of coffee, and she inhaled the steam. "Ahhh, yes, that's the stuff. Thanks."

Her second in command nodded. "So, we have a clear agenda today. Nothing is on fire, literally or figuratively, and most of our open loops are closed."

Tony frowned. "What is that, some sort of business-speak?"

She returned the scowl. "Some of us actually read things other than golf magazines, you know."

"I can't see why. Golf is life. Life is golf."

Diana shook her head. "Quiet, you two."

Rath echoed, "Quiet two," with a small laugh. He had practiced gymnastics on the couch before they'd left and had, for no apparent reason, decided to remain in his tiny form. She had assumed he would become more predictable as time went by, but it turned out that it might actually be the opposite.

Kayleigh swept into the room from the far staircase. "Yeah, shut the hell up, whoever is supposed to be quiet." She flicked her fingers as she approached, and the haptic sensors on her nails sent instructions to the core systems. The screens came to life and displayed several incomprehensible images, maps, and data streams.

Diana paused to regard the tech. Since joining BAM Pittsburgh, she had truly come into her own and abandoned the modest subservience she had demonstrated in DC for a confident leadership that was entirely appropriate. She'd traded in the somewhat formal outfits she'd worn there for something more in keeping with the team, currently blue jeans, killer boots—*literally, given what's hiding inside them*—and a tactical top under a Rush t-shirt. Her demeanor always straddled the line between seriousness and sarcastic teasing, and she shifted across it adroitly when needed. Like Rath, she was both unpredictable and far more than she seemed.

Her attention was jerked back to the moment when Kayleigh snapped her fingers with a sharp crack. "Boss, are you with us?"

She nodded and took a bigger sip. "I have roommate problems. Really bloody noisy video games at all hours, so it's hard to sleep."

Rath added "Pew Pew," and the team laughed.

Kayleigh gave her a look that promised sweet revenge, then gestured at the surrounding information. "What you're looking at is the data from all our surveillance systems around the city. Feeds from the camera grids, from our own sensors, from the Cube's cameras and drones, and even traffic cameras and piggybacks of any live video the tv stations send all fed into our own analysis algorithms."

Sloan, who made a rare appearance, shook his head in apparent wonder. "It's good to know you have eyes on me wherever I am."

The tech nodded. "Eyes and ears, as long as your phone is with you."

Diana waved at the impressive display. "You're showing us this for a reason, I assume?"

"Of course. So you realize how amazing I am." The group laughed again, and she turned serious. "Actually, I wanted you to see all the sources we have so you can judge what degree of credence to give to the system's outputs."

"That's fair. Is there something in particular today?"

Kayleigh nodded and pointed to a map on which several dots moved. "This is a plot of some surveillance that Rath started and Alfred has continued with the drones." She looked at the troll. "The idea of a hidden tag is an excellent one, by the way, and I'm working on it." She laughed. "It's fantastic but also frustrating to have more great ideas to pursue than time to invest."

Diana peered more closely at the display. The moving dots tended to cluster in the same areas and specifically around a group of downtown locations that sold alcohol. The stores were labeled to make sure they didn't miss the point. "It looks like they're casing the places."

"That was Alfred's opinion as well."

Anik nudged Tony and whispered loud enough for the room to hear. "I think Kayleigh's in love with a computer program." Laughter sounded in response.

With a toss of her blonde hair, the tech replied primly, "We're very happy together. Also, screw you. Jealousy is unbecoming." A smattering of taunts followed, and Anik raised his arms in defeat to more general mirth.

Rath chirped, "Timetable?"

Kayleigh gave him a grin. "Finally, an intelligent comment." Diana thought about it for a moment and decided she'd actually been insulted. She didn't have time to make an issue out of it before the other woman continued. "We've picked up some chatter here and there—disconnected stuff, but Alfred is sure there's something big in the works for next week. Bigger than liquor stores, anyway. Our best guess is that it'll happen sometime in the near future."

Sloan nodded. "The thing with Sarah's gang fits that timetable. We're working and rehearsing general plans, but not with the kind of intensity you'd expect if it was planned for tomorrow. Whatever it is."

Diana frowned. "No indication at all?"

The undercover operative scowled. "None, other than it's out of town. This whole situation is pissing me off. They are the tightest-lipped group ever, and my talent only picks up fear of the woman on the rare occasions I get something from someone. She has them really spooked. To be fair, she has me spooked as well."

She understood that perfectly. "Crazy eyes."

He slapped the table. "Yes, exactly—the craziest."

Kayleigh's comment was tentative. "I don't know too much about the whole World in Between, but every time I hear about it, I am reminded that I never want to be there even for a second. It's not a shock that she returned different, I suppose."

Diana banished the memory of tentacles from her mind and changed the subject. "Okay, so, stupid pirate man." Rath giggled on her shoulder. "What's the timeframe?"

"Alfred says that based on the increasing frequency, maybe tonight. Although the weather looks bad for it, so more likely tomorrow night."

"Excellent. New hat for the troll."

Laughter followed, and Diana smothered her grin. "Okay, let's get down to it, then. How can we do better than last time?"

Sloan sighed. "That's my exit cue." He held his phone up to show the text message. "Her evil majesty summons us." He departed with a wave, and the others congregated closer around the display table and the map of the stores.

Kayleigh gestured and percentages popped up over the three locations. Unfortunately, the highest was forty, and the other two were even at thirty. "Alfred doesn't see a particular reason for any of them to be first. They make a rough triangle, so there's no clear progression from one to the next."

Diana nodded. "And, of course, we assume they'll do it the same way as before and strike in sequence rather than simultaneously."

Cara sounded annoyed. "They're idiots. The post-theft rave scene proves that. They'll keep doing what they've been doing. One after the other."

Tony shrugged. "Surveillance on all of them with us somewhere in the middle, ready to roll."

The second in command looked at their boss. "It sure would be nice if we had some kind of moving base…I don't know, like a mobile armory or something."

She rewarded the comment with a scowl. "No, no, and no is the answer I receive every time I ask. I'll keep asking, and you keep hoping, but in the meantime, quit the damn whining, woman."

The woman pouted theatrically. "Fine. SUVs it is. They are way less cool, though."

Three new locations pulsed, and Kayleigh explained, "Alfred says these are the optimal locations for the vehicles to provide the quickest response and best reinforcement."

Tony waved at the map. "There's another option, of course." The others turned toward him. "Drones at all the stores."

Kayleigh interrupted him and held a palm up at Cara. "No one had better be about to suggest armed drones. Even with stun weapons. There are rules, and we will follow them."

The former detective hid his smile under the hand that smoothed his mustache. "What I was about to say was we could let them do their thing at the first place, then meet them at the second. That would give us the element of surprise and either arrive at the same time as they do or even ahead of them if we're lucky."

Anik frowned. "So we sacrifice that first shop?"

Tony nodded. "They haven't hurt people, and we can make sure the fire department is ready to roll. It's only property damage, and while that sucks, it probably sucks less than giving up our tactical advantage."

Diana thought about the various options and saw them play out in her mind's eye. "I think that might be worth it. I don't like being reactive if there's a way not to be. We need to consider our own well-being from time to time, too." She recalled Nylotte advising her exactly that, only in different words. "Is there an argument against simply staging at one and waiting for them there?"

Kayleigh shrugged. "It's always possible that they won't rob the location we choose or that we won't see them coming if it's the first."

Cara laughed. "You have all the surveillance in the world. How would we not see them coming?"

"That's a good point. But things happen, sometimes. Illusions, system failures, EMPs. These are rare but possible." She gestured again and the location at the northernmost end of the triangle lit up. "This is the place with the best odds." The tech spread her hands apart, and the image zoomed in. It was one of the seedier streets in the town with a bar on one side and an abandoned apartment building on the other. It had no entrances or exits other than the front as it butted up against structures on all sides. The metal plates on the sidewalk near the door indicated the lift that led to the underground storage.

Diana clapped her hands decisively. "That's it, that's the one. We'll go with the odds and post there tomorrow night unless we hear something different. Kayleigh, keep your eyes on them and send out the alert if we get any sign they'll move tonight."

The tech nodded, and Cara began to speak. Diana cut

her off. "Shut it. Yes, I know a mobile armory would be perfect for this. You're like a skipping record. Armory, armory, armory." She threw up her arms in mock frustration. "Honestly, go make yourself useful, people. Get some bounties. Hit the range. But quit annoying me, will ya?"

Rath's small hands gripped her ear to move into proper position. He whispered, "Armory. Pew pew." She groaned, and he cackled. *Everyone's against me.*

CHAPTER TWELVE

After the planning meeting about the pirate—*I will so get that hat*—Diana had banished them all to their own tasks for the day. For Rath, that meant foot patrol with Max. The magical train took him almost all the way back to their new house to pick up his partner. They decided to stay in the neighborhood but near the edge where it met the other university.

He'd been surprised to find there was a second school nearby, and even more shocked at how close they were. When he mentioned it to Diana, she'd laughed and explained that there were actually several more near where they lived, and one downtown, a few blocks from their HQ building. Point Park University shared a name with the big green space that filled the area between the rivers as they came together a short distance away from the base. Nearest to their home was Carnegie Mellon, which apparently named after two very rich people from a time long past.

Exactly like the other one, businesses and restaurants

were everywhere. The buildings were fancier than in the streets next to where Professor Charlotte Stanley worked, but none were as eye-catching as the tall cathedral. There was more green space, and with the warm day, more people made use of the expansive lawns. Max dashed and wove between them and he and the small troll who rode with a hand securely gripping the dog's collar generated laughs from the students.

While they roamed more or less at random, Rath kept his eyes peeled for anything out of the ordinary or any areas they hadn't yet explored. He saw one and gave the Borzoi a pat to move him in that direction. It was farther down than they'd been so far, almost at the border between the two schools' territories. A strange-looking old house had apparently been turned into an antique store if the sign in front was any indication. They stood before it and studied the odd building. From the high peak of the sharply angled roof to the ornate wooden banisters that bounded the porches on the ground level and the floor above, it seemed somehow ominous and otherworldly. Dark grey and black paint covered the sides, and the front door was elegant wood and stained glass.

It was also open and only a screen door in front of it separated the interior from the outside. Rath shrugged and prodded Max forward. The dog gave a soft growl, and the troll poked him again with a scowl. When they made it onto the porch, he flipped off the dog's back and grew to his three-foot size in order to clear the way. They stepped into another time.

A long wooden staircase began a few feet inside and led to the second floor. The banister widened from top to bottom and ended in a large horizontal spiral. Beside the stairs on the right was a hallway that led deeper into the building. Rath walked forward slowly and scrutinized the stamped brown tin ceiling, something he'd only before seen in pictures. Light fixtures shaped like candelabras hung from it at equal intervals. The duo turned right and passed through a narrow entrance into the space beyond.

It was an ornate sitting room with a desk in the far corner that held an ancient cash register. A pair of large wingback leather chairs near the front window shared a small round end table between them. The nearest was unoccupied. In the other, however, was a man he'd seen before. They hadn't formally met, though. *He's one of the new Griffins.* Rath knew the group of older witches and wizards didn't actually consider themselves representatives of that august organization, but that's how he thought of them. *And it fits.* His first sight of the person had been with Professor Charlotte and the other members of her team.

The man clearly recognized him, and his silver-bearded face broke out into a wide grin. "Young troll, it is good to finally see you rather than simply hear about you!" He stood and revealed that he wore a light navy robe, unfastened, with arcane symbols embroidered in bright white down the lapels. Underneath, his pants and shirt were both black, and the panels on his wingtips matched the figures above the only break in the pattern. He strode forward and held a hand out. "Emanuel Kensington. Call me Manny."

He shook it with a firm grip and nodded. "Rath." He looked around the room. "Your house?"

Manny laughed and his dark eyes twinkled. "No, my business, actually. I live a few blocks away. It makes for an easy commute, which is important when you're as ancient as I am."

You don't move like someone old. Rath noticed the slight weight in each of his sleeves and judged the man had a wand or some other kind of weapon hidden in them. He approved wholeheartedly. Right now, his collapsed batons and utility belt rode in the saddlebags Max wore. He and Kayleigh had tried to figure out how to safely include grenades but decided it wasn't worth the burden or the potential risk. "Seem young. What is this place?"

Manny spread his arms wide. "This is my shop, where lost and abandoned things wash up to be delivered to new owners." He walked over to a china cabinet and opened it to remove an ornate goblet. "It looks real, right?" The troll nodded. "It's actually a movie prop from when they shot *The Last Witch Hunter* in town. I have quite a selection from that film."

Rath scowled. "Not a fan. *Pitch Black. Riddick.* Better."

The elder wizard laughed. "Fair enough. And I can't argue. I love the silver eyes." The troll nodded agreement. "There are a couple more rooms like this down here, but you might be more interested in the one upstairs. Would you care to see it?" Without waiting for an answer, the man brushed past him and led the way up the creaking staircase.

The troll looked at Max, who had stood in the room's entrance the entire time. "Think it's okay?" He barked once, and he took that as an affirmative. He jumped onto the banister and ran up it to reach the second floor immediately after his host with the dog a few steps behind. There was an open door ahead that led to a bathroom and a hallway that turned toward the front of the house and held two doors on the left. One was closed, and as he passed it, Manny said, "Storage. Here." The next was open, and Rath followed him inside. A tingle of magic skittered over his skin as he crossed the threshold, and he turned to see what it was. Nothing was visible.

The wizard had slid his arms into the opposite sleeves as if to discourage himself from touching anything in the room. *Or making sure weapons are at his fingertips.* He sounded more serious than he had before and nodded toward the doorway. "It's an arcane item that vibrates when it senses magic. I wear a bracelet that is attuned to it, so I know when active powers pass through." He pulled one hand out and held his wrist up to show a chunky band that looked like ivory around it. "You are not technically actively magical, even though you clearly are." He smiled, and Rath's worries fled.

Manny turned toward the far side of the room, momentarily silhouetted in the windows and the door that faced onto the second-floor balcony. There was a trio of display cases there, each heavy wood and metal with thick sheets of something transparent that probably wasn't glass on the inclined top. Rath jumped on a nearby chair for a better look. The man gestured into the container closest to the window. "Wands that have wound up with me in one fashion or another."

The troll hopped onto the case itself and looked down. Red velvety fabric held more than a dozen slender rods crafted of different woods and in a variety of shapes. "Where from?"

He shrugged. "Honestly, I couldn't tell you. I seem to

have a gift for finding things that are lost or hidden. They have come to me in any number of ways." Rath frowned, and the man seemed to read it as doubt. "Truly. I have a knack, I guess you could say. I walk down the street, and I have a feeling. When I follow it, I generally find something interesting."

Rath considered that. "Useful against bad guys."

"At times." He gestured at the next case. "Speaking of which, here are some random weapons I've found." The troll did a flip over to it, landed in perfect balance, and drew an appreciative laugh. Inside were knives, an object that looked like brass knuckles, a tiny club, and a set of wide silver rings. He pointed at them. "Jewelry?"

The man chuckled. "You have a good eye, my friend. Those are eight pieces of a ten-piece collection, I believe. I lack the left pinky and the right thumb." He raised his hands to demonstrate and waggled the fingers in question. "From the outside, they look normal. The inner part is covered completely with etched symbols in a language none of us have identified. They're the only things in the case not for sale. I need to complete the set. It's my main goal before I shuffle off into whatever existence lies beyond this one." The troll looked sharply at him, and Manny shook his head. "No, I'm not in particular danger of dying imminently, at least no more than anyone else. I've merely been at it a long time. If I didn't know better, I'd say the missing parts don't want to be found."

"Is possible?"

He shrugged. "Magic items tend to have a mind of their own, as it were. Even the ones that don't actually have a mind." He wandered over to the last case and stared into it with a sigh. "This piece is also not for sale." Rath vaulted over again and looked down, but saw nothing. The man whispered an incantation and a large bracelet shaped like a lizard appeared, designed so its tail would sit at a person's wrist and the head would rest high on their forearm. "It's a Rhazdon artifact. And, yes, before you say anything, I'm aware that I shouldn't have it. No one should. But as with the Griffins before, it's my responsibility to keep it out of the wrong hands. So it sits here, hidden and unable to cause trouble. Although I do hear it whisper to me every time I come up here. It makes terrible promises."

Rath jumped down. "Keep safe. Keep away."

The man nodded and cast the spell to obscure the object again. A clamor erupted downstairs as the front door slammed and a woman's voice yelled, "Emmanuel, get your butt down here." They both broke into matching grins and hurried down to where Professor Charlotte, who looked cross in her skirt and sweater combo, stood with her arms folded. Max had arrived first and leaned against her leg to regard her with fond eyes.

She gave a thin smile when she saw the troll and absently stroked the Borzoi's head. "Rath, it's good to see you again. It's perhaps even fortuitous timing." She turned her gaze onto the man. "Silas texted us all a while ago. You didn't respond, so I came to check on you since I was already nearby."

Manny clapped a hand to his forehead. "I'm an idiot. I don't actually have my phone with me, now that I think of it."

Charlotte released a long sigh. "You're getting old fast, my friend. First your phone, next your wand, and finally, your clothes or something. Then, they'll lock you up." She gave Rath a quick smile to let him know she was kidding. "In any case, he's heard the same message we all have, and from even more people. All signs point to a significant event happening soon."

Rath nodded. "Pirate Prince. On it."

She shook her head. "No. Something big. There's a buzz. Something on a scale we've never seen is on the way, and we have zero idea what it is."

The troll looked from one pair of wide eyes to the other, then at the Borzoi. "Must get home and sleep. Looks like patrol tonight."

The dog's bark of confirmation sounded worried. *Yeah, Maxie, me too. I feel a great disturbance in the force.* Professor Charlotte held the door as he and Max headed out. *Fortunately, BAM agents are excellent jedis.*

CHAPTER THIRTEEN

Diana crouched in the darkness of the closed liquor store and waited for the action to begin. She nudged Rath, who stood beside her, their eyes more or less on the same level. She layered a Spanish accent. "I hate waiting."

He grinned. "Get used to disappointment."

They laughed together, loudly enough that Anik hissed at them from the other aisle. "Quiet, you two. I'm trying to be professional over here."

Kayleigh had routed the various drone feeds into their glasses. The prince's gang had raided the store Alfred had predicted would be first—points to the AI—and was inbound toward their location. The tech had summoned the fire department immediately, and the blaze was under control and would not spread beyond the targeted building. *That's something, anyway.*

"Croft, status?"

Cara's mic picked up the wind from outside. "No sign yet. I'm ready to do the Batman thing." After their harness deployment from the helicopter, the team had realized that the concept had many other applications. As the most gymnastic ARES agent other than Rath, Cara was the obvious choice to rig a bungee jump from the roof of the building that would allow her to leap safely down the three stories and land on the street among or behind the attackers, depending on how far she flew. She'd have to detach the cord at the right moment, but they'd practiced the move at a local trampoline funhouse and Cara had it down pat.

"Acknowledged. Stark?"

Tony replied, "Hiding in the shadows like some sort of common criminal as ordered, boss." The channel filled with quiet laughter at the remark. He was posted across the road in an alley and had already complained endlessly about the smells involved with the position.

"It suits you," Cara quipped.

He snorted. "Not everyone is expendable enough to be risked on a three-story jump. Show-off. On your best day, you're not half as good as Rath—er, Rambo." The troll had chosen his own callsign, and the team was still getting used to it, and to saying it without cracking up.

More laughter followed until Kayleigh's voice interrupted the moment. "You have thirty seconds, tops, before they get there. At the last place, they smashed the front windows, cut through the security grate with a torch, and looted it fast. Five minutes in and out. There is a large group of them with three trucks this time."

Diana repositioned her hands on the stun rifle and made sure her grip was secure. "Roger." She focused on the drone feeds in her glasses for a moment and decided only one was really useful. "Friday, keep the center feed and lose the other two."

The AI sounded its confirmation tone and the extra windows disappeared. "Glam, roll the fire department when things kick off and the police as soon as you think it's safe to do so." Ideally, they'd require neither support, but it was always better to have and not need than the other way around.

Kayleigh replied, "Affirmative. Enemy arriving now." Another window opened in her glasses to reveal the camera of the drone that hovered high over the scene. As the tech predicted, three large trucks pulled into the deserted street in front of the building. They looked freshly painted in bright yellow. *Hopefully, it cost them a pretty penny to replace the ones we captured last time.* She snorted to herself. *Most likely, they stole these too.*

As they piled out of the vehicles and took position before the windows, Tony observed, "At least there's no back for them to rush out of. Idiots."

Rath laughed. "Stark. Must train more. Run with me and MadMax."

"Oh, hell no, uh, Rambo. This body is made for lov... dating, not running."

Banter time ended as the gang members launched their attack. They fired a spray of bullets at the windows, angled upward to avoid breaking bottles. The barrier, which had been extremely thick glass, shattered instantly. *Those are probably armor-piercing rounds. Criminals don't have to follow rules. I'm glad there's no one above us.* A man stepped forward with a large blowtorch and cut away the metal where the windows had been, while another worked on the grate in front of the door. Her finger twitched with the desire to fire a bullet into the torches' fuel source and end the matter right then.

Anik spoke quietly. "One shot, boss, and boom. Party over. Okay, two, one for each torch. Say the word."

She put an authoritative tone in her voice as if she hadn't desired the same thing. "No, they haven't killed anyone, so we stay nonlethal until it's absolutely necessary not to." Thus the stun rifles and the hollow-point ammunition in their weapons that was the least likely to cause random damage from ricochets. The bars fell away, and the first looters entered the store.

"Party time, people. Go." She kicked it off by stepping around the end cap she'd sheltered behind and fired at the foremost looter, a woman in a bright red blouse and leather pants, with her stun rifle. Her mind flitted back to the raid on the warehouse where they'd first met the pirate's crew. *What the hell? Maybe the apparent eye candy wasn't eye candy at all.* Her target collapsed in a heap and Diana dropped and rolled out of the way of a blast of ice darts that sped toward her as soon as the path was clear for them. They shattered vodka bottles on the rear wall, and the liquor spread onto the tile floor, making movement treacherous.

The caster was removed from the equation by a flying troll. Rath had leapt to the top of a shelf, paused there for an instant, and jumped in a flip and twist to land on the man's shoulders with one foot on each side of his head. He stabbed down with his shock batons and the enemy jerked for a moment before he crumbled. The three-foot troll flung himself aside and into cover behind the cash register counter.

The door banged open, and the first person through met a stun blast from Anik, who had risen and now stalked steadily toward the opening. As he moved, he laid down continuous blasts and trusted the barrage to keep him safe from counterattack. When the line of witches and wizards that had formed outside the window raised their arms together, Diana thought that perhaps his trust was overly optimistic. She shouted a warning and charged.

When the trucks pulled in, Cara watched from her perch high above and waited for the right moment. The initial push didn't inspire her to action, as those below appeared to have it covered. The sounds of stun rifle blasts confirmed her assessment. But when she saw the line of magicals organizing, she knew the time had arrived. She waved at Tony, who had watched her for his cue to move, and took a few steps back.

She ran and launched into space, aiming for the center. In her practice sessions, she'd gone from simple safe landings, which were now as easy as could be, to airborne attacks. The latter still involved some challenge, but what was the point of swooping down like the caped crusader if you didn't deliver some damage at the same time? The first time she'd succeeded using a targeting mannequin they'd brought along, Rath had cheered and called her "human who flies like troll." Diana had explained he'd watched

Dances with Wolves and was renaming everyone. Cara liked it.

For a moment, she plummeted free until the bungee stretched and absorbed some of her momentum. She used the pull to rotate her feet downward and twisted into alignment with the bald-headed wizard in the middle of the line. In one of those strange flashes that happen in battle, she saw Tony hurtle out of the alley with his stun gun aimed toward the witch on the far end. Her target sensed her coming in the seconds before she arrived and his eyes widened as he raised his head.

She slapped the release buckle in the center of her chest, plummeted the last few feet to him, and delivered a powerful kick into his breastbone immediately below his throat. He went down and backward, and she landed with a foot on him and the other on the pavement, then rolled to the side to absorb the impact. The enemies to her left launched attacks directed at the store and the ones on her right turned toward her, three of each.

Suddenly, the criminals on the right were down to two, then one, as Tony's rifle buzzed and disabled them. That was the good news. The bad news was the arrival of a fourth truck at his back and the pounding feet of the rest of the already-present gang from behind her. She raised her stun gun but ran out of time to shoot as blasts of force and lightning made her stagger against the nearest truck as her vest absorbed them. *Shit.*

Rath paused to let any attack that might have followed him

pass overhead before he bounced onto the counter. Anik continued to hold the door against a line of henchmen forced to attack him one by one. Diana rose from her evasive maneuver and fired at the last enemy actually inside the store, a mage who launched poorly aimed blasts of force at her. The result was that even more alcohol spilled over the tile.

Outside, Cara and Tony engaged the wizards and witches, three of whom were already down. He frowned at the incoming mass of attackers, easily a dozen or so, who had apparently been held in reserve. Behind them, in the middle distance, he saw a crazy hat. His lips pulled back in a fierce grin.

The troll vaulted at the enemy Diana was fighting and used the wizard as a launching point to go after one of the witches outside. Hopefully, the distraction would give his teammate the instant she needed to overcome the man. He led with his stun batons and stabbed them into the woman's sides but was immediately hurled away by an explosion of force that radiated out from her. His backward somersault ended in a skid as he landed and charged again. She turned and flung a streak of force darts at him. He dodged several, blocked two more with quick strikes of his weapons, and finally, he was close enough. Rath slashed at her legs with the batons and aimed from the outside and inward. She leapt and delivered a kick to his face that he barely avoided with a deep backbend.

He growled, half in anger and half in enthusiasm for a quality opponent. In mid-air, she launched more darts at him, and he fell on his back to avoid them. She stood over his defenseless form and grinned as she raised her wand to strike a final blow. "Trinity. Help," he called.

Tony stepped up beside her, his stun rifle at head-level, and delivered the answering line with a grin. "Dodge this." The weapon crackled and she went down. The big man nodded but immediately yelped as a blast of lightning knocked the gun from his hands. Rath flipped to his feet and turned to see Cara incapacitate the second to last wizard in the group. The final one, closest to the onrushing surge of hoodlums, launched another electrical attack.

Tony dodged around the front of the truck and lightning scored the paintwork on the passenger door. The witch shifted her wand toward Cara, who was occupied with her own foe. Rath saw only one option. He pushed his batons into the ground to collapse them and hurled them in sequence at the witch. The shock feature required a button press to activate it, but taking a pound or so of metal in the face would still be detrimental. The first missed by a wide margin to the left, but the second connected soundly with her forehead. She staggered back, her head impacted against the truck's side, and she crumpled and fell with a moan.

A sound from his right reminded him of the fourth vehicle and the enemies that surged out of it. Again, only a single option presented itself. He raced toward the closest adversaries and the so-called Prince of Plunder who had his hat and grew to his full size before he plowed into the one at the head of the line.

Diana had an ungraceful moment as she dodged a force blast and slipped on the wet floor to collide with a row of bottles and shatter them. The ensuing waterfall covered her sleeve in bourbon. *Maker's Mark. At least it's top shelf.* She righted herself and fired a stun bolt at the mage, but he deflected it with a force shield and repeated his previous attack. A hurried block stopped the weapon in its path, and she hurled it at him as a distraction afterward. The shouted, "Retreat," rose over the cacophony, doubtless magically amplified by the sonic wizard-pirate. A grin spread across his face. The muttered word that accompanied the extension of his wand was lost in the noise, but the whoosh of flame that followed was instantly all that she could hear or see.

Anik screamed, and she collapsed and summoned a force shield to encase her. The heat intensified as the contents of the bottles ignited, and even though she was protected from the touch of the fire, her mind was gripped with a primal fear of immolation and shrieked at her to escape. Sprinklers activated, far too inadequate to extinguish the blaze. She only noticed her arm was alight when the burning reached a pain point greater than that of the surrounding heat, and she beat at it to extinguish it. The part of her that rightly feared remaining immobile in a blazing building took over and she pushed to her feet and ran, then hurled herself toward the open grate and broken window.

She landed outside in a roll and maintained the tumble to ensure she was no longer on fire. When she finally managed to stand, she scowled at the blisters on her now bare arm and groaned as another wash of agony accompanied her awareness of the extent of the wound. Brighter pain flared, and she staggered as bullets struck her in the back of the vest and triceps as she flung away. *Bloody bastards, now you've done it. But at least they don't all have AP ammo.* "Friday, send ambulances to this position. BAM, weapons free. They've chosen the hard way."

There were a few confirmations and an enthusiastic, "Yes," as she rose in fury and turned to face the enemies that now launched a concerted attack at her. They comprised both firearms- and wand-holders, and in her pained and angry state, she had no inclination to hold back to protect those who had elected to put themselves in harm's way. She reached deep for fire and scythed a wide, thin blast at knee level. The wizards and witches summoned shields and at least one was generous enough to extend it to the mundane pistol-wielder beside him, but her assault brought at least half of them to their knees.

They raised wands, and Diana threw out both hands to release a line of force to take hold of a nearby trash can from the far sidewalk. She hurled the telekinetic missile at the approaching hoodlums from the opposite side. It was almost comical watching the criminals smash into each other as they defended against one attack or the other, only to be struck by the one they hadn't prioritized. She turned to discover that Rath had struck the other oncoming group like a bowling ball and that many were down. The rest had chosen to flee and now piled into the two farthest trucks, which peeled away before she could target them. Anik stood over the downed enemies and stunned them as fast as his weapon could recycle. He looked none the worse for wear other than his dark hair, which appeared a little singed.

"Glam, tag it," she shouted. She heard the high buzz of the drone as it accelerated in a downward swoop and vanished from sight around the corner.

"I have the back one," Kayleigh confirmed a moment later. "They're going too fast for me to reach the first. These are not the most awesome drones ever." She had often complained about the fact that she still used hand-me-down technology on that front because they didn't have the time to develop their own. Allegedly, DC was working on it, but when she'd mentioned that to the tech, Kayleigh had snorted and responded with a shake of her head. "Ems is not interested in drones. He never has been and never will be. He likes the up-close stuff."

Diana sighed and considered using her healing potion but decided she could stick it out for a little longer as Cara wrapped a pressure bandage around her wound. She wasn't sure what the result of taking it would be if there was a piece of shrapnel still inside her and didn't want to risk it unless there was no other choice. "Get to the cars. This isn't over yet."

CHAPTER FOURTEEN

The black SUVs coasted to a stop a block away from where the tagged truck and the other one had finished their journey. Kayleigh had shown the team the location on a map and then with the feed from one of her drones. The vehicles had ducked into a pair of large rental garages in an unexpected area, the affluent Shadyside neighborhood east of downtown.

Occasional streetlights broke the darkness, but there was more than sufficient cover as they advanced on foot toward the house where the drones had detected an abnormal number of heat signatures. *With my luck tonight, we've probably stumbled on a bloody campaign fundraiser for the mayor or something.* The wound in her arm throbbed in time with her heartbeat and made her downright cranky.

Cara jogged beside her as they approached in the shadows with the men behind and the three-foot troll trailing. They'd given up on the stun weapons entirely and held their carbines close to their chests. Now that the enemy had shown a willingness to kill them, they wouldn't hesitate to return the gesture. They still carried standard ammo to avoid harming any bystanders, and each had a mix of those and anti-magic magazines.

Diana didn't appreciate anything about the scenario. "Okay, listen. This will require stealth since they have home field advantage. I hope y'all won't be offended when I say that Stark and Khan are not exactly the most ninja-like of us."

Tony chuckled. "I resemble that remark."

Anik added. "I can be super quiet. I simply choose not to. Um, always."

The quips failed to bring her any amusement. The deep sense of foreboding she felt banished it before it could begin. It didn't feel like a trap, and the likelihood that the prince and his crew knew the team would be waiting for them that night was negligible. Still, this was a criminal who had been around for a while and had probably learned a few things. Plus, he had magic on his side, personal and hired. She shook her head. *Bad. Not good. Very not good. Lousy. Do not want.*

Diana did break a smile when Rath whispered, "Ninja-troll. Stealthiest of all. Let Mortal Kombat begin!"

She chuckled. "Honestly, how do you find the time to watch all these movies?"

He laughed. "Sleep mostly optional. It's good to be a troll."

A somber expression replaced her grin as they reached the boundary of the plot the home stood on, marked by a neatly trimmed lawn surrounded by an ornate stone border. "Friday, scan for alarms." The AI communicated with the drone above and superimposed a white electrical map on her glasses. The house itself was clearly wired, with a pulsing dot at each door and window, but the only exterior devices were motion detectors at the corners of the roof. She tapped the corner of the frames to magnify the view and saw the sensors attached to impressively large floodlights. *That's probably standard issue for the neighborhood, given the property values.*

"Stark and Khan, you're on overwatch. One of you cover front and a side, the other cover back and the other side. Stay in the shadows. Remaining undetected is more important than speed. Glam, more drones if you can get them and create a perimeter in case help rolls in." She received affirmatives and the others moved off. "Friday, are you able to plot the motion detectors?" There was a delay before lines appeared in her glasses. A lane existed that shouldn't set off the sensors. They could move through this as long as they were extremely slow and careful. She crept forward and remained close to the ground, and Cara and Rath followed a step behind.

They reached a low window on the first floor and Diana extended the fiber-optic camera from her sleeve to look inside. It was empty, a small den of some kind by the looks of the large chairs and narrow sofa, but the drink on the end table still full of ice suggested recent use. The electrical pulse of the sensor was vivid yellow in her display, superimposed on the upper sill of the window. She raised the square computer device Kayleigh had added to their kits some time before and held it near the electronic alarm.

The tech spoke almost as soon as Diana's hand stopped moving. "I'm accessing the system now. They have pathetic security. Stand by." There was a pause followed by muttered words that were too low hear. "Okay, I'm in. I have the remotes locked out of the main alarm computer, but they'll think they're getting through because I spoofed the signal." When there was no immediate reply, Kayleigh sighed. "I did a considerable amount of awesome stuff that y'all don't understand because you're trapped in the last century. Go when ready."

Diana exchanged grins with Cara, who also loved doing things to frustrate the blonde genius, and used her telekinesis to flip the latch and raise the window without a sound. She vaulted up and climbed in, followed quickly by the others. A finger to her lips communicated the need to remain silent, and she pointed at the open door leading out before she moved toward it.

She extended the camera again and discovered a long hallway to the left. To the right was the foyer at the front door, and the entrance to another room lay directly across from them. Voices emanated from it, and she scowled as the heat map in her glasses revealed two people walking into the chamber. She held a pair of fingers up, pointed first at Cara and then at herself, and moved when the other woman nodded.

They slipped across the hall and through the opening together, keeping their steps light. The duo of hoodlums saw them as soon as they entered, but the agents had shock gloves at their necks before they could utter a sound and silenced their cries. Each lowered their twitching target gently to the floor, and Diana dragged hers out of the line of sight of the doorway. Cara did the same and stashed her opponent under a couch along the front wall. Rath had run in behind them and guarded the hallway access as they worked.

The glasses' infrared scan was limited and covered only about a dozen feet or so ahead, but it revealed four people in the next area who appeared to be seated at a table, judging by their positions. Diana led her team to the doorway that separated the room from the hallway and snaked the camera around to get a look inside. A book was perched at the top of a cabinet and she flicked it with her telekinesis. It fell with a bang that startled the occupants, and in the moment they all looked toward it, the three infiltrators skipped across the entryway unseen.

Ahead was a staircase to the second floor, and beyond it and to the right, the kitchen area, where several more heat signatures resided. She turned and pointed up, then cocked her head to indicate it was a question. Cara nodded, and Rath agreed. They crept up the stairs and made it halfway before Diana realized her danger sense was prodding her. She'd moved so slowly that it had barely registered. Now, she stopped and looked around but saw nothing. She took another tentative step forward, and the metal band chilled on her wrist. *Dammit.*

She turned and motioned Cara and Rath back and pointed to the illusion detection bracelet. They returned to the bottom of the stairs and huddled in the minimal cover. She took a deep breath, readied her magic for whatever might happen, and whispered, "What is hidden, let it be found." A shimmering line appeared across the stairs, invisible to the naked eye but clear in her glasses, with another guarding every second step going up. *Technological detector obscured by magic. That's damn clever.* Her respect for the Prince of Plunder increased. Then she remembered the name calling and put him right back in the scum category but with a notation that he was also smart.

Diana waved for the others to follow again and climbed carefully over the traps. They reached the top floor and studied the four doors ahead of them. One led to a room with no heat signatures, two opened on areas with two body-shaped outlines in each, and a doubly large chamber contained three horizontal figures that seemed to be overlapped. Her brain put the information together and her stomach twisted at the idea of catching the man in bed with someone.

Someones. Whatever. First things first. She pointed to herself and the nearest occupied room, then to Rath and Cara and to the second. They nodded and prepared to act.

She thought through the moments ahead and decided the time for secrecy had passed. She whispered, "Stark, Khan, there are still a few on the main floor. Go in and go loud. We'll wait until you enter to move. Guard the stairs in case the jerk decides to make a break for it again."

When they heard the doors slam open downstairs, they all burst into motion. Diana darted into the room in front of her and found two wands aimed at the doorway as if they were waiting for her. She yelled, "Trap," and slid to her knees. Force blasts erupted loudly as they struck the wall on the other side of the staircase behind her. She pushed up and fired her own blast of force at the man on the right, but he spun gracefully away to dodge it and put the other enemy between them. A low dresser stood near his new position, and she gave it a telekinetic push to shove it into him and managed to knock the wizard to the floor.

His partner launched another attack at her, and she sidestepped left to evade it. The move was barely in time to avoid the witch who burst through the drywall from the room beside this one, inches from where she stood. The woman crumpled against the far wall. Diana was momentarily stunned and distracted for an instant, which allowed the next force bolt to catch her and hurl her into a structural support behind her. She felt her ribs give, either broken or cracked, and slumped in an orange haze of agony.

The man's grin was huge in her vision as he shifted his wand toward her new position. She braced herself for the blast, but he spun away suddenly as gunfire sounded and bullets drove him bleeding to the floor. The mage she'd struck with the furniture attempted to stand, made it to his knees, and conjured a shield to protect himself. Cara stepped through the witch-sized hole in the wall and her anti-magic rounds punched through his defenses. Two struck his chest and the third embedded itself in his forehead. He toppled backward without a word.

Diana tried to speak but couldn't find her breath. Tears trickled from her eyes, and Cara knelt beside her to smoothly draw a healing potion out of her own utility belt. "Don't panic, boss. We've got you." Rath appeared, and she handed him the vial. "Make her drink this. All of this. I'll end it." Kayleigh must have been watching or listening in, or both, because a window popped open in her glasses to show the feed from Cara's camera. The troll tipped the container against Diana's lips and the liquid slipped down her throat. The magic surged through her and along her blood vessels to reach every part of her body, and she was finally able to breathe. She sipped to avoid choking as he fed her the potion a little at a time.

Cara stepped into the far room and grimaced. The Pirate Prince leaned back against the headboard, his puffy shirt unbuttoned to reveal a wealth of jewelry around his neck. His arms encircled two women, both of whom were dressed like the one Diana had disabled earlier. Cara's rifle appeared in the field of view as she raised it and spoke in a tone edged almost with a low growl. "Anti-magic bullets. Choose your next moves wisely, as they may be your last."

By the time Diana was able to move again with her ribs knitted back together and the wound on her arm sealed, her second in command had the trio handcuffed. The men reported from below that the downstairs area was clear, and she went in to view the bound enemy leader and gave him a nod. He returned it with something like mirth in his eyes. She looked at Cara with a question on her face, and the other woman shrugged. "Who the hell knows? He's a kook."

Rath bounced into the room, raced over and jumped up on the bed, and claimed the man's hat as his own. He put the floppy tricorne on and dashed through the doorway again. Diana shook her head with a laugh. "It seems kooks abound."

The Prince of Plunder spoke for the first time since her arrival. "I'll want that hat back, after."

Cara turned with a scowl. "After what? After you serve a decade or so in the Cube for being a thieving firebug? Sure, we can do that."

He nodded. "After. Remember."

Diana stared at him, but he didn't flinch and merely

gazed back as if interested in her. Her second in command tapped her on the arm. "He's a kook and an idiot. Let's get out of here."

She followed the other woman but couldn't shake the feeling that something was going on, something she didn't see the outlines of yet. *Maybe I simply need a vacation. I wonder if BC likes the beach. Call it a work-cation. Yeah. That'd be good.*

CHAPTER FIFTEEN

The team had taken a few days off after apprehending the Prince of Plunder, and even Diana had gotten some rest, pleading healing to avoid training with Nylotte. The Drow had admonished her to watch her energy and sent her home with a stern gaze that spoke clearly of her disappointment in Diana's sense of self-preservation.

Bryant had invited them all out for a meal when he passed through town on the way to DC, and the team had gathered at a downtown restaurant that specialized in barbecue. They sat at an indoor picnic table with a red-and-white checked cloth and drank local beers, laughed, and shared stories. Even Sloan had made it, although he wore an illusion necklace that Emerson had sent up in case someone wandered by who might wonder what the criminal Tommy Ketchum was up to with such an odd collection of people, not to mention a troll.

The talk was light across most of the table and mainly centered on the food once it arrived. They'd ordered one of everything to share, and there were platters of brisket and three kinds of pork, plus an apple-infused sausage and jalapeño kielbasa. There were sides of mac and cheese, fries, baked beans, and collard greens, and they used paper plates and passed the food like they were in a backyard.

The troll tasted a little of each as they came around to him and reported on whether they were acceptable to Diana. She laughed as he sampled the sausage and gave her a thumbs-up. "Rath, every single thing you've tried so far has been a winner."

He shrugged. "Is good. Must eat."

There was general laughter at that, and she tuned into a conversation that Tony and Cara were having. He said, "Look, just ask him."

Her second in command shook her head. "I won't go over the boss like that."

"But it's the right thing to do. You know it is."

Diana frowned and threw a wadded-up napkin at Cara and caught her on the side of the head. The woman turned, and Diana asked, "What is the right thing to do, exactly?"

She rolled her eyes and looked at her conversation partner. "You're an idiot, you know that?" He grinned, and she faced Diana again. "Tony thinks we need to tell Bryant you're working too hard and he should make you take a vacation for a few more days."

Her frown turned to a scowl. Despite the fact that it was an excellent idea, she didn't like her team talking about her behind her back. She pointed at Tony. "Shut up, you."

From the end of the table, Kayleigh yelled. "They're right. You should totally go away for a couple of days. Far, far away. Hell, make it a week."

Diana banged her forehead gently on the table, once, twice, then a third time for luck, and looked at Bryant, who tried and utterly failed to contain his mirth. She glared at him, and he burst into laughter. "Shut up, you too."

He shook his head, regained control, and wiped his eyes. "You have some great people, Diana. And, actually, this isn't entirely a pleasure stop."

She frowned. "No?"

"No. You and I are wanted in DC. The committee requires a word with us. Apparently, they've been irked since the train incident but have put it off for some reason. Whatever that was, it must be all cleared up because we're officially summoned."

"There's nothing like waiting until the last minute to tell me, jerk." She grinned as she said it, not at all unhappy with the idea of a trip to DC with Bryant.

He took a delaying bite of brisket, followed by a long drink of his beer before he responded. "We were having a good time. I didn't want to ruin it. If I had realized how excited everyone would be to get rid of you, though, I definitely would have said something sooner."

"Again, to clarify, you're a jerk."

"So I've been told, mainly by you."

She grinned. "Well, I am an expert on your particular brand of jerkiness."

He grinned in return. "And yet you keep coming back for more. Why do you think that is?"

Diana didn't rise to the bait. Cara, who clearly had listened the entire time, jumped into the empty conversational space with a voice that carried across the entire room. "The boss is embarrassed to admit it, but she's totally superficial, and you do have a nice ass." There was a moment of shocked silence from the team before everyone burst into laughter except Diana, who was busy banging her head on the table again.

Diana, Kayleigh, Bryant, and Rath were the last to leave the restaurant. Darkness had truly fallen, and she had the feeling that the regional SAC still wanted to talk, so she threw her keys to her human roommate. "Be gentle with my Mustang, woman, and make sure the short trouble-maker buckles up."

The tech's eyes sparkled before she spun and skipped away, the troll at her side. "Let's go before she changes her mind. She never lets me drive." There was a pause as Rath said something Diana couldn't hear, then the blonde's laughing voice carried to her. "I am not reckless. I am an excellent driver. That was the other person's mistake. Both times."

Diana shook her head, and Bryant laughed. He asked, "What's it like, living with those two?"

She grinned. "Actually, it's great. Rath enjoys having another friend around, there are more people to take care of Max, and I feel more secure knowing that her systems are watching the house. Plus, Kayleigh seems to enjoy the company. I get the feeling that she could be a hermit if someone didn't push her out of her spaces every now and again."

He nodded. "That's basically the reputation she had in

DC—really hard worker, very focused, always at HQ. It's good to see her flying a little freer up here."

They crossed the big street that ran alongside the river and stopped at the railing that overlooked the water. On the opposite shore, the moon hung almost perfectly over the baseball stadium. The lights were on, and they could vaguely hear the murmur of the crowd in the distance.

Diana bumped him gently as they stood side by side, looking out at the opposite shore. "What's the deal, Bryant? You're not really you, lately. Is it something I did or didn't do?"

"Nah." He kept his gaze locked forward. "You're good. I'm just...worried, I guess."

"About what?"

He sighed. "About you. About your team. About the remains of the Hartford office. About everyone, honestly. I'm in charge, but I'm not actually able to do much other than run around and offer advice." He exhaled another sigh. "To be honest, it's as frustrating as hell."

She turned and leaned her back against the railing. A slightly taller person could put their elbows up on it and look really cool, but she rarely wore heels anymore since one never knew when trouble would break and so didn't quite have the reach without them. She didn't invade his privacy by looking at him directly but gazed at the city lights instead. "I can understand that. But you're doing what you're supposed to do. What we all need you to do. You'll have to trust us to handle our stuff while you handle yours."

"That didn't work out so well in Hartford."

Now she did look at him and saw the pain in his eyes. "Listen, dumbass. You know in your heart of hearts that nothing you could have done would have prevented that, short of future-telling or time-traveling. If you have those abilities, to hell with you for not sharing the winning lottery numbers." That drew a pained laugh from him. "But otherwise, suck it up, Cinderella. Get out of your fantasies and back into the game."

He looked at her. "You're a hard-ass sometimes, Sheen."

She laughed. "Only towards morons who need a kick in theirs, Bates." She pointed ahead. "Up there is a really nice bar at the top of that tall building. What do you say we take a nice relaxing walk over there, have a drink or four, and catch a Lyft back to my place?"

He raised an eyebrow. "Diana, are you suggesting we should spend the night together?"

She laughed. "In the same house, yes. You get the couch. And you'll make breakfast while I pack for DC since you gave me zero notice. Jerk."

The grin that spread across his face showed that his bad mood had been banished. "Deal. But you buy the first round."

"You probably won't get past the first round, lightweight."

"Oh, please. In this, as in all things, you stand no chance against me."

"Those are fighting words, BC. I don't think you're ready for this." She gestured at herself and struck a dramatic pose.

He laughed. "Bring it on, sister." She strode forward and

forced him to jog to catch up, his chuckles a welcome sound.

This superficial nonsense is over. It's time for you to learn who you're really dealing with, Bryant Classified. Starting tonight. In bourbon, Veritas.

CHAPTER SIXTEEN

They were at the airport an hour and a half before the seven am flight to DC, the only one that would get them there in time to meet with the senators at ten-thirty. Bryant had access to the executive lounge, so they managed fancy coffees—a latte for her, a double shot of espresso for him—and still boarded before the doors closed.

It was a smallish plane with only a few rows of two seats on each side and was empty enough that they each had two to themselves and conversed across the aisle. She leaned toward him and asked, "So, what exactly are we discussing with the oversight committee?"

He sighed and shook his head. "For the hundredth time, I don't know. They called. We answer. That's the entire interaction so far."

"Will that wench be there?"

He barked a laugh. "Do you mean Senator Cyphret?"

"Senator evil manipulative bag of snakes, should be."

"I'd suggest not calling her that to her face."

Diana grinned. "Why not? It might do her some good. I bet nobody calls her on anything."

His expression turned serious. "It's always possible that you'll find yourself on the street—or worse, in the Cube or something—if you push a senator the wrong way. They tend to be very experienced at the kind of games we're bad at, given our preference for direct action."

The corners of her mouth curved down. "They have that much power?"

He nodded. "They do. They really, really do. Most of them are ethical enough not to take it that far since eventually, they'd probably face some kind of consequences for it. But Janet Cyphret...well, I'm not sure about either part. She might do it, and she might get away with it."

"Gotcha. Mental note: don't tick off the senators. Yes, ma'am, no, sir, how high should I jump?"

"Now you have it."

"Sometimes, I think the magic we really need is mind control. Does that exist?"

Their discussion was interrupted by the steward asking for their drink choices. Both selected a Bloody Mary without alcohol. When they had some semblance of privacy again, Bryant picked up the paused conversation. "There's been a case or two, most recently, some scumbag out in LA. But mental powers aren't usually all that effective against magicals, so once the attempt is detected by someone with enough power, it's basically game over." He turned to look her in the eye. "And, of course, we have no guarantee that the senators on the committee are non-magical, even though our research so far suggests they're purely human."

"Well, if Cyphret has arcane powers, they're all evil and nasty. Probably shadow. Tentacles, I bet. Ew." She shuddered dramatically. "Hey, what if I waited at the house while you went and met with the committee?"

He shook his head. "You've been requested specifically. Apparently, you're important and stuff now."

Diana rolled her eyes. "Awesome. This is totally the career I've always wanted. Thank you so much, Bryant, for making it a reality."

He laughed. "You were warned. Fully warned. Don't whine now if you regret your choice."

She closed her eyes and shrugged to try to get comfortable. "The only thing I regret is the third round of drinks last night. Now be quiet while I get myself in the right headspace to meet the senators." *Do not incinerate the oversight committee. Do not incinerate the oversight committee. Do not...*

They were in the same conference room as before but had entered through a different building, separated by several minutes each and wearing featureless business attire as a disguise. Again, there was no coffee and nothing on the walls except a pair of whiteboards and a display. Diana felt entirely unlike herself in the navy suit and low heels. Both Taggart and Bryant wore theirs like they were born to it. *I guess sometimes having no style is a benefit.* She held in both her amusement and her annoyance as the senators filed in moments after they had taken their own seats.

It was the same foursome as before. The pro-ARES

politicos were Sam Somers and Aaron Finley. The anti-ARES jerks were Janet Cyphret and Winston Tomassi. They were all dressed in the politician uniform—dark suits, patriotic colors, and flag pins, one and all. Finley gave them a small head shake as he sat down and looked concerned.

Cyphret set the tone for the meeting with her first words. The woman's beauty was on display again, the suit she wore probably as expensive as any ten things in the fancy side of Diana's closet combined, and her dark hair fell in perfect waves around her flawless face. She had a slight southern accent, whether a put-on for her constituents in South Carolina or real, Diana was unequipped to judge. All she knew was that everything about the woman was annoying, including her happy little Dixie lilt. "So, Agents, we're gathered again in the wake of one of your failures." The senator shook her head in false sadness. "It seems like that's all your agency can manage of late."

Carson Taggart opened his mouth, and she raised a palm to stop him. "Special Agent in Charge Taggart, I have not yet asked a question, so there is nothing for you to say." The man blinked as if slapped, and Diana touched his wrist under the table. She narrowed her eyes and concentrated on the other woman in the hope that her magic warning system would give her something to confirm or deny that she had powers, but to no avail. *That's more a Sloan thing, anyway. I should try to get him into one of these meetings.* She made a mental note to talk to the others about that idea.

Cyphret nodded as the ARES leader remained silent and continued her opening remarks. "You failed to stop the attack on the Army transport, you failed to capture all the enemy leaders, and you failed to keep them from stealing the item you were supposed to protect. Along the way, several Army guards died." Diana was the one who bristled this time at the entirely inappropriate retelling of the assault on the train. Bryant kicked her, and she schooled her face back to neutrality.

The other woman had seen her expression, judging by the shark's grin that covered her face. "Senator Tomassi, do you have anything you'd like to add?"

The neutral-toned Louisiana politician was the scion of a family that had made its money the old-fashioned way through government construction and service contracts involving prisons south of the Mason-Dixon line. He was a perfect male counterpart to Cyphret. *They should be on a yacht in the Mediterranean or something, sipping champagne in the sun.* Diana shook her head at the image in her mind.

He drawled, "Nothing other than to remind everyone that at our last meeting we discussed leadership changes but didn't act on the idea. Perhaps it's time to rectify that error."

The agents had caught onto the game and remained silent, expecting that the female senator would now ask the others to speak. Instead, she looked directly at Diana. "Why did you not intercept the train sooner, before the guards aboard were attacked?"

"We contacted the Army. They told us to mind our own business. Thus, we were unable to intervene until the enemy arrived. We were prevented from earlier action by the rules that govern our operations—the rules your committee have put into place." She shrugged. "Had I possessed full authority, I would have stopped the train as soon as we knew about the threat."

The woman waved her hand. "Impractical. We can't overreact to every one of your organization's hunches." She turned to Taggart. "Do you confirm this story?" He nodded but didn't speak. Cyphret sighed. "Fine, then. Explain, if you would, Agent Sheen, how you came to lose the very thing you tried to preserve."

Answers flitted through Diana's mind one after the next, most of them profane and some deeply so. She found the neutral path between sarcasm and honesty and walked it carefully. "With respect, Senator, it is very easy to second-guess an action afterward. In the moment, our strategy was sound, and would have been successful, in fact, had the enemy not made the unexpected move of sacrificing the leader."

Tomassi quipped in a low voice, "Perhaps that's something our teams should try more often." He shared a dark chuckle with Cyphret. Somers looked angry, and Finley maintained the bored expression he had worn since the beginning of the meeting.

Cyphret shook her head. "So, what you're saying is that your team were defeated by an unexpected tactic. Perhaps Winston is right and we do need better leadership."

Bryant intervened. "I am confident that Agent Sheen and her people acted optimally in all respects, Senator. I have reviewed all the data from the battle, and there is nothing more they could have done. The only action that might have changed the outcome was to have allowed the agents to board earlier and defend against the initial attack, rather than coming in after."

The senator turned on him with a wicked frown. "Agent Bates, we haven't even begun to discuss your failures. Would you care to explain how the ARES locations in Buffalo and Hartford met such dramatic reversals?"

Diana had never seen a look as hard and menacing from Bryant as the one that grew on his face in response to the question. She tensed her muscles, ready to intervene if he did something crazy like jump at the woman. Cyphret seemed to sense the danger. She leaned back in her chair and shifted slightly toward where Tomassi sat.

Bryant, however, mastered himself and spoke in a rough tone. "Clearly, there is an information security problem at the highest levels of the organization, Senator. Our enemies seem to know things they shouldn't. Rest assured, we are working on this matter with all our available resources and will act accordingly once we've gathered appropriate evidence." She heard the threat in every word, and by the way that Cyphret and Tomassi paled suddenly, they did too.

Guilty consciences, Senators? If there is a leak, I really, really hope it's both of you so we can throw you into prison cells right next to each other.

Finley slipped into that moment and took the conversation in a different and more productive direction, and the pair of antagonists were more or less professional for the rest of the meeting. Bryant's face never lost its hard expression, though, and Diana looked forward to helping him find the leak and to assist in plugging it with a level of violent vengeance appropriate to the crime.

Nehlan waited outside the building where the enemy agents were meeting. The elf was unhappy to be on Earth and deeply frustrated that his superior had not permitted him to call upon one of his own underlings for this task. "It's too important, Nehlan," he had said, followed by, "This is vital, Nehlan."

Yes, we'll see how vital it all is when your magical essence is added to my necklace. He had already decided to betray his master, to withhold the antidote and allow the poison to do its work. Anyone from the council would be better as a boss, given the attitude the wizard now held toward him.

He was wrapped in illusion, of course, and had taken on the guise of an elderly man who sat alone. The elf had scowled away several efforts by others to speak to him and kept his attention focused on the door the woman had entered through hours before. The plan had been worked out in advance and the tracer spell was ready. He'd only needed the time and the place. Their contacts had provided both. Now, it was merely a matter of waiting for her to appear.

He had requested permission to simply kill her and be done with it, but no, that was not to be. His master wanted to make a statement of one kind or another—or relished the drama of the act or some such nonsense. Nehlan snorted to himself.

Fools. All of them fools. It's unfortunate that they do not see that the most direct path is almost always the best path. His subordinate Kergar had died at the hands of the woman, a loss that still rankled. Not due to the absence of that particular being, no, but what the dwarf had represented— the projection of the elf's power on this accursed planet.

She stepped out, part of a trio in similar outfits. The older one separated and strode away, and the woman and the man who'd been seen in her company previously walked past about ten feet away. He staggered up and lurched forward a little, like an old man would, muttered the incantation, and waved his fingers at her. He targeted the purse she carried on her shoulder as he felt it was safer to place a spell on the bag rather than directly on her.

The woman stopped and looked back suddenly, and he gave her a gap-toothed smile before he tottered away in a different direction and mumbled incoherently all the while. She continued to gaze around, then shrugged and resumed her journey.

Soon, woman. Soon, you will get what's due to you. He changed direction and began the long walk to the nearest secluded spot, already thinking of the meal that awaited him at his bunker deep in an Oriceran forest and away from the horrible beings that surrounded him on this planet. *When the tracking spell stops moving and darkness falls, you will be mine.*

CHAPTER SEVENTEEN

Being back at her old MMA studio as Lisa's guest, rather than the other way around, was utterly bizarre. *A sign of how things have changed for us both, I guess.* She tied her belt in place and turned to see her best friend doing the same. There was a sparkle at her neck, and Diana laughed.

She snagged her half-heart necklace and held it up to Lisa. With a grin, the other woman extracted her own and completed the symbol and the words *Best Friends*. They both tucked them away with smiles on their faces.

Lisa pointed at her. "Don't embarrass me." Diana remembered the times she'd said the same and shook her head.

"I've missed you, you idiot."

"Me too. Witch."

"Wench."

"Shut up and get in there." Lisa pushed her out of the dressing room and into the main space of the dojo. She bowed, stepped on the mat, and began warming up. She noticed right away that while her kicks and punches were as powerful as before, her flexibility had decreased since she'd headed north. *Dammit. Not enough training simply for the sake of training. I need to do more stretching or something.* She and Rath had done evening yoga in front of the television for a while, but things got busy and their house was destroyed, and... *And then and then and then. Excuses, all of it. Get your act together, doofus.*

Lisa broke her concentration when she launched a kick that stopped an inch from Diana's nose. Her level of trust in this familiar space was such that she didn't react, having given and received similar attacks countless times over the years. "Good one. You're improving. Hella slow, but there's progress."

Her friend extended both middle fingers but hid them quickly behind her back as the school's senior teacher and owner appeared out of nowhere. He was tall, very dark skinned, and movie-star handsome. *Hey, I'm not actually his student anymore. The no dating in the dojo rule doesn't apply.* Diana gave him a flirty grin, even though she'd never really try to get between him and his also-a-kick-ass-black-belt wife. "Hello, Jackson."

"Welcome back, Diana." His voice was deep and sexy, and she still enjoyed the sound of it exactly as she always had. "Your friend there is basically trouble on two legs."

She laughed and stuck her tongue out at Lisa, who fell backward onto the mat with her arms spread wide as if she'd been killed. "Right? I'm surprised you haven't kicked her skinny ass out of here yet."

He gave a slow smile. "There's a place here for anyone

who wants to train, regardless of booty size. You know that."

She laughed again. "I do indeed. That's the thing I've always liked best about you. Come one, come all."

He nodded and raised a fist, and she bumped it. *Just like old times.* He wandered over to the next set of pupils and she took the few steps to stand over Lisa. "Get up, slacker."

"Go away. I'm dead. You killed me. Seriously. Your flirting skills are so terrible they actually stopped my heart."

The assistant instructors clapped to summon the students to line up, and Lisa bolted up like a rocket to run to her place. Diana was still senior by belt rank, so she took her place higher up in the order. The teachers led them through a brisk warmup, then separated them into sparring pairs. Everyone hurried to don their combat gear, which consisted of half-gloves that only protected the knuckles from punches, shin guards, and foot protection in case someone failed to stop their blow early enough.

Lisa had pulled some strings to put them together and lined up across from Diana. An instructor senior to them both watched over their bout. He was no-nonsense and towered over them both. "No groundwork until I call it."

They nodded, and her opponent grinned through her mouthpiece. "You're going down, cupcake."

Diana's laugh was poorly timed, as the man started the match before she was ready. Lisa's first kick flashed in her face, and Diana guided it past. She stepped in to discover that the real attack was a spinning sidekick that tapped her on the ribs before withdrawing. *Stupid. Get your head in the game.* A part of her mind whispered magical options to her as she blocked, kicked, and punched. She wasn't sure whether to be happy or upset that her arcane abilities had become so entwined with her physical ones.

Lisa's foot was in the air for a round kick to the face when the instructor set them free for groundwork with a yell. Diana grinned and grabbed the leg, then stepped in to knock Lisa off balance with a body block. The woman fell, and Diana made sure to land on top of her. The elbow that would normally have struck Lisa's solar plexus poked into her stomach instead at only partial force but still drove her breath away for an instant.

She didn't realize it was a trap until her friend had locked out her arm and wrapped her legs around her knee. Lisa bent against the elbow and Diana tapped the mat with a grin. She rolled off and clapped as the other woman rose. "Damn, girl, nice job!"

The blonde nodded. "I am awesome."

It struck her for the first time how similar Lisa was to Kayleigh. They shared a sassy attitude that encapsulated an optimism she envied. Her mind wasn't wired for that sort of relentless positivity, apparently. *Which is probably why I'm drawn to them both when you come right down to it.*

She shook the thoughts away with a grin. "Okay, awesome woman, let's see if you can do it twice."

They sat at the bar of the Beagle in the same chairs they used to virtually own. Diana had been shocked to find them vacant when they arrived but caught the wink the bartender threw at her friend and realized she must have arranged it in advance. Lisa ordered, but Diana didn't get the chance to speak before Julia appeared and gave her a glass and a hug. A taste of the drink proved that the server's skills in selecting beers she'd like had not atrophied, and she thanked the woman, who retreated into the crowd.

Lisa shook her head. "This place never changes. I don't come here nearly as often since you moved away."

"Where do you go instead?"

She shrugged. "Nowhere, really. It turns out, now that I have a nice house that's not under and over annoying neighbors, I like chilling at home."

"Not alone, I hope."

She laughed. "Not always. But I'm a little gun-shy after Steve, to be honest. I don't get serious as quickly as I used to."

Diana swiveled to lean one elbow on the bar and face her. "That might be a good thing, given your checkered past."

She made a face at the insult but sounded okay with the situation. "Agreed. I think for a while there, I believed I needed another person in order to be happy. Now, I feel like I can probably be happy either way. Not that I'm closing the door or anything. Especially if Jackson ever leaves his wife. Damn, that man is gorgeous."

"You are not kidding." Diana laughed. "But maybe the dojo should be a refuge for you like it was for me."

She nodded. "I get it, now. I mean, I always got it, but before I dated Kenneth and made things at the school uncomfortable for a while, I hadn't really realized what having that safe space to simply focus on me was all about. Now I do, and I want to keep that protected."

Yeah. It would be nice to have that again sometime. But there's stuff to do before that can happen. She grinned. "Rath will be so impressed when he hears you were able to take me down once." The rest of the bouts had all gone Diana's way as a result of her depth of experience both in and out of the training space.

Lisa pouted. "You could have let me win at least once more so everyone didn't think it was a fluke." Her pout evaporated into a relaxed giggle.

"First, I never let anyone win. It's not in me. Second, no one paid any attention. And third, someone watching you train would know you're the real deal."

"Honest?"

"Cross my heart." She touched the necklace, and Lisa laughed.

"I went past one of those vending machine stands in the movie theatre—the ones with the candy and the stupid trinkets and stuff—and there was a box that had jewelry for a dollar. I happened to have four quarters, and I thought I'd give whatever came out to one of the kids hanging out nearby. But that was what I got, and I decided it was a sign that it was meant for the two of us."

"Big spender, you."

She laughed. "You know it, sister."

"Are you a partner yet?"

Lisa frowned and motioned for a refill of their drinks. "No. And it's looking more and more like I won't ever be. I tell you, there's something happening there. I have no clue what it is. Hell, maybe all the partners are having affairs or are in a polycule or involved in some swinger group and they simply don't want to 'fess up. But it's like secrets on top of secrets now." She took the new drink as it arrived and swallowed a third of it. "I really thought I would be there forever, but these days, I honestly doubt it."

Diana's spirit dropped a little, even though Lisa seemed less upset that she would be if the situation were reversed. "I get the secrets thing. When we're someplace private, remind me to tell you about the senators. They suck, with a capital S."

Lisa raised her glass. "To sharing secrets, but only with those we trust."

Diana clinked it. "To best friends."

At the corner of the bar, unobserved by the two women, a man in a business suit watched them using a hidden camera on his phone that pointed sideways instead of forward. He'd been ordered to track them while the brunette was in town and deliver all the information he gathered to his boss, who would then send it on to his boss. The person at the top of the chain was a mystery to him. All he knew was that his superior referred to him as Spock when they talked about him, and always with a laugh.

He recorded the time they entered and noted that they were on their second drink. His fingers moved rapidly as he made a show of texting and tried to portray himself as a man waiting for a date and, eventually, a man who was stood up by his date, if needed. When the women left, he followed a couple of minutes after and saw them climb into the blonde woman's car. They headed a few blocks up and took a turn, and he smiled.

He called his boss, who picked up after a single ring. "They're on the way home to the location you mentioned earlier."

"Perfect. Our part is done. Come on down and have a drink."

He killed the call and put the phone back in his pocket with one last look in the direction the women had gone. *I don't know what's in store for them, or when it's supposed to happen, but I can't imagine it'll be good. It's too bad, too, because they're both fine-lookin' ladies.*

CHAPTER EIGHTEEN

With Diana out of town, Rath and Kayleigh had spent quality time together, both at the office and at home, and discussed his particular needs for gear. He had pushed for a suit of armor like Iron Man's—the cool one that came out of the briefcase in the second movie—and had evidently decided that he could wear something that would hold it. *At least until nanotechnology is ready for Iron Troll.*

Kayleigh had suggested it might be something of an overreach given their budget and staffing, and Rath had grudgingly surrendered on the matter during their drive to the HQ building. Once they were comfortably seated in her domain, the conversation turned to the flight gear. The tech asked, "So, is the interface between Gwen and the equipment fast enough? The data I've reviewed looks good."

He nodded. "All things Gwen are shiny."

"Are any improvements needed?" She smiled.

"More grenades."

Kayleigh shook her head. "You'd have to give something up for them. There's no space and no weight to spare." She'd suggested he might want to remain a touch smaller so the wings could carry more load. Rath was unwilling to change from what he considered optimal, so they'd moved on. "Okay, how about the grappling hook?"

The troll shrugged. "Cables are a little floppy. Otherwise fine."

"Yeah, that has been a problem for everyone. I think I have a solution for them but I'm not sure how we can do that for you. Creating a breakaway tunic is more difficult than it seems."

"Velcro. Works everywhere else."

She nodded. "That's the idea, but you're last on the list for that, I'm afraid. It's a minor issue anyway, right?"

"Yep."

"Okay…so AI, flight, and grapnel gun are all good. Three boxes checked. How are the batons?"

"Bigger shock is great. Fewer shocks is not awesome."

The tech shrugged. "It's all about the weight. If you want to carry more batteries, I can make the charges last longer."

He shook his head. "Have to be able to move."

"Then you get what you get. Quit complaining." They laughed together. She pulled out a wide black strap secured with Velcro at the front and a host of other things attached. "But I have done some work to optimize your utility belt, so that's something." He leaned forward eagerly as she spread it flat on the table between them. "We still have the essentials. Here and here are the loops for your holsters. Flashlight, zip-ties, air supply for the grapnel gun, and comm repeater are all in the usual places. I've managed to shrink version two of the compressor a little."

Rath nodded. "Excellent. Every bit helps."

She gave him a smile in return. "That's what I like about you. Always looking on the bright side of things."

"All problems can be solved with Maximum Effort."

"From *Serenity* to *Deadpool*. Quite a shift there, my friend." She shook her head and pointed at an item on the belt. "This is an even smaller version of the computer interface I designed for the others. If you use it, you'll need to stay reasonably close as it doesn't have the range." She looked up. "Tradeoffs, right? Always tradeoffs."

He nodded, and she slid the device back into its pouch and pushed the Velcro seal down to secure it. She retrieved a flat black rectangle and showed it to him. "I've been concerned that you don't have a fallback weapon like the others, but clearly, a Ruger isn't the proper choice size-wise. I asked Ems for help, and he created this." She handed it over.

Rath accepted it and turned the object over in his palms. It wasn't particularly heavy but was clearly composed of metal. Two buttons adorned the top, left and right near one end, and a groove that a curved finger fit into perfectly had been shaped on the underside.

Kayleigh pointed at the front. "You have two shots. The range is fairly short since the barrels are so small. The indentation in the bottom is the safety and it must be filled to fire. Pressing the button shoots. It takes standard anti-magic rounds."

"Ooh. Nice."

Kayleigh looked uncomfortable. "Be careful. It's gone

through a fair amount of testing, of course, but is probably less safe than a larger gun would be."

He nodded. "Gotcha. Thanks to Emerson."

"I'll tell him you said so." She accepted it from him and slid it into its narrow pouch, then pointed at two other thin receptacles. "For potions, if Diana ever gets her act together and finds you some." She sighed. "I know. It's not her fault. Troll physiology is different. But you'd think that since the damn things are magical and you're magical, acquiring one would be easier rather than harder."

Rath tilted his head. "Are you okay?"

The tech crossed her arms on the table, set her chin on them, and looked him in the eye. "I'm fine. But sometimes, it's a little hard to be safe here when y'all are out there and risk your lives. I want to be sure you're as protected as possible."

"Doing all you can."

"Yeah. I know. But I'm coming to the uncomfortable conclusion that I might not be able to handle all this myself, despite my total awesomeness and all."

The troll laughed, and after a moment, she joined in. He patted her on the arm. "It takes a village. Not a Batman." Her chuckles turned into real laughter and she raised her head again.

"All right, movie man, I get your point. So, we've been over the holdout pistol. It doesn't have a field reload—you basically have to take it apart to rearm it. So use it wisely." He nodded. "One last item for the belt, and I think you'll like it." She retrieved a thin tube, about as big as a collapsed baton, with a cap on one end, a hole on the other, and a button on the top. "You wanted an invisible tracking method and you got an invisible tracking method." She pointed the open side toward the far wall and pressed the button. There was a soft puff of air, then nothing. She handed him another device, which resembled a half-size smartphone. On the screen was a map with a small dot.

"Nice. Truly invisible?"

She shook her head. "We can see the trace with our glasses as long as they're in the proper mode. It's a harmless radioactive liquid. The carrier evaporates almost immediately when the tiny bubbles that contain it burst and leave the signature behind. You have to be reasonably close to detect it, and the residue only lasts an hour or so, but it'll do what you want. I'll upgrade the drones as they cycle through maintenance to add detection capability. They should provide good coverage once we have them all reconfigured."

He nodded. "Excellent. Could not be better."

She grinned. "Oh, you're wrong there, it could be better. Which is why I made these for you." She reached under the desk and pulled out a boot, which looked like it would reach just under his knee. "Yes, I know, weight. This is obviously only one of a pair. But they're really light, all things considered. They have armor plates on the shin and instep to make your kicks hurt more. Throwing knives are tucked in the back, just in case. But neither of those is the best part. In fact, there are two best parts."

She set it down on the desk between them, grabbed the sides, and pulled. It telescoped apart and the metal frame extended in all directions. "They'll grow with you, unlike the rest of your gear, if you need to go big." Rath reached out to touch it, impressed at the construction.

"Still strong?"

Kayleigh shrugged. "Not as strong as when in compact mode but still substantial enough that they shouldn't fail under most normal situations. And yes, normal includes kicking and punching and jumping and all the other crazy stuff you people do." She wore a wide grin now, and he couldn't help smiling with her. *She's happiest when she's doing good things for us. A perfect teammate.* The push of a button on the side shrank it down to a size appropriate for his most common form again.

She paused and looked him in the eye. "Here's the best part. And before I show you, know that Diana will likely hate this, and we'll probably have to work together to convince her that it's a safe thing and a good idea." She grabbed the matching boot from under the desk and set the two beside one another, then snapped the inner sides of the heels together like Dorothy clicking her ruby slippers.

A pop sounded and both boots bounced up simultaneously. Rath put his cheek on the desk to look, and his eyes widened. "You didn't."

"I did."

He grinned. "Roller troll! How many wheels?"

"Four on each, big enough to keep you moving but not enough to hinder you setting down your toe or your heel. You'll need to practice with them." He nodded and pushed back the urge to grab the boots and put them on right there. "Also, they're wireless, so Gwen can deploy or retract them for you if needed."

"Amazing. Awesome." He looked toward the door, and Kayleigh laughed.

"Take them and go. I'd suggest practicing in the tunnel. It's fairly flat and there isn't too much stuff around to destroy if you crash into it."

He snatched the boots and hugged them to his chest, then turned to the tech. "Thank you."

She waved at him. "Get out and quit bothering me. I have work to do." She couldn't hide the huge grin on her face, though, and Rath knew she felt good about this accomplishment. As he left the room, he shouted "I feel the need. The need for speed!" Kayleigh's groan followed him into the hall.

CHAPTER NINETEEN

Rath checked with Max to ensure that the new belt wasn't too heavy for him, but the dog seemed fine with it and barked happily once he was fully outfitted. The Borzoi's harness now held the quick-draw holsters for his batons, tie-downs for his folded-over utility belt, and the collar rings for the troll to use when riding. His interface necklace was carefully stored in a pouch on the side with his full-sized comm gear.

They were running at the moment, purely for fun. The world passed by in a blur as Max dashed along in the grass between the University buildings, headed for the antique shop again. Rath looked forward to seeing Manny and had received an invitation to visit by actual mail at the house. Diana had asked how anyone knew his address, and he'd shrugged. "Professor Charlotte has her ways." *Or maybe Emanuel considered me another lost thing he somehow magically found, and the address is part of that.*

In any case, the man had expressed a desire to see him whenever his schedule allowed, and today was mostly free now that Rath had tired of testing his new boots in the parking garage tunnel. He regretted that they were too heavy for Max but knew they'd be valuable additions to his nighttime solo patrols. As they emerged onto the sidewalk on the far side of their shortcut, a small chime sounded in his earpiece.

Rath frowned and jumped down. He grew to his three-foot size, put away his tiny earbuds, and donned his headset and AI interface. As soon as he settled it into place, Gwen's feminine tones announced, "There's a problem in your area."

She's never alerted me like this before. That's weird. I thought when she wasn't being worn, she wasn't active. Guess not. "What is?"

"Silent alarms from the bank nearby. One indicates a break-in. The other says there are hostages involved."

"Not good."

"Agreed. The authorities are on their way."

He turned to his partner. "Should probably leave it to police. Right?"

The dog growled, as clear a negative as Rath had ever received from him.

"Excellent. Agree. We go in." He looked around. "Gwen, which direction?"

"Thirty-seven degrees to the right, two blocks. That will bring you in from the back of the building."

"Perfect." He donned his belt, pulled the batons free from the dog's carrier, and slid them into the holsters on each leg. "Let's move."

Rath ran toward the bank. The AI had provided a vector that routed him out of sight of the public, so he didn't need to worry about anyone acting strangely over a speedy troll. Max kept up without a problem and they were soon at the building. He frowned at the back door which had no apparent means of entry. "Gwen?"

"Scanning." He tapped his foot during the slight pause that followed. "Scan complete. There is an electronic keypad hidden under a metal plate that requires a key to open. It is likely the access to unlock the door."

He frowned. "Connect to Kayleigh."

After another pause, the tech spoke in his headphones. "What's up, Rath?"

"Bank break-in. Going to help. Need lock assist."

"Should you do that? Wait, never mind." Like Diana, the technician was sometimes a little overprotective. And, like Diana, she was working on it. "We're talking something electronic, right? Because I can't do much for you otherwise."

"Yep."

"Okay, first things first. Pull out the computer block." He did, and she chuckled. "Wow. The exterior security camera network is lame. They're offline already, anyway. Put the device as close as you can and stay beside it." Rath crossed the small alley that ran between his hiding place and the bank's rear entry and placed the compact black rectangle against the metal panel. "Okay, I have the electronics. Let's see if I can get in there." Her fingers tapped on a keyboard, the only sound in the short silence that ensued. "Sheesh, damn, that thing's ancient. It's not hackable. But it might be possible to short it out. Is this the only option?"

He looked at the featureless wall above him and knew

he couldn't go in the front entrance because they'd be watching it. Not to mention the police and probably TV people. "Yep."

"Okay. Put the block away so you don't hurt it and strike the plate with both your batons. It has a reasonable chance to work. This is exactly why most banks upgraded their systems a decade ago." He pictured her shaking her head in disgust, and it made him smile. He stowed the device and flicked his weapons open, placed them against the panel, and pressed the buttons together.

After the loud snap when they activated, the door clicked. Rath pulled on it, and it swung free. "I'm in."

Kayleigh's concern was clear. "Don't do anything stupid, okay? Diana would never forgive either of us."

"No worries. Only going to help if I can."

"You're not Batman, remember."

"Iron Troll."

"Not even. Far more squishy than that."

He dropped the banter as he snuck inside and Max padded along behind him. Rath trusted that Gwen and Kayleigh would let him know if there were electronic alarms or traps and focused on remaining stealthy. He crept through several office areas, then slipped into the last one to peek around the corner into the lobby.

The bank had a three-story ceiling with a transparent roof. *Couldn't be glass. That would be really stupid.* A metal grid crossed it about halfway up to provide support for the fancy lights that hung down on chains. The result was a brightly lit marble public area with ancient-looking barred teller stations. Three men in masks were positioned behind a wall of innocents who stood near the front windows.

Through gaps in the line, the street beyond was visible, filled with police cars flashing their red and blue strobes.

Kayleigh's voice sounded in his ear. "SWAT has arrived. I'm watching and listening on the police feeds, and I've sent a drone your way. They'll call to negotiate soon." Rath didn't reply and simply kept his eyes and ears open.

One of the men gathered money from the tellers' drawers into a big duffel bag. Another had disappeared down a flight of stairs with a hostage a moment before, presumably to access a vault below. The third marched behind the cover provided by the bank patrons and kept them in line by yelling threats and promising injury to anyone who failed to obey.

The troll looked at Max, who sat quietly near him in the office. "I'll take a look downstairs. You stay here. If there's trouble, run away. If you see me wave at you, run away. If you see me pretend to clap my hands together like this"—he demonstrated—"I want you to bark and run away. Got it?" The Borzoi licked his hand once in reply, and Rath patted him on the head. "You're the best partner ever, Maxie."

Kayleigh spoke over the comm. "Police said the thieves have disabled the cameras inside the building too, so give the criminals credit for that, at least. If they only turned them off, I should be able to hack them if you get the block close enough. If they killed the power, there isn't much I can do. In a place like that, they're probably recording on VHS or Beta or something." He peered up into the corner and saw one of the rectangles with a small lens on the front and a light on the top that apparently should have been lit but was dark.

Ahead, a railing prevented people from walking into the area where the stairs led down from the opposite direction. It was an expensive-looking, ornate golden barrier, and would make what he was about to do that much more difficult. He retracted and holstered his batons, took a moment to wish he'd carried some of his night gear, especially the grapnel, then let it go. *Must live in the now. I am rooted in the me that is on this adventure.* He laughed quietly at his own joke, and as the man who gathered the money bent behind the counter, made his move.

The troll dashed forward and leapt at the barrier, gripped the top, and used it to flip over, then released it with a twist to face back the way he had come. He landed softly about three-quarters of the way down the staircase and descended the rest with quick steps so he wouldn't be seen from above. A small guard desk, unoccupied, stood off to the side of a large circular door. He ducked to put the furniture between him and the vault and peered over it.

Inside, a man in a suit opened boxes for the masked robber who transferred their contents into a wide bag. Given the lack of sophistication of the operation, the troll half expected to see a huge white dollar sign on the black sack, but it wasn't quite that cartoonish. There were no shadows to hide in, so his timing would have to be perfect. Obviously, the police couldn't move against those above without putting the innocent man in the vault in danger, so it was up to him to act.

He waited until the criminal shifted to empty the next container. In the moment his head was turned away, Rath hurtled around the desk and angled for the doorway. His feet slapped against the hard tile of the vault floor loud enough to be noticed, and the man pivoted and the gun in his near hand arced sideways toward the troll. His foe's face filled with shock as it rotated to see what approached, and Rath vaulted, led with his feet, and aimed for his target's mouth.

The man drew in a breath to shout, but the troll's heels impacted with his jaw and cut his warning short. He fell in a heap and the pistol spun from his hand to career across the vault and thunk into the containers on the far side. Rath landed beside him and pivoted to kick him in the temple so he wouldn't get up. His eyes rolled back in his head, and the troll stared at him. *Idiot. Should have had backup.* The fact that he was downstairs alone occurred to Rath, but then he grinned. *I have a partner. He's on the lookout upstairs.*

He turned to face the stunned bank employee and raised a finger to his lips. The hostage nodded and looked pale, so the troll patted the ground beside him and gestured for him to sit. He complied and ran a trembling hand through his thinning hair. Rath thought he looked a little like a younger Vincent Price from the horror film channel. He tossed a pair of nylon ties at his feet, pointed at the downed enemy, and received a nod in return.

Satisfied that the bank employee would make sure the criminal was secured, he turned away and crept into position behind the desk to study the stairs. There was nothing to see from that vantage point, unfortunately. He tapped the button to activate his mic and asked, "Update?"

Kayleigh replied instantly. "The police are on the phone with one of them. He's yelling a lot and has threatened to kill the hostages. They can't get a clean shot because he's hiding behind the civilians. They'll send some officers around to the back entrance, although they expect it'll be watched since the criminals know the police are on scene."

"Maybe not. Amateurs."

"I'll make sure they know that. Is there anything else I should tell them?"

"One downstairs. Knocked out."

"Okay, stay out of the way and let the police do their thing."

"Will." He clicked his microphone off and crept up the stairs to see what was going on. The scene was the same, although the man who had gathered the money was no longer visible. He took a couple more steps to get a better angle, but the criminal wasn't behind either of the counters. He realized that staying on the staircase was a terrible plan, but had no idea where to go since he didn't know the other enemy's location.

A loud noise at the rear of the building was immediately followed by the sound of gunfire. Rath heard noise from the street side as well and crept higher when he saw a black shadow flit across the top of the stairs. He continued and peered through the railing at an angle. The man who had been near the front now faced the back. The robber held a gun to the temple of a terrified older woman, someone probably Professor Charlotte's age. Incoherent screaming resulted in a stalemate, and the criminal threatened to kill her in thirty seconds if the police didn't leave. The officers remained in place and continued to try to reason with him.

In his ear, Kayleigh murmured, "They apprehended the second man on the way in, but they don't have a clean shot on the third one from the front. They're worried his gun might fire if their shot isn't perfect. The situation is stuck for the moment as no one will buckle."

He whispered as softly as he could, "Tell them not to react."

"Done."

Rath took a deep breath, judged the angles, and climbed carefully onto the marble banister that ran along the stairs. He walked it to the top, then turned and used it as a runway to race forward and launch as high and as far as he could. He drew his batons in mid-air, flicked the left one out to full extension, and hurled the other one down and to the right.

The metal weapon clattered on the marble floor, and the man ahead of him jerked his head around. The troll's extended baton struck the gun and shoved it away from the woman, and when the criminal pulled the trigger, the round fired harmlessly into the corner of the room. Rath careened into the robber and the railing at the same time. His adversary pitched forward on his face, and the troll flipped over the obstruction to land awkwardly on his side. He rolled left as soon as he recovered his wits, out of the way of the swarm of police officers who charged the downed thief.

He rose slowly and painfully to his feet, careful not to appear as a threat. The woman seemed stunned as she was led away by a pair of policewomen. Rath moved quietly toward the rear exit, collected Max from the office, and headed to the door. "Could have used a bark there maybe, partner. I think you need a comm." He looked back once before he exited, and one of the SWAT troopers gave him a thumbs-up. With a brief nod in response, he departed before anyone decided to stop him for a chat.

A half-hour later, he was in the antique shop drinking tea with Manny, who congratulated him on the successful operation after Rath explained why he was late. The old man looked at him with a smile in his eyes and said, "Young Troll, if the Griffins were still around, there is no question that you would be one of them."

Rath grinned and thanked him. *More like, if the Griffins were still around, they'd want to join BAM.*

CHAPTER TWENTY

The coin had begun to burn two hours before when Sarah was out handling sensitive negotiations with a supplier that had required her direct attention. Her lieutenants had both attempted to solve the issue, but the man with the weapons they needed had been steadfastly unwilling to come down to an acceptable price. He no doubt considered himself a capable businessperson, able to sense when his clients were under time pressure and take advantage of it and them.

Fortunately, the man's second in command had been far more reasonable after witnessing the shadow tentacles tear the man apart and spread the pieces around the storage garage that was their meeting place. The woman had simply removed the dress shirt she'd worn over a tank top, used a clean part of it to wipe the remains of her former boss from where they'd splashed her neck, and thrown the garment aside before she asked, "So, what would you consider an appropriate price?"

Despite the opportunity to use the new situation to

their own advantage, Sarah had stood firm on her previous offer and the bargain had been struck. The woman's underlings packed the truck for the transit to the warehouse, but formalities required her to stay and oversee the transaction to its conclusion, conscious all the while of the warmth of the metal where it lay against her chest.

She considered herself fortunate that the wizard could not—or had not chosen to—increase the heat with each minute that passed before her response. *I would have. And if I couldn't, I would have figured out how to and then done it.* She had ordered her lieutenants to call their underlings together as soon as possible, then pulled Wysse aside to drive her, leaving Mur to ride with the truck, and they had made haste to the main base. The weapons would be delivered to a holding point where their own people would then take possession of them. Secrecy was important, even from one's alleged allies.

Sarah walked calmly but with a purpose through the warehouse, already filled with the quickest responders or those who happened to be nearest when the call came. A couple of individuals offered respectful nods that she returned, but she didn't deviate from her direct path toward the steel stairs leading upward. She maintained her pace, stepped up two at a time, then closed, locked, and warded the door behind her. *With much better protection spells than Vincente ever used, that's for sure.*

It was the work of a couple of minutes to prepare both herself and the objects required for communication. She took a deep breath and arranged the strands that had come loose from her long ponytail behind her ears and slid the coin into the depression. The magic flowed upward, climbed the twisting spiral of the statuette, and formed into the form of Dreven, who was her conduit to the will of the Remembrance. *For now, anyway, until I find someone more...amenable to my particular perspective.*

His voice was deep, arrogant, and excited. "Sarah."

"Dreven, sir."

"Everything is in place, as we discussed. Are your people ready?"

She nodded. "They are on their way here as we speak."

The tiny image paced a small circle before her, its face still hidden from view. "Excellent. You must be in transit within two hours in order to meet the deadline."

"We can be. What is our objective?'

"You are to travel to Philadelphia, to a location that will be shared with you en route. At about nine-thirty, you'll mount an attack at a public event. The call will go out to scramble their Anti-Enhanced Threat force, and probably the city's Special Weapons and Tactics troops. Possibly, if we have good fortune, the Paranormal Defense Agency may make an appearance as well. When they arrive, you and your people will destroy every last one of them."

She grinned and the idea generated a wash of pleasure that started at her toes and warmed every inch of her on its way to her brain. "Thank you for this opportunity. We won't disappoint you."

He raised thin hands to lower his hood so she would be able to see his face. He grinned, a bloodlust that matched her own visible in his expression. "You must not fail. The consequences would be beyond dire. This is but the first of a series of actions, but a setback in any of them might derail the entire plan. Understand that failure will result in the elimination of any who manage to survive the encounter."

A bite of sarcasm entered her voice as she spoke. "So, in other words, come home with our shields, or on them?"

He offered a slight bow of acknowledgment, but his eyes never left hers. "As historical references go, it is apt."

She nodded. "Understood."

"Good. After this, we have something even bigger planned for your city. But more on that once you have successfully completed this task. Go now, and expect instructions when you arrive. Another underling of mine, Nehlan, will coordinate the evening's activities. Obey him as you would me."

The image vanished suddenly, and she kept her expression neutral until the statue and coin were again locked away. Then she snorted. *Obey him as I would you. As if. I will, as always, make my own choices. Hopefully, our wills will be aligned this night.*

She headed to the door to hurry the weapons shipment along. The items were required sooner than expected, which in the end was to everyone's benefit. As long as they made it to the objective when they were supposed to.

When they'd been called back only hours after the morning training session, Sloan knew something was up. It had been almost a week since the meeting he'd attended at the HQ, and most of the intervening time had been spent practicing tactical maneuvers to turn the magical and non-magical groups of Sarah's followers into a team. *Well, two sets of people who can work together for short periods, anyway. That's not really my definition of a team.*

Teddy had picked him up outside the bar since the fiction was that Tommy Ketchum couldn't yet afford his own wheels, which put him further under the power of those above him. Sloan took some consolation in the fact that they seemed to find it almost as annoying as he did. The man's decrepit sedan wheezed as it climbed the small hill to the warehouse, and the tires spun a little as they lost traction in the gravel. It knocked and pinged for several seconds after they closed the doors and started walking toward the entrance.

Inside, the atmosphere was thick with tension. Everyone had the same excited vibe, the expectation that something big was about to happen. Sloan cast about for Mur and saw him standing at the base of the stairs, speaking with the lead witch. He poked Teddy. "Look at that."

The man followed his gaze and coughed to cover the choking sound he made. He turned and faced away from them. "She gives me the creeps, man. It's like she wants to crawl into the boss's skin or something."

"Mur's?"

"Hell no. The boss boss. Sarah." He shuddered visibly as he said her name.

Sloan nodded. "I know how you feel, man. I'm totally right there with you. Any idea what's going on?"

He hadn't brought it up in the car and had simply played dumb. He guessed that Teddy was both in the dark and scared because of it, and he wasn't doing much better.

The other man shook his head. "Mur texted, said get everyone down here and be ready to move tonight."

Sloan cursed inwardly. It was a moment of decision, and he was still worried after the little witch had identified the turncoat and the big witch had brought about his demise. He pulled out the low-end smartphone he carried, called up the keypad, and dialed in a ten-digit code. The phone blanked and was now essentially bricked—no one would be able to get anything from it as the data would permanently scramble itself. It remained good for only a single thing—transmitting what it heard in tiny encrypted packets onto a specific Internet site, one monitored by Kayleigh and her AI.

If the transmission was discovered, he could say he'd picked the phone up and found it broken, which would give him some weak deniability. Any examination would conclude it was only a damaged cell trying to get a signal from the nearest tower. The feed would also act as a location beacon as the device would constantly transmit. He'd carried similar devices on undercover assignments before but had never needed to use one. *Maybe I'm overreacting. The likelihood that anyone would be capable of discovering my secret is minimal, at best.*

The black-clad witch appeared at the head of the stairs and walked down slowly. She gazed at them possessively, like they were a herd of cattle. *Or pawns on a chessboard. Likely sacrifices, either way.* She stopped halfway down, where every eye in the room would have a good look at her, and her presence was such that every eye was locked on her. Teddy nudged him, but he ignored the man and kept his gaze glued to the woman.

"People, it is finally time to put all the excellent training you've done into practice. We are called upon tonight for one of the most important tasks we have ever been given. We have the honor of making the first move in a larger offensive, and at the end of it all, there will be abundant rewards for everyone."

A half-hearted cheer rose but quickly fell silent. She didn't seem to notice the interruption. "There is some room in a couple of trucks for those who want to ride inside. Otherwise, we take individual cars. We are headed across the state to strike at an enemy that has long interfered with the actions of people of power here on Earth. Under the guise of law and order, they have repeatedly oppressed our kind, both those of us with magic and those of us who choose not to follow all of society's weak rules."

She was stirred up and spoke quicker as she delivered her speech, and the crowd responded to it. *Damn, she has charisma in proportion to her crazy. That's so not good.* He wondered if there was a way for him to slip out and had gotten as far as looking around for an exit before she said the words that sealed his immediate fate. "Get to the vehicles now. We are headed for Philadelphia, and before we leave the City of Brotherly Love…" Her tone was viciously mocking. "We will turn one of their most famous icons into nothing but rubble, dust, and blood."

CHAPTER TWENTY-ONE

Kayleigh had put the call out as soon as Sloan's phone went into ghost mode and the team was assembled to check gear and await the command to deploy. Diana was eager for the same, ready to go another round with the scary witch who'd taken charge of the criminal organization when BAM had captured their leader.

For now, though, she waited for the monitors in front of her to light up with feeds from the other essential participants in the afternoon's discussion. The one on the left illuminated first to show the concerned face of Carson Taggart, Special Agent in Charge of ARES. Next, the one on the far right activated, and she grinned to see Bryant, even in this circumstance. He responded with a smile and a professional nod. *Sure, sure, pretend to be all supervisory. After rounds of drinks with you, I know what you're really like.*

The middle display came to life with the image of a concerned-looking woman. She wore the uniform of the Philadelphia Anti-Enhanced Threat team. She had short black hair, only an inch or so on top and shaved on the sides. Diana guessed she was in her early to mid-thirties by the few lines that showed on her makeup-free face. Her features were sharp, and her entire demeanor echoed the look. "Thanks for taking the time for this call. I'm Kendra Michaeli. What's going on?"

Taggart, as the initiator of the conference, took the lead. "Our Pittsburgh bureau has received credible information that there will be an attack in your city today. All we are sure of is that it will be something big. Our intelligence intercept caught the word 'icon,' but our analysts caution that it could simply be hyperbole."

The woman nodded. "We deal with threats like this every day. What makes this one such a cause for concern?"

Bryant replied, "The nature of the opposition. They have worked on a regional basis before and attacked simultaneously in several cities. In this case, they appear to be bringing help in from other locations to act against yours. That is something you should be highly concerned about."

"Do you have any idea why?"

Diana shook her head. "All we know from our...intercepts is that the Pittsburgh group has been deployed to attack you by someone above them in the criminal hierarchy. This is the group that was responsible for the attack on the Army train a while back, so they are not a force to be taken lightly."

The woman's face settled into a scowl. "I heard about that. It sounded like a major mess from start to finish."

All three ARES agents winced, but it was her obligation to reply. "It was. There were issues. Let's all agree to blame military bureaucracy and move on from there, shall we?"

The AET officer gave a dark laugh. "Yeah, I hear you.

So, in summary, there's a team of heavy hitters who have targeted our city, probably tonight, and probably someplace notable. We have all the usual activities going on for a Friday night, plus a couple of concerts and a baseball game."

Bryant asked, "Who's playing?" *As if it matters.*

The fact that she didn't have to look up the answer kicked her up a notch in Diana's estimation. "Phillies vs. Red Sox at Citizen's, Taylor Swift at Wells Fargo, and GOT7 at BB&T."

He frowned. "What the hell is a GOT7?"

Diana laughed. "K-Pop band. Crazy popular."

"How the hell do you know that?"

"Rath likes them."

Taggart and Michaeli watched them with odd looks on their faces, and Diana returned to the topic. "It seems like any of those could be a legitimate target."

The AET officer nodded in agreement. "I'd probably assume that GOT7 is the least likely if they mentioned a Philly icon. It's technically not in the city." She held her palms up and shrugged. "Honestly, though, if we include historical monuments, there are too many to name. Not to mention museums, the aquarium, and that sort of thing."

Taggart sighed. "A plethora of options. Diana, any indication of where they might strike?"

She shook her head. "None." The Remembrance leader had made the strategically sound decision to require cell phones to be left at the warehouse. All they received now was the sound of a few caretaker hoodlums watching the place and grousing about not being included in the operation. Kayleigh was personally offended at the lack of data and was already talking loudly to anyone in proximity about implanting trackers in all of them. *We're all frustrated at the impending action and at the fact that one of our own is involved. Some of us merely have more creative ways of working it out.* She rocked her neck back and forth to crack it. *Me, I'm looking forward to shooting something. A tracker's not a bad idea for Rath, though.*

Bryant looked and sounded angry. "Okay, what can we do to upend whatever these bastards have in mind?"

Diana put a fist gently into her other open palm. "My team is down for a road trip. But we've already lost a lot of time."

Taggart nodded. "There's no way you can drive. We'll borrow a transport from the Air Force Reserve base near you and fly you in. You'll need to carry your own gear as there's no chance to have supplies routed there today." Diana glanced down and typed a quick text to Cara to instruct her to start the team packing. "DC has its own obligations tonight. Bryant, is there anyone else we might bring in?"

"Negative. They're all busy getting back on their feet." The AET officer looked confused, but no one chose to explain the comment.

"Okay, then. It's up to AET, Philly SWAT, and ARES Pittsburgh. Diana, tell your people to play nice with the other organizations, please."

She laughed at the joke. "Boss, we're always nice. Except to the enemy, of course."

Michaeli shook her head. *She probably thinks we're all totally insane. We have her fooled. We're only mostly insane.* "We'll put our ear to the ground for any clues and prepare for your arrival. Thanks in advance for helping us keep the peace."

They said their goodbyes, and the woman dropped from the call. Taggart's concern was visible on his face and audible in his tone. "I don't like this one. They've been all about acquiring magic and suddenly, they're taking a detour into domestic terrorism? It doesn't smell right."

Bryant asked, "If the orders are coming from someone on Oriceran, is it really 'domestic?' I mean, it's not international, but maybe interplanetary?"

Their boss sighed. "Bryant, I understand that you're trying to be funny to lighten the mood, but you're not good at it, so you should stop." Diana snorted, and her regional supervisor grinned. Taggart simply shook his head and looked equal parts amused and exasperated. "You people need to take this stuff more seriously."

She shrugged. "What's the point? We're doing all we can do. A little dark humor between friends soothes the soul."

He seemed about to argue, then surrendered by shifting topics. "If this is like every single other thing they've done, it won't be a one-off."

"Agreed. Everyone should be on their toes. I'll make sure the Cube and PD are aware here."

Bryant growled his frustration. "I'll warn Hartford. Do you think it's worth sending out a regional terrorism alert to make people alert for trouble?"

Taggart nodded. "I do. I'll check in with Finely to see if he agrees."

"And if he doesn't?" Diana asked.

"We'll have Bryant do it so I have deniability with the oversight committee."

The other man's voice was laced with syrupy sarcasm. "Gee, thanks, boss. It's awesome how you provide cover for us and all. Maybe you should consider becoming head of the CIA so you can show them your unique brand of support by sharing the names of all the agents with the media or something." The jibe made everyone laugh, and Taggart shook his head in disbelief.

"Every time I think you can't be more stupid, Bryant, you step up your game. It's truly amazing."

BC sounded very pleased with himself. "And worth rewarding with a raise and some additional vacation days?"

"Worth rewarding with a week training in Siberia, maybe."

"If you were head of the CIA, you could probably arrange that for him," Diana quipped,

Taggart threw his hands up in surrender. "We're done here. Diana, be safe and kick some criminal butt. Bryant, try to make yourself useful."

The call dropped, and she shook her head. "Friday, put me on intercom." A small chime acknowledged the order. "We roll out as soon as possible, people. Finish packing and get it in gear."

Forty-five minutes later, the team drove out of the garage in a caravan of SUVs filled with agents and equipment. Local PD held the intersections for them to join the highway and blocked the ramps to give them an unimpeded route to the reserve base. They pulled the four vehicles up the ramp of the C-130H Hercules transport, and Air Force personnel rushed to secure them to the deck under the shouted orders of the loadmaster.

Diana hopped out and waved her team into the jump

seats mounted in the front of the aircraft. She continued forward to talk to the pilots. "How ancient is this thing? Did you have to take it out of the actual mothballs for this mission?"

The man with the grey crewcut on the left laughed. "She's not that old. Late forties, early fifties. Age, not build year."

The younger woman in the right seat nodded as she made a mark on her checklist. "We have any number of people who spend most of their drill time making sure she's good to go. We'll get you there, no worries."

Diana grinned. "I have no doubt. I'm busting your chops, that's all. Is there anything I need to know?"

The first one spoke again. "Nope, relax and enjoy the ride. We have priority clearance for both departure and arrival and should be on the ground within two hours of wheels-up."

She patted them both on the shoulders. "You rock." When she headed back, her team had strapped in and left an open seat between Tony and Cara for her. She sighed and looked at Anik and the Air Force officers, all of whom avoided eye contact. "Does anyone want to trade seats? Anyone? Please don't make me listen to those two for the whole flight."

CHAPTER TWENTY-TWO

"Thirty minutes out," called the loadmaster from the cargo area of the plane. "Pilots say weather is clear now and you can do your thing."

Diana popped the harness holding her in her seat and strode toward the back of the transport, the rest of her team a step behind. They'd talked over the mission for most of the flight and were all as frustrated as she was about the long wait for action. Even Kayleigh, linked in through the comm equipment in the SUVs, sounded irked about the delay.

They opened the four rear compartments and withdrew the crates inside, each almost as large as the area allotted for it and requiring a pair of agents to extract it. They set the cases on the deck and strapped them down, then popped the lids to retrieve their equipment. The first held something Kayleigh had promised for a while but they hadn't had time to train or deploy in yet. Their new tunics were tight and designed to be worn under their other tops. The wiring that connected the vest capacitors to the shock gloves passed through built-in channels with a connector dangling at each end. A thin fiber-optic camera tube ran down the left inner forearm.

The neck was contoured to follow the line of the AI collars that she and Cara wore, ensuring that the devices could read their vital signs. The tunics had that capability as well, for redundancy and to track the team members who didn't have the other equipment yet. Diana twisted her arms to look at the channels and admired the way her muscles rippled through the tight material. "Kayleigh, damn, nice work."

The tech's voice was tense. "Glad you like it. All the tests have been good. Even if something goes wrong, the only loss is the shock gloves, really."

"Nothing will go wrong. Your gear is always amazing."

Tony growled and flexed in imitation of a bodybuilder to make those around him, all of whom were in better shape, laugh and tease the stocky man. He took it in stride and traded pleasant insults with them. They all slipped into their heavy knife-resistant pants and shirts and replaced their footwear with combat boots. All the street clothes went in the case, which Anik and Cara returned to the first SUV.

Next was the container full of defensive gear. Tony retrieved the shin, thigh, forearm, and upper arm guards and passed them around. As she sat to buckle them in place, Diana missed being able to help Rath into his equipment. She hadn't felt good enough about the mission to bring him along and wanted him safely away from whatever nonsense the Remembrance was up to tonight.

I guess Nylotte's warning has taken a deeper hold than I

expected, both for me and where Rath is concerned. Besides, if they saw a troll with us, they might figure out we weren't local, which could out Sloan.

She looked around at her team and thought again that they needed at least one more fighter. *And another tech, someone with magic to complement Kayleigh. And maybe a driver for the mobile armory we don't have.* She snorted to herself. *Actually, we should ask for a plane as transport and negotiate down to the truck. But one a little newer than this one.*

The aircraft bumped, no doubt in turbulence, and the team exchanged alarmed glances, then broke into shared laughter. Cara nudged Anik with her boot. "Nervous, puddy tat?"

The demolitions expert flashed a grin and looked around with wide eyes. "How did I end up here? I must have taken a wrong turn at Albuquerque."

The woman grinned. "No, you let Diana talk you into becoming a part of something ridiculously dangerous because you're an adrenaline junkie, exactly like the rest of us."

He blinked, then nodded. "Okay, actually, that's on point."

Tony nodded as well. "Yep. That says it all." He turned to face Diana. "Way to turn our dreams into nightmares, boss."

She laughed. "You're the only nightmare around here. Should we discuss the museum incident again?"

He raised his hands and spoke loudly. "So, more equipment then." He retrieved the vests and passed them out, then replaced the lid on the empty crate. They all stood to don them and assisted each other to hook the connections up between vest and tunic and thread the cables through the small grommets that had been stitched into their shirts and trousers.

The next one held their utility belts, holsters, and other straps and pouches neatly laid out in custom indentations cut into grey foam rectangles. She retrieved hers and set it on top of the case. The belt fit snugly around her waist as she snapped it closed with the thick fastener in the front. She tied the holster down to her right leg and attached the grenade-holder strap on her opposite hip. The holster for the Ruger was already in place to the left of the small of her back, and she touched it to confirm the location.

Her flashlight was on the belt, as was the thin tube for captured enemy wands. Zip-ties and magic-detecting shock cuffs rested in their own pouches. The comm repeater and remote-computer-gizmo filled out the rest of the slots, except for two magazine containers and two grenade holders. She put pepper in one and sonic in the other. The strap on her leg received two flashbangs.

The final container was filled with weapons. Diana retrieved her set, again packed into custom foam cutouts. She checked her carbine and slid home a magazine loaded with standard ammunition. The blue-striped ones filled with anti-magic bullets went into the slots on her vest, and she slipped an extra set of standard ammo into its holder on her belt. Her Glock received one of the blue-striped mags, and she secured the pistol in her holster. The remaining three magazines, two standard and one containing special presents for enemy magicals, slotted into the few empty places on chest and belt.

She raised her backup revolver and opened the cylinder

to ensure it was properly loaded with blue-dotted rounds. It was, and she closed it and stored it in its holster. Finally, she pulled out the large Bowie knife and held it up to the light to admire its edge. She bent her arm back and slid it up into its sheath, giving it the extra push needed to secure it into the grippers so it wouldn't slide free without an effort. The act of arming herself was mind-cleansing, and as always, she emerged from the process with more clarity than she entered it with.

She turned to face her team, who had grown quiet as they readied their own weapons and perhaps traversed the same mental steps that she did. They felt her gaze and faced her, one after the other, until the only sound was the shuddered vibration of the airplane's descent. "I want you all to remember something tonight. Your survival is every bit as important as the mission. Prioritize it. I'm not saying you should hide from a fight, that's not what we're about. But we can rely on AET and SWAT for support. We don't need any particular heroics from anyone at this moment."

They nodded, and she stared at them for a couple of moments more. "I'm not kidding."

Tony was the first to break into laughter, and Anik and Cara followed. The former detective patted her on the shoulder as he headed toward the front of the plane. "Very inspirational, boss. Such leadership. Much wow." Diana groaned and grabbed his hand to apply leverage and bring him back near the open cases. "Ow, ow, ow."

"You, sir, are a chucklehead. As such, you get to stow the crates. The other two can help. And don't forget your damn masks."

She snagged her own headgear from the pile. The fabric

would show only their eyes, which would be covered by their glasses and so leave the enemy with no clues to their identity and hopefully preserve the secret of their inside information. Diana strode forward and buckled herself into a seat near the loadmaster so she could at least have a few moments of peace. *Those three can sit together and annoy one another for a change. It serves them right.*

CHAPTER TWENTY-THREE

The plane bounced once as it touched the tarmac, then rolled quickly to taxi speed. The team unbuckled immediately and got into the two rearmost SUVs, Diana behind the wheel of one with Anik by her side, and Cara driving the other. When the transport stopped, the loadmaster triggered the rear ramp and waved them out as soon as it was down.

She reversed, turned, and sped down the auxiliary runway toward the gate at the end. The Air Force cleared the path for them and swung the barrier open as they approached. Friday whispered directions in her ear as she drove, and Diana spent the intervening moments setting plans for the action to come. "Kayleigh, do you receive vitals from all of us?"

The tech sounded harried. "Yes. The signals from you and Cara are the best. The sensors in the tunics are not as effective as the ones in the collars, plus your AIs are doing some processing locally."

"Okay. Is that a problem?"

"No, sorry. TMI. It's all good." The tech sighed. "It doesn't look like I'll be able to give you drone coverage. I've been trying to link up with AET's systems, but they're not willing to grant me full access and the crap connection they have given me is the next best thing to useless."

Diana laughed. "Let's hear it for inter-agency collaboration, right?"

The tech grunted dismissively. "I probably wouldn't want to let them into our computers either, but honestly, it's a messed up choice at this point."

"It's okay, Kayleigh. Chill. This is merely another mission."

"You know, it seems like that, but it also doesn't seem like that. I have a bad feeling here. There's something that's not right."

"I have that too. But the only way out is through. So I guess the question is, what can you do from there?"

She blew out a sigh. "Okay, here's what I have. I can watch your vitals, all good. I can keep you connected by comms to the other groups, also good. I'm setting that up locally for you, rather than routing the signal through here, so there should be no delay. That's easy stuff." The sound of keys clicking continued as the tech worked her systems. "No drones, because the AET techs are assholes." She paused and exhaled another sigh.

"Fine, yes, they're only doing their jobs. I get it. Okay. I've gone over the highway cams on the turnpike, and I think I may have spotted them. I can't be sure, of course, but there are a couple of trucks that have shown similar patterns of behavior often enough that Alfred's flagged them. He will keep an eye on them wherever he can, and if it develops into something, I'll let you know."

Diana asked, "What about the stuff going on tonight. Any inspiration?"

The tech sounded disgusted. "There's actually a lot more things happening around town than the AET chick said in your call. But I think that the most likely options are Independence Hall, if they're looking for a political statement, the Taylor Swift show if they're looking for the easiest carnage since it's an indoor venue, and the Phillies game if they're only there to cause visible trouble."

"Alfred hasn't come up with a priority list?"

She barked a laugh. "No. He's being a loser about it. Thirty-three percent each. He did ditch the K-Pop band, though."

The AI has good taste in music. "Why?"

"His algorithms are fairly complicated, but if I had to summarize, it's because the place is smaller and not in the city proper. There's probably a reason that the witch specified Philadelphia and not Camden, right?"

Diana shrugged. "It's as solid a guess as any."

A crash filled the comm, and Cara interjected, "Is everyone all right there?"

Kayleigh sounded disgusted. "A helmet prototype fell."

"Fell?"

"Fell, was hurled across the room and then fell, whatever. It's not important."

Diana kept her voice neutral despite the concern she felt for their brilliant technician. "Maybe the time has come for you and I to join a martial arts studio together. We can release a little pressure now and again. Some have suggested that I'm a little high-strung, and I could use a partner."

"I'm sure Rath would love to do that with you. It could be a bonding experience."

"Well, your other option would be talk therapy, I guess."

Another crash echoed through the channel. "Fine. I'll go."

Cara asked, "Um, not to break into a tender moment, but what was that noise?"

"Test 3D print of the helmet. It also fell, although it made it further than the other one." The agents laughed, and Kayleigh finally gave in and joined them. She sounded more like herself as she apologized. "I'm sorry. I suppose the pressure is getting to me. I always had Emerson to look to for leadership, and now I don't have anyone."

Diana groaned. "Thank you for the vote of confidence."

The tech's sassy attitude returned. "You know what I meant. Not everything is about you."

Cara's grin was apparent in her tone. "Now that's the Kayleigh we all adore. So, back to the issues of the moment, how can we help you to help us?"

It took Diana a few moments to follow the phrasing. The tech got there first. "Well, it depends. If you're in the AET HQ and you feel confrontational, you might try to convince them to give me drone access. If you're there and you feel subversive, you could find an open cable port and hook up the computer block, or put it close enough to a server for wireless access. Assuming neither of those appeals, keep an eye out for ports to plug it into when you get wherever you're going."

She nodded, even though Kayleigh couldn't see her. "Got it, we'll do what we can."

The connection was interrupted by a ping from Diana's AI. "Go ahead, Friday."

"AET is requesting commlink."

"Grant it."

A moment later, Michaeli's voice came over the line. "Divert to the stadium. We received a call that suspicious activity has been seen in the surrounding blocks. We'll meet you there. It looks like we should arrive at about the same time. We'll stage about a block away, to the south."

"Affirmative. Kayleigh, did you get that?"

"Yep. I'm looking for cameras now. Stand by."

Anik, who'd listened in, nodded when she looked at him. Friday told her to turn, so she wrenched the wheel to the left, driving faster than was wise on the city streets she was navigating. With a curse, she slowed to an appropriate speed and got the car under control again. "When we get the damn mobile armory, it needs to be self-guided."

Cara laughed. "I like the when part, rather than if. And we could always find a new teammate who is a good fighter and a good driver, unlike you. You know, someone more like me."

"We already have one witch on wheels. We don't need another."

The other woman tsked. "Diana, you shouldn't put yourself down like that." Kayleigh's laughter was salt in the wicked wound.

There's too many of them. I can never win at this rate. So it's time to stop playing fair. She grinned. "Okay, this round goes to you. My vengeance will be sudden and brutal." Then she made another turn and saw the AET mobile command ahead. "Let's put that thought on pause for the moment. Time to go to work."

Kayleigh returned as they walked toward the AET post. "I'm into the traffic cameras in that section of town. It looks like we have a large enemy contingent, more than only the Pittsburgh crew."

Diana peered forward as if they might be visible if she tried hard enough. "That's not a good sign."

"Definitely not. There are two groups, both on foot. Our friends are coming from the East, and the rest are inbound from the North." The AET vehicle was parked to the south of the ballpark, between it and the football stadium. *They're right next to each other, like in Pittsburgh. I wonder who did it first.* Michaeli stepped out of the truck and extended her hand, and Diana gripped it with a nod.

The AET officer was calm but concerned. "Your tech informed mine that you know some of these assholes. Do you want 'em?"

Diana nodded. "We could use another foursome if you have them to spare."

"Can do. We've had people from SWAT training with us for a while. They can fill in the gaps." She grabbed the walkie talkie clipped to her shoulder. "Send Team A out to join our new allies."

"Glam, what are the numbers like?"

The tech's response was immediate. "Somewhere between three to one and four to one odds against you.

The other group is bigger, but Philly has more people so it's about the same ratio."

"Okay. That works. Can we intercept them before they reach the park?"

"Negative. They'll get inside at least a minute before you get there. And that's if you run."

Diana sighed, then let the worry go. "Okay. It'll be what it'll be." Four AET troops ran up to stop beside her team, and she nodded. "We're on our way. Friday, link the four comm sources nearest us into our network." A chime announced that the task was complete. "Welcome, y'all. Time for our evening jog." She led the way and covered the ground between their position and the stadium in a measured rush.

The explosions and screams began as they jogged through the entrance on the first base side of the park. They shifted into an all-out sprint and reached the stairs leading down to the field in time to avoid being stopped by the panicked crowd fleeing to the exits. Groups of the enemy had already deployed on their side and in the outfield. *I hope AET is moving fast, or we'll be overrun.* They reached the bottom and leapt over the low fence onto the field. She issued a brisk order. "Stop them from hurting the fans, whatever you have to do."

The AET officers dropped to one knee and aimed their rifles at their opponents. Diana's team arced out to the left and right of them as they ran forward to avoid their firing lines. Anik's footfalls were close behind her, and Cara and Tony were on the far side. They had agreed on the way in that taking care of the magicals would be their primary focus. Several of the rifle-wielding enemies fell, but shimmering shields appeared between the AET officers and their foes. They switched magazines quickly, no doubt to load in anti-magic bullets, and resumed their fire.

As if they'd waited for that cue, their opponents ran in different directions and spread out to make them harder to engage in multiples. One of them ran into Diana's path, and she caught him with a bolt of force that catapulted him ten feet away. *Shit. I need to conserve my power. I was a little excited there.* She reached out with her magic to steal a wand from a witch who faced in the other direction and chuckled until the wizard beside the woman twisted and sent a wash of fire at her.

Diana cast a shield, and Anik stepped inside it for protection. The flames failed to penetrate and subsided quickly. The enemy's strategy became obvious when they more or less stopped moving in unison, turned, and launched attacks at the four officers who still kneeled and fired. Magical assaults hit them first, each targeted by at least one foe and some by multiples. Auras glowed around them as their anti-magic deflectors absorbed the incoming energy. Bullets followed, but their heavy vests and helmets weathered the initial blows, and they continued their fusillade and reduced the enemy numbers with each volley. *Damn. That's some stone-cold discipline.*

Diana and Cara launched their own arcane assaults on the magicals and eliminated several before their adversaries realized they were under attack. Anti-magic barrages from Anik and Tony accounted for a few more. She had a moment to glance across the field to where the PDA, AET, and SWAT response proved effective against their group of attackers, too. Her attention quickly returned to her own battle and she deflected an incoming bolt of ice with a curved buckler to launch it back at her attacker. Her success brought a surge of accomplishment. *All right. It looks like we have this.*

The thought had barely found life when the second wave of enemies appeared.

CHAPTER TWENTY-FOUR

Cara was the first to see them, and after a quick yelp of surprise, she spoke calmly. "Enemies coming down from the mezzanine." Diana looked up and saw them —witches and wizards and ordinary people with guns— marching down the stairs on both sides of the park to surround them. The criminals on the ground moved as the new participants appeared and dashed for the outfield, and were quickly bolstered by additional reinforcements from the northeast.

Diana's team and the AET force backed away from the newcomers and fired as they went until they were arrayed in a wide circle in the middle of the field, as far from the attackers as they could get without bunching up and making themselves vulnerable to a single attack. A gloating voice shouted loudly enough to be heard across the stadium from where she stood behind the plate.

"It's so good of you to join us, Philadelphia SWAT and AET. We put this little show together just for you, after all."

Diana exchanged glances with Cara, and the other woman nodded. She'd wondered where the lead witch from the Pittsburgh gang of Remembrance idiots was during the initial fight, and now she had her answer. *Dammit. That should have been a clue that something was up. Idiot.* It meant that Sloan was probably somewhere nearby as well.

As traps went, it wasn't a bad one. The enemy had the advantage in both numbers and position, and as long as they kept their attacks angled downward, they were not in danger of crossfire injuries. Diana studied the park systematically, section by section, in search of any possibility to turn the tables but found none. Michaeli's voice rang out from somewhere across the circle from her, possibly facing third base. "How about you all surrender now and we can end this before anyone else gets hurt?"

Sarah laughed, a sound on the border between condescension and insanity that slid toward the latter at a rapid pace. "I'm afraid we'll have to decline. Hurting you is the whole reason for this gathering. Any last words?" She paused, but the AET officer didn't respond. "Very well. Goodbye."

She shrieked something Diana couldn't make out and a wave of magical attacks emanated from all sides of the encircled officers and agents. A series of popping sounds was added to the noise of the assaults as anti-magic deflectors were consumed. Diana countered as many of the spells as she could, deflected some, shielded against others, and spun like a dervish to keep up with the ongoing strikes. She wracked her brain for a method to shield everyone at once and hoped to think of a way to bring them all into position for a counterattack but was distracted when Michaeli's voice shouted over her comm.

"Everybody drop—now, now, now!"

Diana flung herself down as a loud buzzing filled the air. Large military-style drones swooped into the stadium over the outfield wall and fired stun blasts as they circled in a line around the venue, then whirled for another pass. The enemy that hadn't been hit in the first barrage reacted quickly. Spells and bullets careened to intercept the flying vehicles and caused several to crash into the grandstands and onto the field. The remainder continued and lined up for the next strafing run.

"Cara, Tony, Anik, with me. Let's go get that witch."

Diana sprinted toward the fence to vault into the seating area. Ahead, members of the gang she recognized from the surveillance they'd done on Sloan raced toward the mezzanine. The BAM agents surged after them, Cara an aisle to the left and Tony and Anik angled for the next one over. Five people—two witches and three men with guns—were in Diana's line of sight and had almost reached the end of the stairs. They cut to the right when they reached the flat area that was the main path around the stadium, but a flaming drone hurtled in from that side to collide with the top row of seats and cartwheel into the mezzanine. The impact expelled shrapnel into the walkway and instantly started several fires.

They turned and ran the other way, and Diana grinned. *That's right. Get between us, you scumbags.* She reached the top and a barrage of bullets welcomed her, and she barely had time to conjure a shield to deflect it. A food stand nearby offered some cover and she flung herself over the counter and hoped the brickwork wasn't merely painted wood and could hold up against the incoming gunfire.

She yanked the flashbangs from her thigh and threw them, then followed with the pepper and sonic grenades. Sounds of weapons fire came over the comm, as did Cara and Tony calling out warnings to one another. Her hurled bombs detonated, and she vaulted over the counter and charged into the swirling dust, smoke, and debris, coughing as the acrid mixture met her lungs. She was shocked to find double the number of expected enemies and realized that they'd posted a rear guard. Worse, they had the rest of her team pinned down with rifle fire. *Well, let's even that out.*

She spread her hands and a wash of flame emerged and spread in a thin fan as it closed the distance to her adversaries. Sarah laughed and cast a counter-wave of ice that intercepted and defeated her attack. Diana flicked force bolts at the witch's face, but her opponent skipped adroitly aside and returned the favor with a cascade of shadow orbs. She sidestepped to avoid them, and the spheres changed trajectory to track her. With a growl of annoyance, she crouched behind a force shield, and the orbs impacted with surprising strength and required her to expend additional power to maintain the defense. The smoke had intensified, and despite the sprinklers, visibility was minimal and she lost sight of the enemy leader.

Bullets pounded against the shield, and she increased the flow of magic to it. In frustration, she realized they could probably keep the assault up more or less forever as long as the fire didn't bring the roof down on them all. *Not good. Okay, time to turn the tables.* She drew her pistol with her right hand while she maintained her defense with the other. With a long, slow breath to focus her mind, she stood and extended the barrier to cover top to bottom. With it held at arm's length before her, she charged the enemy through the smoke of the fires all around. Her comms returned to normal from the protective silence initiated by the grenades, and she heard her team coordinate attacks on enemies on their side.

Diana had expected to find Sarah directly ahead, but the ranks had reshuffled somewhat and she encountered a pair of men with pistols instead. She pounded the closest of the two in the face and torso with the force shield as she took a step away from the other to clear the space, then shot him twice in the chest with the anti-magic bullets. Blood blossomed from the wound and he fell, so she restrained her finger from pulling the trigger to put a third round into his head.

The man on the opposite side of the shield had recovered and fired into it to drain her power further. When his gun locked empty, she released the magic and stepped in to deliver a left hook to his jaw. The shock glove discharged with a loud snap and he fell without a word.

She rushed ahead and angled toward the stadium seats. The sounds of the nearby battle increased. The thick smoke cleared for a moment and she saw that Anik was face-down on the cement, Tony fired whenever a target appeared through the haze of the battlefield, and an exhausted-looking Cara dodged attacks while she cast her fire darts at enemies. Several non-magicals on the ground with burning holes in them testified to her efforts. Her unpredictable movements had kept her preserved from major damage so far, but she stumbled a little, clearly slowing.

The attack that would have finally caught her was intercepted when Diana cut in front of her and used the curved force buckler to reflect the incoming ice bolt back at the witch who had cast it. It felled her and left six of their adversaries suddenly revealed by the swirling smoke —two witches, a wizard, two men with rifles, and one with a pistol. Sarah shouted a word and raised her wand, and a wall of shadow appeared behind Diana to cut her and Cara off from Tony and Anik. More walls dropped to her right and on the far side of the enemy line to box them in with the witch and her allies.

She was glad for the mask that covered her team's faces so Sarah couldn't recognize her. They would be merely two more Philadelphia officers, albeit ones with magical aptitude and training. The witch would probably assume they were with the Paranormal Defense Agency. Diana lowered her voice and yelled, "Give it up. I don't know who you are or what you're up to, but it ends here."

Sarah scoffed at her in reply. "Your teams are dead, and any who aren't are cut off. Look around you. You're outnumbered. It's you who will end here."

Cara stepped beside her and made a rude gesture at their enemy. "You think too much of yourself, bitch."

The witch laughed, and her henchmen followed suit. One of the laughs sounded familiar, and Diana's eyes widened as she really looked at the rifle-wielder on the far left for the first time. It was Sloan, his expression deeply worried. *He probably has an idea that it might be us but can't be sure because of the masks. Dammit. I should have seen this coming and set up a password. I suppose if necessary, I'll break his cover so he can assist in defeating them.*

The witch pointed at Cara. "You die first." As if it was a command, all the enemies attacked at once. Sloan's rifle barked but was angled up so it didn't hit anything. The incoming rounds deflected from the shield that Diana threw in front of her and Cara, but the move left her unguarded against the shadow orbs that curved around the opposite side and powered into her. Her vest absorbed the magic and shattered all her deflectors at once. The energy was enough to thrust her backward. *Damn, that wench is strong. Well, she's not the only one.*

The other witch had attacked Cara and lightning reached over, under, and around Diana's shield to wreath her in power. Her second in command was preserved from damage by the deflectors until the shield fell and the enemy's magic went to work on the resistors. A pistol round from a perfect angle avoided the barrier and caught her vest, and she spun away to fall heavily. Diana raised her carbine, flicked it to full auto, and depressed the trigger with a shout.

Both witches summoned shields to block the rounds as the barrage swept over them, but they weren't Diana's target, merely along the gun's path to the one she really aimed at. The man had raised his rifle toward Cara. He seemed reluctant but did it just the same. Her bullets jerked him back and he collapsed as her weapon clicked empty. *Three or four, anyway. He's out of the fight.*

She let the carbine fall and flicked her hands out to attack the bald pistol-wielder with a burst of force that hurled him back against the far shadow wall. It sizzled as it met his flesh and dragged a scream of pain from him. Without meeting Sloan's eyes, she yanked his rifle away and hurled it into the magical barrier behind her. He wisely ducked out of the midst of the battle and evened the odds.

Cara stepped beside her again. The woman's vest still smoked from the lightning it had absorbed and dissipated. Her voice was filled with scorn. "You people aren't very good at this, are you? Poor leadership, I assume." The weak taunt hit home, and Sarah scowled. Diana dug within for her fire, coaxed her power forward, and allowed it to flow and gather without releasing it. The pressure built inside her, like fighting to hold your breath when you desperately needed to take another. The enemy leader said something, but she couldn't hear it. When the witches raised their wands together, she sighed with pleasure and set the energy free.

She thrust her hands forward in a double straight punch, and fireballs erupted from her fists, one aimed at each of the remaining opponents. There was no time for them to cast, distracted as they were by Cara's efforts to occupy their attention. The flaming spheres expanded as they traveled the short distance to their targets, and the witch on the left was engulfed. Her shout of alarm transformed into a scream of agony as the flames covered her. She dropped and rolled to put them out but the magical assault proved impervious. The witch fell silent and the blaze still did not cease until nothing remained but ash. It took only seconds.

Diana was so entranced by the unexpected and horrific

spectacle that she didn't register the effects of the attack on their other adversary. Fortunately, Cara did and knocked her legs out from under her before the witch's counterattack could make impact. The steel beam the woman had ripped from the ceiling whipped through the space her head had occupied. Diana jerked her gaze back to Sarah and saw that an aura of flame covered her, separated from her skin by a thin barrier of shadow. Her lips were pulled away from her teeth in intense anger as the fire fought to reach her and the darkness prevented it.

The witch raised the beam again with a gesture from her wand, and Diana summoned her telekinesis to hold the giant metal object suspended over them so the woman couldn't attack them with it. She siphoned off some of her magic—all that wasn't needed to keep them safe—and gathered it for a force attack in the hope that she could knock Sarah off balance and make her lose focus on the attempt to destroy her and Cara.

Suddenly, the pressure ceased and the beam spun away. The witch made a strange movement with her free arm and in almost the same moment, held a wand in each hand. She gestured upward, and dust filtered down as the roof creaked. When she twirled the second wand to create a portal beside her, Diana released the force bolt. The witch made a final movement with her other wand to strike from top to bottom, and the ceiling above them shattered and fell. Diana's last image of the woman was her skipping into the rift with a triumphant grin.

In the seconds before the steel, wood, and stone of the mezzanine roof crushed them, Diana created a force shield over her and Cara. They were already conveniently intertwined from the other woman's flying tackle. She raised another over Sloan as he dove on top of the bald man who had staggered beside him. Then she lost sight of everything except dust and debris, and the only sound was the roar as the ceiling descended upon her.

It took almost a full minute to settle and after another minute to be sure it was all truly over, Diana threw off the collapsed structure with her force powers to free herself and Cara from the wreckage the witch had dropped on them before she'd portaled out. Dozens of feet away, Sloan supported the older bald man as they ran back toward where the enemies had come from. "Did anyone see if Sloan was wearing a vest?"

Kayleigh responded immediately. "I have him on a drone. He is."

"Front and back?"

"Yes."

"Croft, shoot him in the vest. Shoulder."

"What?"

Diana looked at Cara, who shifted her rifle forward in reflexive obedience to the order. "We have to keep his cover intact. There's no way he wouldn't have been hurt."

Cara growled something unintelligible and laid on her stomach to sight carefully. Diana magnified her lenses, ready to cast a spell if anything went wrong. She focused hard to summon her magic and deliberately slowed time as the bullet left the barrel. It rocketed toward their teammate, and although she was prepared to nudge the round in one direction or the other, additional action proved unnecessary. She released her magic and collapsed, spent, as the projectile impacted his shoulder and pitched both him and his companion to the ground.

The team's Face staggered to his feet and pulled the other man with him. They reached the exit and stumbled out of sight. Diana managed to mutter, "Good shot," before she lost consciousness.

CHAPTER TWENTY-FIVE

In the week that followed the operation in Philadelphia, Sarah had been sullen, Mur had been maudlin, and Teddy had vanished, most likely among the dead in the attack. When they arrived at the warehouse, she had been waiting and seemed dismayed to discover how few of her followers had returned. She'd thanked Mur for his work, mumbled something about needing to replace Wysse, and disappeared out the front door to walk away into the night.

There was no contact from the organization for several days after that. When he did receive a call, it was confirmation from Mur that Teddy hadn't survived. He informed Sloan that he'd been promoted and was now his number two man, which would have been impressive if there was anyone left to lead. There was only one remaining member of the old gang, and he'd climbed into a bottle the day after the battle and probably wouldn't climb out anytime soon, if ever.

Sloan rotated his arm with a wince. He wasn't sure at first who'd shot him as he couldn't see through all the dust and debris and had wondered if he'd been wrong about who they were fighting. But when he picked up his replacement phone from the Post Office box they'd arranged when he went undercover and made contact with Diana, she'd confirmed that it had been Cara and a deliberate choice to help maintain his cover.

That plan paid dividends, as the injury sustained while rescuing him put Sloan solidly in Mur's confidence. Since that first call, Mur and he spoke regularly and the ARES team listened in. The man complained a lot but also talked about the possibilities that opened up as the Remembrance focused ahead. He'd told Sloan to wait outside the bar at a certain time, and he'd agreed.

When he pulled up in a new pickup truck, far nicer than the one he had owned, Sloan was genuinely surprised. He climbed into the cab and slammed the door behind him. "Nice ride, Mur. Did you win the lottery or something?"

The bald man was dressed better than before, too. All in black again, but better quality fabrics. Less blue collar, more white collar. *Heh. Let's call the style powder blue.* His face was where the most notable difference was visible, though. Before, he'd been generally cheerful and not particularly confident. He'd been more focused on showing he was a leader than actually being a leader. His time with Sarah had changed that. Mur had proven to himself and others that he was up to the task of running the human side of the group while the other leaders were imprisoned, and he carried that knowledge with him. It caused him to sit straighter and to meet Sloan's eyes more readily. Frankly, it looked good on him. *Too bad you work for a totally evil sleazeball.*

His voice was the same, with its ever-present edge of humor. "No, only some payment for our efforts so far and decided it was time for an upgrade."

"So, you bought it legit?"

Mur chuckled. "I wouldn't go that far. It's used but only slightly and may have been erroneously reported as destroyed to the insurance company."

Sloan laughed. "Ahhhh. Nice scam."

"It is, isn't it? You can't do it too often, but it seemed like the right moment since I have a friend in an insurance company and a friend in the DMV."

"You have a lot of friends these days."

Mur looked at him, a serious expression on his face. "You do too, Tommy, after what you did in Philly." He turned to watch the road. "It's not write-your-own-ticket level friendship or anything, but you're on your way up. Keep yourself pointed in the right direction, and you'll be good. I told Sarah all about your efforts there at the end."

The fight had been an absolute nightmare for him. He'd been unable to warn anyone and unable to stop it from happening. He hadn't even been informed of the whole plan and so had no idea it was actually a trap to destroy the AET and possibly the PDA in the city until it unfolded. *And I still don't know why we did it. Honestly, it doesn't make any sense.*

He realized he was shaking his head, too deep in his thoughts, and covered it with a comment. "Nah, man, I didn't do anything special. I was only looking out for my own." He had done so in truth and fired always over the heads of those he aimed at and on a couple of occasions, saved those around him from immediate death by pulling them out of the way of attacks.

It wasn't the first time he'd been in the situation where he had to act against his own side in the short term as an investment for the long term, and he tried not to let it bother him too much. As long as he didn't actively hurt anyone and didn't help others to do so, his conscience was generally okay with it. There were one or two times when he'd strayed way too close to the line, and once he'd had to do exactly what Cara did—short-term damage to solidify his cover. The officer whose arm Sloan had broken never really forgave him for it, though.

Mur pulled into the gravel lot after a few minutes of silence. He killed the engine, which obediently ceased operation and lapsed into silence. The leader looked forward without moving. "You know, Tommy, I think whatever we're about to do, it'll be even huger than the Philadelphia thing. Which is scary."

He nodded, careful not to break the spell in case the man revealed something valuable.

Mur shrugged. "Think about it. We blew the hell out of a baseball stadium. How can we go bigger? That's the question. But still, that's the impression I get from her."

Sloan barked a laugh and lightened his tone against the ice that materialized in his stomach at Mur's words. "Is she any less scary when you know her better like you do?"

The bald man turned to him and shook his head gravely. "No. Far, far more scary. The more sense you have of what she's capable of, the more you realize you do not want to piss her off. Ever. In any way."

He swallowed hard. "Right. Point taken."

"Let's get inside." They walked side-by-side through the open sliding door of the warehouse, which was notably emptier of both people and things than before their efforts across the state. At the bottom of the stairs stood a dark-skinned witch with large gold hoop earrings, spiked neon blue hair that was shaved on the sides, and the odd fashion choice of a scarlet kimono with a dragon on it overtop a black tank top and matching jeans. Her arms were folded over her chest, and her black wooden wand tapped the opposite arm every so often like a threat to those around her or one side of a conversation only she could hear.

Sloan nodded at her. "New top witch?"

Mur gave a grunt that he took as affirmation. She didn't seem likely to be as fawning as Wysse had been, and he couldn't say he was upset that the alleged empath was no longer among them.

A loud bang sounded from the second floor as the door struck the metal walls of the office and once again, Sarah entered the presence of her underlings with a reminder of how far above them she was. She descended halfway, reviewed the people before her, and stepped down another few steps. Her face looked gaunter than it had previously, and her eyes more furious and energetic. Her hands twitched as she stood in silence, clenched into fists, and relaxed, again and again. *I wonder if she realizes she's doing it. I wonder if she realizes anything that happens outside her own head.*

"My people. You have persevered through challenges to be here. You have seen the loss of your friends, of our brothers and sisters who sacrificed themselves to advance the goals of the Remembrance. I am here to tell you that it was worth it. It continues to be worth it. Our success in decimating the authorities in Philadelphia has proven our value to those above us."

Sloan frowned. *She sounds crazier than usual. And that's seriously saying something.*

"We have been rewarded with our biggest task yet, one that will launch us to the top of the groups fighting to continue the ideals of Rhazdon, fighting to claim our rightful places on both Oriceran and Earth."

Wow. Laying it on a little thick, aren't you, lady?

"Soon—very soon—we will receive the tools we require to make our next accomplishment a success. It will take effort, of course. It will take loyalty. It will take all the power and ability present in this room to ensure our ultimate success. But we can do this. We will do this." She pointed a finger at them and swept it across the room. "The first step is to find more warriors, more people who believe as we do. In the past, I have refrained from doing so for fear of our secrets escaping. But no longer. Now, as we are about to come into the light, it is time to abandon those restrictions."

That's not good.

"Go, now. Go out to those you know, to those people who crave more, who desire a greater say in their lives and who need the life-changing opportunity our vision offers. Bring them to me two days from now, and we will judge them, appoint them, and make our plans together with them.

"Soon, my people, we shall be ascendant. So it has been promised, and so it shall be." She turned with a flourish and stalked up the stairs. No words were spoken until the door had slammed shut, and even then, the crowd was largely quiet as they filed out. He opened his mouth to speak to Mur, but the other man shook his head.

The return trip to the bar was silent. When he climbed out of the truck and headed for home, there was only a single thought in Sloan's mind. *I have to warn the team that something enormous is on the way.*

CHAPTER TWENTY-SIX

Diana had spent the week following the events in Philadelphia while healing. Nylotte had left the kemana and visited her at home to chide her for expending her power too freely. When she'd protested that the enemy had more or less dropped a baseball stadium on her head —*okay, some exaggeration, but still*—the Drow had merely given her a stern look and reminded her that perhaps it would be smarter not to get into such situations in the first place.

Well, it's not like she's wrong, per se.

She'd stayed at home mostly, and although she'd communicated with the others electronically, she'd generally rested. When her physical strength returned after a couple of days, she started jogging and did some light sparring with Rath, but the truth was that she had taken a significant amount of bruising in the last few months and it had caught up to her. So, when fate or the universe or whatever granted her in-between time, she took it.

Then the downtime ended, and it was game on again.

The change started with a call from Kayleigh. "Dead drop marker was up today." After the action at the baseball stadium, there was no word from Sloan after the initial contact and they had assumed he was probably worried about whether his cover was blown and so kept things on the straight and narrow. He hadn't sent an alarm code, and they'd tracked his movements through the device, all of which looked more or less normal.

Yesterday, the equipment placed him at the warehouse again, so they'd anticipated there might be some form of communication. He didn't put the phone into ghost mode, an indication that he felt reasonably safe. *As safe as an undercover agent among a group of renegade magicals led by a witch whose mind was broken in the World in Between can be, anyway.* Diana had spent the time since then waiting for the other shoe to drop, and the marker was it.

They sent Cara out as her fieldcraft was good and she was generally the least visible of them. Diana arrived at the core before she returned with the note, a series of numbers corresponding to words on a specific webpage—in this case, one dedicated to the works of Sir Arthur Conan Doyle. A book-based cipher for the electronic age. When Alfred decoded it, the message read only, *Something big afoot in the near future in our city. Recommend maximum caution.*

The three women looked at each other, and Kayleigh summed up their shared opinion. "Damn. That doesn't sound good."

Cara nodded. "Do you think they'll go after the stadiums here, too?"

Diana shook her head. "I really don't. It seems that was

all about misdirection. I imagine what they really wanted was to wipe out the defenses against them in Philly. It's probably a prelude to making a power grab of some kind. But I can't see them doing the same thing here since they know we're around. It's actually odd that they sent people from Pittsburgh there, isn't it?"

Kayleigh jumped in with an answer right away. "I've worked on that idea for a while. I can see two main possibilities. Option one is their Philadelphia team was doing something else that night, or there weren't many of them and they needed supplementing."

Cara tapped her temple. "Those are some deep thoughts there. Couldn't you come up with anything more obvious?"

The tech made a gun with her fingers and pantomimed shooting the other woman. "Option two—and this is the one I prefer—is we're looking at a situation like the mafia in movies, where a single person is in charge of a city. They don't have all that many top people in the game, so they don't have many cities with a strong presence."

Diana nodded. "The last one might make some sense. Although it could also be that there's enough activity going on in so many places that they're working regionally."

Cara replied "Uh-uh. I don't buy it. I think it could have something to do with what you both have said, but that's granting them too much deliberate choice. Maybe they make it up as they go along. Some of this seems fairly random, you have to admit."

The discussion was ended by Tony's arrival through the door from the parking garage. He hurried over to them. "I didn't want this on the radio, even the encrypted ones, but the Warden says there's something going on in the Cube.

That Vincente dude, his human follower, and a group of Kilomea all seem more animated and are chatting more. She's allowed it for now but can shut it down if we need her to."

Diana shrugged. "As long as we listen in, we might as well see where they lead us, right?" The others agreed.

Her second in command asked, "Hey, Tony, how's the dumbass pirate doing in there? I still regret not shooting him for being an idiot."

The former detective shook his head with a disbelieving look on his face. "So, this is about the best story of the day, really. They put him on the fourth level—where Vincente is—which basically means solitary confinement. Warden Murphy didn't want him to talk to any of his followers in there, which is logical. Well, after the tranquilizers they'd given him wore off, he freaked out and acted like he had a seizure or some garbage. They brought him to the infirmary and checked him out, but found nothing."

Kayleigh made a tsking sound. "Was he merely being a baby?"

"I'm almost there, hang on. So, he's going down in the elevator, and the guards can see him getting worse with each passing floor. He was okay on the top, began to itch on two, trembled on three, and freaked out again on four."

Diana realized what he was about to say before he said it. "No way. He is not."

Tony laughed. "He is. He really is. The Prince of Plunder is a bonafide magical creature. He's apparently used his magic so often it's part of him now, and he can't function normally without its presence."

Cara blinked. "I did not see that coming."

"No one did, least of all the workers at the Cube. So he's been moved to level five and now hangs out with the guard-bots, seemingly as calm as can be. No wands permitted, of course."

Diana had that odd feeling again of a big picture she couldn't quite see. *Damn, woman, you're paranoid. Knock it off.* "This town is weirder and weirder. I vote we move. Who's with me?"

Kayleigh snorted. "You just made me come here. No leaving."

"All right, fine. Let's put a proverbial pin in this and return to it when we have more information." She stared at them and they didn't move, so she made shooing gestures with her hands. "Clueless people, this means you need to go and get more information. Off with you."

They departed, laughing, and Kayleigh gave her a one-finger salute before she left. Diana shook her head. After she'd learned of the troll's roller-boots, she and the tech had downed a few drinks and engaged in a heart-to-heart. It hadn't gone quite the way she'd expected, as their new roommate shared some very deep and insightful thoughts on the things they needed to do to allow their resident troll to reach the heights he wanted to reach. Diana had been convinced, but Kayleigh went a step too far when she suggested rocket boots. She'd gotten blustery, and the tech had departed for the basement with mocking laughter at how well the provocation worked following her all the way down.

She activated the buttons to isolate her comm and connect it to her phone and dialed Bryant. He picked up after one ring. His voice was concerned. "What's up?"

"No hello? No how are you doing?"

He chuckled, but the worry didn't leave his tone. "Hello, Diana, so lovely to hear from you! I pray that you are doing well. What inspires your ever so welcome call on this fine day?"

She laughed despite her effort not to. "Have I told you you're a jerk lately?"

"I merely insert those words mentally every third sentence or so to save you the trouble."

"Okay. You win this round, but I will have my revenge. The word around town is that something big will go down in the not too distant future."

"Like stadium big?"

"Uncertain."

He sighed. "Damn."

She nodded. "Yep, couldn't have said it better myself."

"What do you need from me?"

She laughed. "A mobile armory." He sputtered, and she finished quickly. "I think it'd be good if you were in town."

"Okay. You got it. I'll be there tomorrow at the latest."

"Perfect. Thanks, Bryant."

"Is that your sincere voice?"

She blew out an exasperated breath. "No, this is, so listen carefully. You, Bryant Bates, are a jerk." She hung up to his laughter and wondered if calling him in was overkill. *I really, really hope so. But I doubt it.*

CHAPTER TWENTY-SEVEN

I t had cheered Rath up when Diana finally went back to work a few days before. He had been worried after the battle out of town and both disappointed and illogically ashamed that he wasn't there to protect her from getting hurt. *Partners should stick together.* Still, he understood that there was no way to dependably disguise him and agreed that risking Sloan's cover would have been bad.

Despite that, a voice inside whispered that he'd failed somehow.

He and Max had patrolled with a purpose the last few days, both in their neighborhood and in the downtown area, looking for clues or leads or anything that would be of some use. The ominous sense that something big was about to happen hung over everything. He even thought that the average person on the street looked a little more tense than usual.

The troll spent hours each night doing the same thing with Gwen instead of the Borzoi, but not a single piece of the puzzle had shaken out yet. His biggest accomplishment in the last trio of days and nights was intervening to shoo away a couple of mangy dogs that had cornered a cat in an alley. The feline hadn't even been grateful for the rescue and tried to claw him. He'd growled, the cat panicked and ran, and that had been that.

His mood was low as he and Max wandered through their old neighborhood, headed for the Cathedral where Professor Charlotte now worked. He figured that he could at least spend some time in the ancient-looking common area, or maybe in one of the classrooms decorated in the style of a different culture. He particularly enjoyed the Irish-themed room and had more than once heard a child whisper, "Look, it's a leprechaun," as families toured the spaces.

But when he saw the Professor and Manny walking together toward the coffeehouse with the delicious bubble tea, he and Max diverted to follow and caught up with them about a block before the entrance. Both of their expressions were uncommonly grave, and they greeted him with only a nod and a gesture for him to precede them into the store. Booths made up the wall the door was on and the one to the left, and Max selected a table to lay under. Rath slid in, and shortly thereafter, the older folks returned with a bowl of water for the dog and tea for the rest of them. Professor Charlotte sat beside him, and Manny took the opposite side.

"Why upset?" Rath's sense that things were heading in the wrong direction had intensified upon seeing their faces and grown with every second since.

Emanuel shook his head. "We all feel like something bad is about to happen. Each of us thought we were the only one but then we talked about it and discovered we all shared the same dread."

The troll nodded. "Me too. Other shoe."

Professor Charlotte replied, "Exactly that. I'm not sure what the first shoe was, but it truly feels as if another one is about to fall. And land right on our heads."

"Attack in Philadelphia. Remembrance."

Manny blinked, startled. "Really? The news merely said it was a freak accident."

"Coverup. Bad guys."

"Holy cow. That's…bad, I guess is the only word for it. But very bad."

"How can we help your group, Rath?" she asked.

He looked at Max, but the dog didn't have any ideas either. "Not sure. Keep lookout. Tell if you see something." He raised his eyes to the man across the table. "Hide artifacts."

They both nodded. The troll took a sip of his tea, but even the tapioca bubble filling his mouth with sweetness failed to lighten his mood. The others sensed it or felt it themselves, and the gathering quickly broke up. Rath and Max headed home to be ready in case they were needed.

Reflecting back upon it, Nehlan thought that never in his life had he been as angry as when Dreven denied him the opportunity to kill the woman after he'd tagged her. His plans had been set and his weapons prepared, all in readiness to eliminate her that very evening. He was sure that when his master contacted him, it would be to wish him good fortune on the elimination of that particular threat.

But no.

Instead, his increasingly hateful superior had told him to wait until the moment was right. Nehlan had argued vehemently about the benefits of catching the woman unaware while she believed she was safe with her friend. He'd made the case that they would never, ever, have her more defenseless than that night. His logic was flawless. He was positive he would have his wish.

But no.

"You will wait," was all Dreven had said before his magical representation vanished, leaving the elf sitting at his table, the deactivated statue in front of him, completely stunned and more furious than he had ever been. He'd called his human servants in and planned to kill them in her stead, but the fact that they had no minds left to resist with made it a futile gesture, and he sent them away with copious curses instead.

The intervening time had been spent uselessly. His mind was locked on the woman, obsessed with vengeance. Killing her would get him back into the good graces of the Remembrance leadership, and to have it delayed was maddening. His brain went around and around and made arguments that his imaginary superior denied one after the other. He managed no sleep, only unconsciousness when his body stopped responding after several days of wakefulness.

But today, finally, his journey to vindication would begin, even though it was to be far different than his imagination had painted it. When given the new approach, he'd done his reconnaissance and located a secluded space close to his target's house that he could portal into. His contracted subordinates had watched her for days, ready to alert him if she should do something unexpected, but her routine was like clockwork. While the middle of the night would have been his choice of timing, the orders were to make his move in the late afternoon. That was not optimal but doable. At least it was a weekend day, so she would be at home.

He stepped through from his Oriceran bunker to a park around the corner from the woman's house. The space had been cleared in advance by his human employees. He'd considered letting them take care of this step of the process, but his anticipation of defeating Agent Diana Sheen had nagged at him for so long that he couldn't pass up any part of it, no matter how small.

With an incantation and a wave of his arm, his features changed into those of the old man he'd used before. He walked slowly down his target's tree-lined street and admired the houses and watched the traffic, prepared to slow his approach or abandon the action for another walk around the block should any human authority appear. Nehlan scanned extra carefully for one of the dark, supposedly unmarked government vehicles that were nonetheless surprisingly easy to distinguish from any other cars that might be near them.

There was nothing to see. The time was right. His heart beat faster at the thought that finally—finally—things were about to begin. If he played his cards right, if it all went according to plan, Diana would give her power up to become part of his necklace, which inched ever-closer to completion. *Soon, my magical strength will surpass Dreven's, and then we will see what we will see, oh yes, indeed.*

He glanced forward and back at his hirelings whom he'd posted as lookouts on the corners, and neither signaled him to stop. The old man walked up the small flight of stairs with a totter appropriate to the image he presented and rang the doorbell. His wrinkled face tilted to smile at the camera mounted above and held up the package he had brought as an excuse, printed with the words, *A gift for*, followed by the target's name.

She opened the door, kept the chain latched, and looked through the gap. "Hi, I don't think I know you." Her hand was hidden, and for a moment, he worried she might have a weapon and be about to attack. Then, he smiled. *Maybe if it was the other one. But not her.*

He grinned wider, and even though he knew he should continue the charade, he simply couldn't wait any longer. He stood tall and allowed the illusion to fall away, and the woman's jaw dropped. She started to push the door closed, but a blast of power knocked it open, shattered the chain, and threw her across the room. The woman slammed into a small wooden dining table and tumbled over it to land in a heap on the far side.

Supremely confident, he stalked inside slowly and gestured with a hand to shut the door. He'd seen that she had no weapon hidden, so now it was merely her skills against his power. He held no fear that she might win. *Again, maybe the other one, but not her.*

The woman's blonde hair was the first thing to emerge from behind the table, followed by a very angry face. He nodded. "You don't seem afraid. You really should be."

"Of you?" she replied. "Come closer, pointy, and I'll kick your ass right back to your own planet."

He laughed, deep and long. "It figures that the best friend of Diana Sheen would be as overconfident and disrespectful as the woman herself." His target paled when she realized that he desired to not only hurt her but to use her against one she cared for. *It makes the effort even more delicious. Perhaps, before I kill him, I will thank Dreven for changing the plan.*

She yelled a battle cry, vaulted the table, and charged at him. Nehlan let her get close so she'd imagine she was doing well, and when she jumped to kick him, he slapped her aside with a fist backed by his power and catapulted her into the couch at his side with enough force to topple it. He circled slowly and looked at her where she lay blinking and dazed on the floor, her temple bleeding. A small gesture applied gentle magical pressure to the blood vessels in her neck until her eyes rolled back in her head.

He crossed to the door and leaned out, then beckoned for his hirelings to join him. Things had to move quickly now if they were to close the trap on the vexing agent.

Diana had come into work on Saturday because she couldn't stay at home any longer. She and Rath drove each other nuts and both of them fed off the other's sense that something was in the works. They talked about it but had arrived at no solutions. They'd sparred, gone for a run, and even tried playing board games, but nothing would push away the funk that hung over them.

Even Kayleigh wasn't immune to it and had locked herself away in her basement apartment with her video games and essentially remained disconnected from the world. The only thing Diana could think of that might have helped was a training session with her magical mentor, but the relationship with the Drow was still very much one-way. Unless it was a dire emergency, Nylotte called her, not the reverse.

She replayed the footage fed back by their glasses from the battle in Philadelphia to see if there were any clues at all in it. Alfred hadn't found any, so she wasn't particularly confident about her ability to do so, but she had to do something. When her phone rang, she instantly hoped it was the Drow somehow reading her thoughts, then reconsidered. *If she can read my mind and knows what I think about her during training, I'm basically screwed.* When she saw Lisa's name, a small smile managed to crack through her stress.

She forced a light tone, not wanting to burden her friend with her worries. "Hey, girl, what's up?"

"I'm sorry, Lisa can't come to the phone right now." The voice was deep and menacing.

Diana's blood turned to ice. "Who the fuck is this, and where's Lisa?"

He laughed. "Oh, Agent Sheen, there's no reason to be that way. After all, it's you we want. And your friend is unharmed. Well, mostly. For the time being, anyway."

She growled a rumble of anger. "I promise that I will end you in the most painful ways I can find if Lisa comes to harm."

"A fair response. Noted. However, it is up to you whether she does or not. In three hours, you must be in the exact center of the football field in your former city's stadium. Right on the feathers of the logo. I'll be nearby, and when I see you, we will make a simple trade—you for her. Do not even consider bringing assistance. If anyone appears other than you, your friend dies in agony."

Diana gritted her teeth as her mind raced, but she had no ideas. Nothing but white rage filled her brain. She said shakily, "I'll be there. Remember my vow."

He laughed again, the condescension so antagonizing that she had to fight to keep herself from screaming. "You do not scare me, woman. But know that your insolence has earned you days and days of torment before you die." The line dropped and Diana released the pent-up scream at the top of her lungs to vent the fury.

Panting, she dialed Bryant. "Someone's taken Lisa. I'll go to deal with it. But this might be the start and I need you here to lead the team."

"Done. Go."

She dragged in a breath and rushed to her locker. Working by instinct rather than by conscious thought, she retrieved her Glock and its waistband holster, two extra magazines of anti-magic bullets, and the leather jacket she always kept at work. While she gathered those, she tapped the activator for her microphone. "Alfred."

The cultured tones of the AI replied through her earpiece. "Yes?"

"Red Alert. Get everyone in. Tell Cara she's in charge until Bryant gets here. Confirm, please."

"Red alert. All personnel to report to headquarters. Agent Binot has command until Special Agent in Charge Bates arrives."

"Good. Execute."

She waved her hands and summoned her magic. *These bastards will wish they'd never laid eyes on Lisa.* Glyphs glowed on both her bare arms as she created a connection between the base and the training area in the basement of the Drow's shop. She stepped through, already shouting for her mentor.

CHAPTER TWENTY-EIGHT

The Drow was at her side in seconds, the shop's warning system no doubt having alerted her to the presence of magic that wasn't her own. "What has happened?"

Diana paced, unable to stay still as she shared the story with her teacher. She finished with, "I need a way to kill him and anyone he brings with him."

Nylotte tapped her finger against her teeth, her expression thoughtful. "No, that would be to play into their hands. If you were thinking clearly, you would have realized this already. What we must do is strike when they don't expect it. This three-hour mark…there's no reason for it."

"To get into position?"

She shrugged. "They can portal wherever they desire to be, I'm sure, assuming they've done even the minimum of planning. No, this is probably something else. Some part of their plan to defeat you. We need to reverse the scenario and change from prey to hunter."

Diana shook her head. "We can't risk Lisa. It's my fault she's caught up in this."

Her teacher slashed a hand through the space between them and raised her voice. "Diana. Clear your thoughts. Fault doesn't matter, and Lisa is already at risk. If you truly believe that the enemy will simply give her back, you are fooling yourself."

The white haze crept in at the corner of Diana's mind again, so she stopped pacing and took a deep, intentional breath like she had so many times before in this space. It felt good, so she did it again. Her brain began to work properly, and she realized her teacher was right. "Okay, how do we turn the tables?"

Now, Nylotte was the one in motion. She seemed to have a conversation with herself and muttered all the while. Diana reached absently under her t-shirt and pulled out the half-heart to rub her thumb over it while she made silent promises of vengeance against whoever had taken her friend. Her reverie was interrupted when the Drow snapped at her. "What is that?"

She blinked and raised the pendant. "Lisa gave it to me. It's one of those silly high school friendship things."

Nylotte stepped to her and held it in her hand. "Does she have the other part of it?"

"I can't know for sure, but we've both worn them basically all the time since she got them for us."

The Drow yanked and the thin chain holding it in place snapped.

"Hey—ow."

Her teacher rolled her eyes and extended her other hand to summon an ornate brown wooden platter with runes etched around the outside and a pair of scarlet cushions. They spun into the center of the space and settled in a line. The Dark Elf sat on the closest one with the plate in front of her and placed the necklace inside it. "A scrying pool would work better, but I don't have one handy and every second probably counts." She closed her eyes and waved her hands over the jewelry as Diana lowered herself onto the other pillow.

Misty images appeared in the air over the platter and reminded her of an early scene in *Star Wars*. The small voice in her mind managed a laugh despite her gnawing fear. *Help me, Nylotte. You're my only hope.* A bare room of chiseled stone wavered into view, apparently seen through Lisa's eyes judging by the visible arms wrapped around jeans-clad knees and running shoes. She whispered, "Is that her right now?"

Her teacher nodded. "There is enough resonance between the pieces of jewelry that I could use that connection to seek her. Fortunately, they were once a whole that was then cut in two. If they had been made with separate molds, this wouldn't have worked." Her voice was as intense and focused as Diana had ever heard it. "Now to find out where she is. Those blocks look Oriceran."

She thought they merely looked like stone but wasn't about to argue. The viewpoint rose, and she had a glimpse of Lisa before it passed through the ceiling and out of the building. She recognized nothing but her teacher apparently did. "Clever. They are hiding in the dark forest. But not clever enough to take the basic precautions of stripping one's captive so they can't be traced. Your foe is an arrogant fool."

Her heart did flips. "So you know where she is?"

The Drow nodded.

"And you can get me there?"

She shook her head, and sickness suffused Diana for an instant. Then, her mentor smiled. "I will get us there. I have a professional obligation to meet someone who's this big an idiot personally. Call it research."

"I'm ready. Let's go."

"A moment." She muttered an incantation that caused the pendant to glow, then rose and crossed to the supply cabinet and withdrew potions, two each of energy and healing. Finally, she reached into a small box before she returned to Diana. "I assume you were too stupid to bring potions, right?"

She cringed but nodded and accepted the single vial of each type that her teacher handed her. The woman dropped two charms into her hand. "You'll like these. The first creates mirror images of you—a simple illusion. I don't know how many it will make, but it could be handy in the right situation. The second generates a cloud of smoke." She had Diana repeat the trigger words several times before she nodded and removed the robe she wore in the shop to replace it with a long leather jacket that her trainee hadn't seen before. It covered down to the woman's thighs.

Diana was immediately filled with fashion lust for the coat and couldn't resist asking, "Where did you get that?"

The Drow raised an eyebrow. "Even if this were the time and place to discuss my sartorial choices, I still wouldn't tell you. Some secrets are too valuable to share." Her smile vanished as she squared her shoulders and rolled her neck. "It is my assumption that we will enter the enemy's stronghold. There will probably be defenses and defenders to try to stop us. Are you ready for that?"

She slipped the potions into her back pockets and checked the draw on her Glock. Satisfied, she zipped her leather jacket—which was one of her favorites and had seemed really cool before she saw Nylotte's—closed at the neck. "I'm more than ready. Let's teach this asshole that you don't go after people who aren't playing the game."

The Drow nodded and waved her arms to summon a portal that led to the room revealed through Lisa's eyes. When it materialized on the opposite side, they both leapt through, prepared for anything.

The room they landed in was not the one they'd seen through the portal. Diana assumed that had something to do with the wicked wrenching she'd experienced partway through. She stumbled but didn't quite fall and spun to look at Nylotte. The woman merely looked irritated. "Magical wards. They couldn't stop us but could redirect us." She lifted the pendant. "It's warm, which means your friend is close by. Apparently, his arrogance is such that he hasn't sent us far."

"I didn't know that was possible."

She laughed, her amusement short but sincere. "The list of things you don't realize about magic could reach to the moon and partway back, Diana."

"Which moon?"

"No more nonsense." She pointed toward the closed

door at the far side of the room. "Let's not try to be subtle, since our quarry certainly knows we're here. We need to move fast. Destroy that."

"With pleasure." Diana channeled her power into a force blast, still her strongest attack, and reduced the exit to splinters. They strode forward into a long hallway that turned in the distance. Halfway down, a pair of enormous rats charged toward them. The creatures were bigger than Great Danes and had large fangs and evil eyes.

The Drow sighed. "It's amateur hour." Two wicked spikes of ice rocketed down the corridor and impaled the animals. They convulsed in their death throes as the women strode past.

Diana looked at the blind angle ahead. "I should have brought some grenades."

Nylotte didn't reply until they were near the corner and then snapped, "Shield." She summoned her own of shadow, and Diana created a buckler of force, ready to expand it if necessary but tried to minimize her energy expenditure lest the Dark Elf turn this adventure into one of her teaching moments. She realized that she'd walled away the anger that had threatened to overcome her, thanks to her teacher's guidance, and was now filled only with purpose. *As training sessions go, this might turn out to be a good one. As long as Lisa's safe at the end.*

Turning the corner resulted in a hail of darts fired at them from a short distance away. Diana reacted by extending her shield in time to block them before they struck. *Okay, maybe trying to save power wasn't so clever.* The hallway turned again several feet ahead, and Nylotte sighed as they approached. "It's a labyrinth. This is ridiculous."

She stopped, spun in a circle, and held the pendant in an outstretched hand. "I have the bearing. We need to take this turn. Shield again."

This time, when they rounded the corner and took a step, flame erupted all around them. Diana yelped and started to expand her shield into a bubble, but her teacher cast ice barriers on all the surrounding surfaces with a gesture to seal the holes and halt the attack. She pointed at the left-hand wall, about a third of the way down the long hallway. "That one. Destroy it."

A dozen snarky comments leapt to mind but she discarded them, cupped both hands in front of her chest, and generated a large ball of force between them that she sculpted with circular movements. When it was the size she wanted, Diana hurled it forward and it detonated against the stone and shattered it. Cries of pain issued from the area beyond, and they stepped through the rubble to find a human on the ground, bleeding from a multitude of cuts from the shrapnel. A pistol lay near his outstretched hand.

Diana turned to her teacher. "Did you know he was back there?"

She shook her head. "No. But it is convenient. Two birds with one stone."

He made a weak movement toward his gun, and Diana kicked it gently down the hall and secured him with zip-ties before she grabbed the pistol and shoved it into her waistband. "Where to next?"

She pointed at another section of wall on the same line as the one they'd stepped through, and Diana blasted it away. They repeated the process three times before they emerged into what appeared to be the final room of the labyrinth. It had much thicker-looking walls, an exit door, and a pair of humans whose nervous looks were probably the result of the sounds of the explosions coming nearer. They reacted quickly to raise and fire their pistols.

She flung herself to the right and into a roll, drawing her Glock as she moved. It struck her that the comforting weight of her chest armor was absent. *Damn. Did I really leave without my vest? I'm an idiot.* The voice in her mind was argumentative. *You were freaked out. It happens. Perhaps you should focus on the moment. Oh, and try not to get shot.*

When she came out of her tumble, she stopped on one knee and focused her eye along the iron sights on the top of the weapon. *It's a waste of good anti-magic ammo.* She pulled the trigger twice, struck the man in the chest with both, and he fell. As she shifted her aim to the second target, a trio of ice bolts stabbed deep into his torso and hurled him into the wall before he, too, collapsed.

She stood and strode to the door with a questioning look at her teacher. The Drow brushed some dust from the shoulder of her fine jacket, checked the locator, and nodded. Diana disintegrated the barrier and stepped forward, a full-size force shield leading the way. There was nothing on the other side except a corridor that extended in both directions and a featureless wall in front of her.

Nylotte stepped beside her. "She's moving. We need to hurry. Go left."

Diana ran and the Drow kept pace behind and called orders. They cut through a dining room and another hallway. Their path was blocked by another door but she ripped it from its hinges with her telekinesis and hurled it aside before she darted through the opening. Lisa was there and appeared mostly unharmed although her arms were bound at her back and a man's hand latched in her hair. *No, an elf's hand.* There were two humans with him, and in the moment, they didn't react but kept their guns aimed at the floor.

The elf grinned, and she recognized his voice from the phone call. "You are too late. Make a move, and she dies an instant before my friends here shoot." Lisa's head rose and Diana was elated to see the anger and determination in her friend's eyes. She focused on the band securing the captive's wrists and pictured exactly where she would apply her magic to snap it.

Nylotte stepped through the door. Her tone was ice and exasperation. "Nehlan. I knew you were an idiot, but this far exceeds my expectations." She extended her fingers, and the pistols jerked out of the humans' hands and clattered into the hallway beyond.

The elf sputtered and yanked at Lisa's hair at the same moment that Diana broke the bonds around her wrists. His former prisoner transformed into an immediate threat as she reached up for the hand that held her, grabbed the wrist, and spun. The sound of the elf's arm fracturing as she snapped and twisted the limb downward was a pleasure to hear. Lisa kicked him in the side of the knee and toppled him before the men near her lunged to defend their employer.

In a move far too fast for Diana to see the details, Nylotte summoned a portal, reached out with her magic to grab Lisa, and hurled her through it. She let the rift close, then folded her arms and nodded. "So, Lisa is safe at my store. I believe you might have some business with these people, no?"

Diana cracked her knuckles and looked at the two men who had apparently discovered their courage and interposed themselves between her and the elf who whimpered as he pushed himself to his feet one slow inch at a time. She pointed two fingers at the humans. "Surrender?"

The goon on the right gave an arrogant laugh. "To you, princess? No thanks. Let's see what you're made of." He raised his fists like a boxer, and she couldn't help but snort at the scene.

She pulled her right arm back and thrust it forward in a punch, and a blast of force lifted the man from his feet and propelled him into the wall behind him with a satisfying crunch of breaking bones. The other used the moment to attack, and Diana stepped forward smoothly at an angle and chopped her hand across at throat level. His block protected his windpipe and saved his life, but the blow still threw him off balance. She pivoted and landed a jab in his ribs, then delivered a left hook to his temple. It connected, and her foe went down in a heap. It was all over in ten seconds from start to finish.

The wizard rose with a snarl on his face. "You have been in my way for far too long. Die, woman."

Magic exploded from him, a combination of shadow and flame that she had never seen before. Together, they rippled in an ethereal wave as they washed toward her. The fear that shadow magic always inspired in her appeared, but she welcomed it as a familiar companion and relegated it to the back corner of her mind. Diana summoned a force shield and maintained it as the attack flowed around her.

The raw power of the elf's assault was unexpected, and she weakened under the barrage. Her mind went to the energy potion in the metal vial in her back right pocket, but she was uncertain that she could get to it without allowing the attack through. She turned her head to look at her teacher, whose expression showed a complete lack of concern.

Diana mustered her strength and pushed against the magical barrage. Her shield shifted forward, but it was too much. She'd never get to him before he battered all her energy away. The voice in her mind sounded exasperated. *Since when are you about power, anyway? Remember who you are, stupid.* She grinned. *You're right. And when you're right, you're right. And you? You're always right.* Her grin still in place, she flicked her fingers at the mage and yanked his damaged arm, and his assault floundered and vanished in a cry of pain.

Tears streamed down his face as he raised the undamaged arm to attack her, and she jerked the wounded limb again and brought him to the ground. She walked over to stand beside him and stared with a cold expression. "You crossed the line when you attacked my friend. I am justified to end you, right here and right now. You have one chance—one—to survive beyond the next minute." He nodded, and she reveled in the fear that shone in his eyes. "Tell me why you did this."

His words were interspersed with sobs of pain and mental anguish. "Ordered to. Council. Remembrance."

"Why three hours?"

"Wasn't told."

"Take a bloody guess, you idiot."

He coughed, and blood stained his lips. "Probably... timed with attack." He managed a disgusting grin. "Your people...dying by now."

Diana turned to Nylotte. "I have to go."

The Drow nodded. "You do. I will deal with him and watch over Lisa. Go, and remember that you've already used some of your power."

She didn't react to her teacher's words as she cast a portal to headquarters and raced through it. *Hang in there, y'all. I'm on my way.*

CHAPTER TWENTY-NINE

Her comm crackled to life with the sounds of her team discussing logistics as soon as she arrived, Bryant's deployment orders chief among them. Alfred gave driving directions, so she assumed she wasn't that far behind. When there was a gap in the discussion, she asked, "What's the status, people?"

Bryant's voice was full of relief. "Is Lisa okay?"

"Yes. Thanks for asking. Nylotte is a bloody treasure. Now, status."

He chuckled once before he sobered. "There's an attack underway at the Cube again. We're en route and are waiting for an update from Warden Murphy. The attacking force portaled in on all sides and are gathering at the moment. It's unlikely we'll make it before the fun kicks off."

Kayleigh added, "They have drones up now." A window opened in her glasses to show the scene. Mixed groups of humans, witches, wizards, Kilomea, and what looked like dwarves were visible as they closed in on the area in a rush.

Another pair of drones swooped into view and fired stun blasts at the oncoming enemies but they were absorbed by magical shields. "They're planning to deploy lethal ones shortly."

Rath sounded far more serious than she liked to hear him be. "We all felt this coming."

Diana nodded. This had to be the event they'd been waiting for. *Which means that Sloan's in that mess somewhere.* "Glam, warn Murphy that we have a friendly among the attackers. She should limit her lethal attacks to non-humans when possible, but not to make it too obvious. We don't want to compromise Face's cover either."

"On it."

Diana banged her locker open and changed faster than she could ever remember doing, leaving her other clothes in piles on the floor wherever they landed. She pulled the vest on and tightened it, then slipped her AI collar over her head. Next came the gloves, and she spent a moment making the necessary connections between her equipment. She popped the partially used magazine from the Glock and replaced it with a full load of anti-magic rounds and stored it in its holster. As she sat to buckle on the armor pieces, she asked, "Why do they think this attack will go better than the last?"

Tony replied, "I asked the warden that at the start. She has no idea but imagines that given all the talk inside, they're hoping for a riot or something. Based on that, she put the Cube in full lockdown the moment this all began. Barriers are in place to separate the levels from one another, and the prisoners are all locked away in their cells."

She fastened the last strap, stood, and selected her grenades. She chose sonics and fragmentation on the assumption that if she needed fire, she could use her magic. The energy potion went into her belt beside the healing potion that was already there, and she set the spare health draught into her locker. *I'm sure I'll need it eventually.* She slammed the door closed and moved to the weapons wall. "How long until you're on site?"

Alfred replied "Three minutes, twelve seconds."

She shook her head at the prissy AI. "Excellent. What's the plan, Hannibal?"

Bryant put a trace of the A-Team leader into his voice. "That depends. Will you join us?"

"I'll be there before you."

"Okay. We'll go in together. Meet at the East side behind the enemy, near the far wall of where the office building used to be. We'll approach from that angle and see what the situation is. If we're able to identify Face, we can direct the Warden's drones so they're more efficient."

"Roger." Diana slipped her Colt M4 carbine strap over her head and slotted the spare magazines into place, exclusively anti-magic rounds. She stared at the versions loaded with armor-piercing ammunition with a distinct longing but shook her head. *Too dangerous. There will be guards and prisoners who aren't part of this. I can't do it.* "Glam, what else can we do here?"

"Not a thing, boss. The PD is blocking traffic, emergency services are on standby, and the Air Force reserve has choppers inbound."

"Armed?"

"Yep. I'm assured it's merely a backup plan in case things go to hell."

She imagined the scene of a mini-gun opening up inside the city limits and shuddered. "Let's make sure they don't, then, shall we?" She opened a portal to a location near where Bryant had set the rally point and strode through.

Diana jogged up as the others bailed out of the SUVs. She stepped beside Bryant and together, they looked ahead toward the prison. Searchlights swept the grounds and revealed the enemies encircling the building. A low hum persisted behind the general noise and seemed to come from the center of the circle. Flaming wreckage from several drones was scattered around the perimeter. She shook her head. "What are they waiting for? And what happened to the drones?"

Kayleigh was the first to reply. "Fireballs took them out. They're not all that nimble, all things considered. They'd probably be better with an AI on board for defensive maneuvering."

Tony snorted. "And six months later, Skynet. No thank you."

Warden Murphy's voice joined the channel. "We have a situation inside." The earth trembled beneath Diana's feet, and she noticed that the humming had increased. She put it together an instant before it happened and yelled, "Get away from the cars." The team scattered as she dashed to the side and the ground heaved and dirt erupted in random explosions. Their vehicles bounced, then settled.

The humming noise had built into a shriek, and their earpieces dampened in response. She could still hear the warden shouting something but couldn't make out what it was. Another heave convulsed like the earth tried to throw them into space, and a fissure appeared at the border of where she knew the Cube to be.

She read Bryant's lips as he cursed, and she nodded. The enemy troops scattered as the tear in the soil grew and spread toward the ARES team's location. It ended about halfway to them, and Diana launched forward as the nearest opponent leapt into it. The sounds had stopped and the comm was audible again. Warden Murphy sounded apoplectic. "That stupid pirate is behind this. He set up some sort of resonance between his magic and the stuff outside, even though we took his wands away. And he's on the bottom floor, where there aren't any anti-magic emitters." Pieces that had gnawed at her subconscious like square shapes she had tried to force into small round holes finally assumed their proper configuration.

Diana now saw clearly how extensively and effectively she'd been played. The scenes flashed before her—how easy it had been to track the Prince of Plunder and how calm he'd been when they'd discovered him. *He wanted to be captured. And if he's doing magic without wands, that means the bastard has pretended to be a wizard and used the wands like I use my bracelets when I'm bounty hunting.* For a moment, she was actually in awe of the masterstroke that had gone exactly as the enemy intended. Their plan had been to literally break the Cube apart in order to free their people with one of the most unusual forms of magic generated simultaneously from inside and outside the prison.

The moment passed, and anger surged. "Okay, people. I've had it with these assholes, one and all. Any prisoner who resists, eliminate them. Every person you see inside who's not in an inmate jumpsuit or a guard uniform is fair game."

Kayleigh interrupted, "Except the warden. Please don't shoot the warden."

Cara snorted angrily. "Tell her to keep her scrawny ass upstairs and coordinate, then."

Diana nodded in agreement as she raced downward into the split in the earth. Ahead, the formerly underground structure of the Cube towered over her. The fissure ran down at a steep angle to the bottom floor where the not-actually-a-wizard pirate had been housed. All five stories were visible above and a crack through them opened each level to the newly created canyon. On the top level, guards fired into the mass of onrushing enemies, but the Remembrance troops had already penetrated the middle levels. She assumed the Prince of Plunder had made his escape shortly after he'd blasted the place open.

"Okay, folks, we'll have to split up. Rambo, Hannibal, and I will go in on the fourth level down. You all go in on three. Our primary targets are the people we put in here. The main target is the male wizard leader. Second is the man he had leading his human followers. I'm sure the witch is around here somewhere, too. If you see her, don't hesitate and pound her with every single thing you have. You do not want to play with her."

She received a chorus of affirmatives from everyone. "Glam, can you give us feeds from inside?"

"Negative. The place wasn't built to handle having one of its walls blown out, apparently. Everything is down. Main and backup power are both gone." There was a pause accompanied by clicking keys. Diana slid to a stop and found a rough ledge to climb on that would lead her toward the fourth level. Ahead, several enemies took position in the gap, their rifles and wands facing outward. The tech sighed. "I have no eyes, no ears, and no access. Our own drones are inbound."

Cara said, "Be sure to have someone waiting outside the escape tunnel. They should probably bring stunners and shoot everyone who emerges, regardless of what they're wearing. Sort it out later."

"On it."

Diana considered that the prisoners might subdue the guards and take their uniforms, then decided it didn't really matter. She'd trust no one, and she'd recognize the targets they were after on sight. Anyone else who got in her way...well, they'd better lay down fast or they were in for a world of hurt.

"Stay safe, people. If they escape, it'll suck, but we'll catch them again. Now, get in there and kick some Remembrance ass."

CHAPTER THIRTY

C ara led the way up the side of the fissure, then stopped and knelt. The men trailing her did the same. "Upstairs. Let's clear those idiots out." They'd all loaded anti-magic magazines into their carbines on the drive over, so it was about to be an expensive barrage. *But a necessary one if any reinforcements are going to get in there to help us. Also if we want to avoid getting killed on our way in, which would be nice.*

She sighted through the compact scope on the top and aligned the green reticule with the chest of the witch on the right side. She threw fire at a target on the surface level, presumably at guards the Cube had called in or the Police Department. *If someone up there is smart, maybe the Army.* She squeezed the trigger three times, and the woman staggered. No blood flowed, which indicated the enemy's intelligent decision to wear vests, but she stood close enough to the edge that she fell and bounced down the steep slope to land a couple of feet behind Bryant, who looked up and tipped his hat to Cara.

"Watch out, they're wearing vests." Tony and Anik opened fire, and she chose her next target. Before the enemy realized what was happening, they'd wounded, killed, or driven back everyone who'd stood on the first-floor gap. She let her carbine fall against her chest. "Let's go, double-time."

Her arms pumped as she ran up the incline and alternated between keeping her gaze forward in search of enemies and down to preserve her footing. Halfway toward the opening, an enemy appeared on their level, and she had zero time to react before the bullet struck her chest and she staggered into the dirt on her right. *Thank God that hit me on the wall side.* She threw darts of fire at the shooter, and they struck and burned through his leg, vest, and face.

Cara willed away the wooziness that accompanied the use of her power and ran on to vault into the Cube through the giant V that had replaced its east wall. She crouched and raised her rifle, traversed it through a one-eighty-degree arc while her teammates joined her, then rose. "If I remember correctly, there are cells around the corner to the left and right, and a guard post ahead, with the recreation area beyond it."

Tony replied, "I recall the same."

"Okay. Glam, any clue as to where the Remembrance jerk we put away was stored?"

Kayleigh's voice was scratchy. Something in the Cube's construction apparently interfered with the comms. "He was to your right. But every indication is that the enemy had a plan, and they've been in there long enough to set the prisoners free."

Cara sighed. "Do we know how they intend to get out?"

"The warden's best theory is that they'll use the escape tunnel on three. They'll probably try to hold inside the entrance so they can deal with the guards or whoever one at a time."

"Okay, I guess that's our target. Quinn, give me the quickest route there." Her AI put a map into the corner of her glasses and a dotted path headed directly ahead into the recreation area before it cut to the right. "Copy that to Stark and Khan." She advanced in a crouched walk, setting one foot carefully in front of the next with her rifle up and ready.

She was prepared for anything except the ambush that triggered as soon as they reached the guard tower.

———

Diana and Bryant walked side-by-side, their rifles in position, each of them responsible for one part of the area as they made their way through the fourth floor. Several enemies with weapons appeared and quickly ducked again as the duo delivered shots to center mass and kicked anyone still functioning in the head to keep them down.

Rath trailed them, and every now and again, when she turned full circle to check behind them, she saw him swing his batons as if itching for someone to hit with them. *I know the feeling, my man.* She kept the potential appearance of the clever pirate at the forefront of her mind, ready to make sure he understood exactly how she felt about him but truly didn't expect him to show. The one she really wanted was the enemy leader, Vincente.

Not only because he'd tried to throw her into the World in Between, although that was high on the list of reasons. He had been a thorn in her side and a risk to her city since the first day, and it was time for him to be permanently removed from the equation. After the failure of the Cube, Diana planned to argue that the worst of the worst should be sent to Trevilsom prison because keeping them around was clearly too dangerous.

Let the experts in magic punish those who abuse it the most. That punishment is appropriate. We'll keep the lesser offenders and their henchmen in the Ultramax.

They'd chosen to travel along the right side, not really trusting the structural integrity of the middle portion and a little alarmed by the way the turret in the hall to the left kept momentarily coming to life and shutting down again. Despite a list of worries as long as her arm, it felt strangely good to have Bryant with her again and to know that Rath was nearby.

Ahead, short hallways led off to the cellblocks, and she'd have expected noise from within them. There was none. She stuck her head around into the hall and saw that the individual cell doors had been warped, likely from the same sonic blast that devastated the building's structure. *We'll be lucky if it doesn't collapse with us inside.* "We have to check them. We can't leave them unsecured behind us." Bryant nodded, and they cleared the first set, which was empty of prisoners. In the second hallway, they found one prisoner, a wizard, cowering in the corner and muttering to himself. "Dammit. We can't leave him here, and we can't take him with us." The three looked at each other, and then both she and Rath stared at Bryant.

He rolled his eyes. "Fine, I'll take him back to the entrance and toss him out of the building. Will that make you happy?"

Rath grinned. "Don't break."

He let out a long sigh. "No, I won't break him. Try not to get killed before I get back, okay? If Diana gets a beat down, I want to be there to see it, at least."

She snorted. "Nice. Love you too. Go." She waved for Rath to accompany her and they crept forward slowly and eventually reached the door that led to the recreation area. Sound came from inside—laughter and shouting—and she slipped her camera tube around the corner near the floor and under the barrier.

The window in her glasses revealed that the space was full of criminals who systematically stripped and donned the clothes of the guards who lay unconscious or dead nearby. Diana spoke softly into her mic. "Enemies putting on guard uniforms on four." She pointed the camera more carefully. "Friday, snap pictures of these guys and upload." The expected chime confirmed her command. She panned the lens to include all of them and caught motion in the corner of the room.

"Oh, how cute. The witch and wizard reunited." She watched as Sarah handed Vincente a wand and the mage took it reverently, pointed it at a downed guard, and ejected a cone of fire at the prone form. Diana twitched, ready to attack, but there was nothing she could do for the burning figure except hope he wasn't conscious for the experience. *Okay, no more prisons for you two. The worlds will both be better off without you in them.* She whispered to Rath, "This one looks ugly, buddy."

He clicked his batons against each other. "Partners. Together to the end."

She nodded. "You know it."

Bryant came around the corner and dropped onto the floor beside where she crouched. He breathed as if he'd run all the way from his previous task. "It's getting bad outside and more enemy reinforcements have arrived. Word is that the choppers might have to join the battle, and they're calling up the National Guard to set a perimeter in case."

Diana frowned. "I didn't hear that."

He nodded. "There are comm issues inside the building. Kayleigh has promised to create a portable base station or something like that. Who knows? There were a lot of unfamiliar words."

She laughed. "There always are with her. Don't feel bad because you're stupid. We won't judge." She paused and when he tried to speak, interrupted him. "Okay, the room inside sucks. Sarah and Vincente are both there, along with a ton of goons. There may be friendlies alive but all are down, which rules out frag and incendiary grenades. So, here's what we'll do."

After a minute of planning, they were ready. Diana held a sonic grenade in her left hand and crouched in front of the door. Rath pressed his back against the wall beside the metal barrier with a flashbang in each hand. Bryant stood on the other side of the door, his carbine raised, and braced to dash into the room. The plan was to eliminate the leaders in the first barrage while they recovered from the grenade attack and before they could bring their magic to bear. *Especially their shadow magic.*

She looked at her teammates. Bryant smirked and Rath

gave her a double thumbs-up around the grenades before he pushed the primers down. *I couldn't ask for better people. I hope the others are okay.* She pushed all worry out of her mind to focus on the moment. "Here we go. Three, two, one...."

CHAPTER THIRTY-ONE

The turrets mounted on the guard station spun to life as they advanced and the two nearest their position swiveled to face them. People in street clothes appeared inside the partially transparent diamond-shaped room with wicked grins on their faces at their clever play.

Cara reacted instinctively and flung herself forward and away from the turrets and to the right of the defense post. She hadn't accounted for the weapons on the back, which rotated to face her. Anik, quicker on the draw, grabbed Tony and pulled him directly against the side of the tower and below the guns' deflections to keep them both safe. They kept their chests pressed against the bullet-proof glass as they sidestepped around toward the door that led into the structure.

She rolled onto her knees, released her carbine, raised her hands, and fired flaming darts at the turrets on the far side before they could acquire her. The bolts of fire sliced through the gun emplacements and they sparked briefly before they fell quiescent. She stood and her legs wobbled

a little. Her intention was to break the door open and eliminate the criminals inside, but the steel barrier that separated the elevator lobby from the hallway to the recreation
center retracted to reveal a cluster of foes behind it,
arranged in pairs. The first duo held rifles aimed at her
head.

"Oh, hell. A little help," she yelled. A quick flip of a
switch set her carbine to full-auto, and she knelt and
released a volley at the enemies at the same time that they
pulled their triggers. She counted on them being amateurs
and not allowing for recoil, and they luckily obliged. Their
initial shots went high and the next ones even higher. She
rode the weapon's pushback and used it to drag the rifle
from lower left to upper right and stitch the pair with
bullets.

She fired until the magazine ran dry and annihilated
the first four in moments. The criminals behind them
clambered over their bodies and flooded into the room.
Tony came around the corner firing, and Anik turned to
the guard post windows, held up a claymore so the
enemies inside could see it, and made sure they saw him
slap it against the doorway and place a trigger. His grin
was audible. "That'll keep the bastards bottled up unless
they want to eat steel."

Cara decided the nearest ones were too close for her to
free her pistol in time to stop them from overrunning her
position. She stepped forward with her left foot and
brought the right around in a crescent to drive the closest
one's weapon aside. Before he could respond, she turned
her motion into a spinning sidekick that hurled him back
into his allies. Tony double-tapped foes one after the other,

and in short order, none remained in the hallway. She ejected the magazine in her rifle and replaced it with standard rounds, then knelt and emptied it at the turret ahead to leave it a smoking lump of metal.

Tony looked at her with a grin. "Did you have something in particular against that one? It bullied you in school, maybe?"

She groaned. "Honestly, you're an idiot."

He laughed. "I know. But you love me anyway."

"Is that what that sick feeling like you're going to throw up, is? That's good to know." She reloaded with anti-magic bullets and led them forward. "Okay, recreation area ahead and tunnel entrance off to the right. Don't get too comfortable. These guys didn't have vests, but we know some of them do now. These were total cannon fodder. There will be something more dangerous waiting for us."

Anik chuckled. "I'm not locked in here with you. You're locked in here with me."

Cara groaned again. "Okay, you're both idiots." The sound of the two men exchanging a high five followed, and she shook her head with a grin. *If you're going to risk life and limb, it's good to be able to do it with people you like.*

Diana gathered force in her cupped palm, then pitched a fastball at the metal door before her. It rocketed off its hinges and into the room beyond, and she had the satisfaction of hearing a shout of pain from one of their adversaries when it smashed into them. Rath threw his grenades around the corner, set for short-duration, and they detonated as they landed about halfway across the large space. Hers flew in an instant later and did the same.

Bryant was in motion immediately after the grenades and ducked into the room, and Diana was right behind him. Her glasses and earpieces dulled the impact of the flashbangs and preserved her from the effects of the sonic grenade, although the concussion still rattled her teeth. She couldn't hear the bullets leaving Bryant's gun but saw the witch summon the dented door and position it in front of her and Vincente to protect them from the barrage. Bryant shifted his fire to deliver rounds into the chest of the nearest enemy. When the woman didn't fall but returned several shots from her pistol, he lowered his rifle and shot her in each leg before he moved on to the next target.

Diana's initial force attack had also been blocked by the metal barrier, and she wasn't up for another game of tug o' war with the heinous witch. Instead, she used her telekinesis to take hold of the tables that had been pushed to the perimeter of the room and hurl them at anyone other than Bryant who still stood. She ran out of fresh ammunition and reused the ones that hadn't broken from the first use. Enemies fired at her, but she maintained a full-body shield while she worked. The energy drain was substantial, and she recalled and quickly discarded Nylotte's warning. *Maximum effort, like Deadpool would say.*

In her peripheral vision, Rath hurtled forward and weaved through the chaos toward the two primary enemies. She launched random shards of furniture toward them to cover the troll, and he slid along the slick floor with his batons raised, then stabbed them into the feet of the witch that were visible under the barrier. He rolled aside as the door's bottom clanged down, and Diana saved him from being crushed with a force push that shoved him out of the way of the toppling metal and out of immediate danger.

Sarah snarled at the pain from the shock Rath had delivered, but otherwise, didn't react. The man beside her smiled. "Agent Diana Sheen. I have longed to see you again."

"I'm happy that my pain can be your pleasure. I had hoped never to see your ugly face again."

"Well put. Your pain will be my pleasure, and I dearly hope you'll last a long, long time as I carve the flesh from your bones."

She turned to Bryant. "You heard that, right? Did he actually say that?"

He nodded. "Yep. It's like evil villain primary school in this place."

Diana laughed and faced the wizard again. "Are you cranky? Do you need a nap? Maybe a juice box? Listen, you can be honest, I won't tell anyone. do you have Mommy issues?"

Vincente's face had grown steadily redder, and the last comment broke the dam that restrained his fury. He raised his wand, and a fireball rocketed at the troll. His other hand clenched into a fist and tentacles of translucent darkness erupted from it. All eight of them moved unerringly toward her. She summoned a shield, and the wizard's satisfied smile grew large in her vision as they bent to the left and impaled Bryant, two in each limb, and hoisted him off the floor. His scream of pain rang in her ears, and she dashed toward him. She skidded to a stop as a line of shadow orbs from the witch forced her to conjure a buckler that wasn't nearly fast enough and staggered as the magical attack consumed half her deflectors.

She met Rath's eyes and saw determination in them. "Go help Bryant." He nodded and broke into a run. Diana reached deep for her fire, envisioned the shape she wanted to form it into, and let it flow. Her shield was replaced by two large fans of flame that extended from her hands, the edges sharp and rounded. She sprinted at the tentacles that held Bryant, ducked under them, and spun to sever the translucent limbs one after the other. Her twist ended on the far side with a telekinetic burst that lowered him gently to the ground. Rath was there in an instant, and she protected them both with a force bubble seconds before Sarah's magic covered them.

Her left hand was free, and she acted without conscious volition to draw the Ruger and empty the six chambers into the woman. The witch's eyes widened, and she called upon the shadow skin she'd used before, but the anti-magic rounds were not impeded. The bullets struck her in the hip, twice in her chest, once in the shoulder, and once in the arm she'd raised in defense. The final bullet missed because the witch was already falling, out of the fight for the moment at least.

She holstered the weapon in time to raise her own arm against the table that careened toward her face. *Dammit, I hate it when the idiots use my own tactics against me.*

CHAPTER THIRTY-TWO

Cara led the way into the recreation area, which was unexpectedly empty. She stepped in, moved right, and swung her rifle to cover that part of the room. Tony did the same for the center and Anik the left-hand portion. Only echoes greeted them.

She sighed. "That's weird."

"Right?" Tony replied. "It sucks when you get all dressed up to annihilate criminals and they don't show up."

The other man's voice had lost its playfulness. "This means they're ready for us somewhere else, doesn't it?"

Cara nodded toward the door that led from the right side of the room. "Probably. What do you think the chances are that they left a present behind on the other side of that door?"

The demolitions expert moved to it without answering, extracted a rectangle with a display screen, and ran it from the bottom to the top. "Yep, there are explosives somewhere around."

Tony asked, "Could it be from the gunfire?"

"No. I detect the signature of C-4. The enemy must have brought some along." He stowed the sensor and dug into the pouch on his thigh, withdrew three small bricks of explosive, and pushed them into place at the top, middle, and bottom of the door on the side opposite the hinges. Anik pulled three compact chips from a separate bag and inserted them into the soft beige compound.

He disappeared into the hallway they'd come from and stuck his head out. "Unless you're really looking for a close-up view of things going boom, you might want to join me." They did, with hasty steps.

He extracted a black cylinder from his belt with a large yellow button on top covered by a plastic cap, with three colored buttons on the side. A twist of its upper and lower sections in opposite directions caused the top button to glow. He pressed the red one. "I'm selecting the detonator group."

Tony sounded concerned. "What if you didn't use all of them? Wouldn't the ones in your pocket blow up?"

He chuckled. "Of course not. They need to be armed on the device, then they need to be armed with this. Double safety. Plus, there's a distance lockout so if the detonators are within three feet of the trigger, they won't go off. So, triple safety." He flicked the cover open with his thumb. "Fire in the hole."

He pressed the button and a large bang sounded from the next room, followed by an even larger one. Cara stuck her head around the corner and saw that the door, plus part of the wall, no longer existed. "Wow. That was certainly something."

Anik tucked the device back in his belt. "What can I say. I'm good at what I do. All the things I do." He put a lecherous lilt in his last sentence and both Cara and Tony broke into laughter, which teased a dramatic frown from the demolitions expert. "What? I am."

She shook her head and advanced toward the room, trusting the others to stay on her six. Once she entered through the demolished doorway, she made a right toward the double-sized door that guarded the emergency exit tunnel down the corridor on the left side. An arm appeared, and a pair of grenades rolled at them. She uttered an undignified scream and called, "Grenade," but knew she couldn't get away from them. Her mind offered her only one idea, so she ran forward and kicked each of them as hard as she could. They were halfway down the hallway when they detonated and spread flames onto all the surrounding surfaces.

Tony muttered, "That was so stupid," as he ran past her toward the entrance that sheltered the attackers. Anik stalked past on her other side, and added, "So, so stupid."

Cara sighed. "An artist is always unappreciated in her own time. Now, let's shove some grenades down these bastards' throats."

She turned the corner to where the other agents were already firing, and the enemy stumbled backward. Ahead, she saw the man she'd personally put into the Cube holding a pistol in his remaining hand. He aimed it at her and fired three shots. She spun to avoid them but took the next trio in the back of her vest. The force of impact slammed her forward into the wall. She let herself fall and roll into a backward somersault, tried to ignore the grinding sound and sensation of her newly broken nose, and lurched to her feet.

Another two grenades clattered in their direction, and Tony yelled, "Out." They dashed around the corner in time to avoid the shrapnel that erupted. The group paused, waiting for more to appear, but none did. Cara bolted back into the room, her eyes watering from the pain and the dust and debris, and watched the steel door separating their section from the next slide closed to shut out Marcus's wide grin.

Tony limped up beside her and stared at the barrier. "Why didn't you do one of those run and dive things? You totally could have made it."

She turned with a glare. "That opening was like a foot wide and ten feet away."

He shrugged. "You're small and agile, Croft. I'm disappointed, frankly."

She held two middle fingers up to his face and waved them there to make sure he had a good look, and they laughed together.

Anik came into the room in time to see the finish and shook his head. "You people are insane, you know that?"

Tony spun to address him. "So what you're saying is that you joined the right team?"

He broke into a grin. "Absolutely."

Cara jogged past him, headed for the large crack in the building. "We need to let Kayleigh know they're going through the tunnel. Then, we should check the higher levels and make sure the warden and her people are okay." The immediate footfalls of her comrades beside her were a balm against her frustration. *You had the advantage this time, my one-armed-bandit friend. Next time, I'm gonna rip the other one off and beat you with it.*

The table crashed into her upraised arm and the impact shoved her toward the wall. She gathered her wits in time to use her own hurled debris to deflect other pieces that were pitched at her by the damn regrown tentacles. A shadow blast exhausted her deflectors as she focused on the dual needs to protect her teammates and annihilate Vincente. The wizard's arms were in constant motion to both direct the tentacles and throw things at her.

"Okay, enough. Rath, grab Bryant and hold tight." The troll obeyed, and Diana slid them out of the room through the opening she'd created earlier with a gentle shove from her force magic. "If you see anyone, let me know right away."

"Will."

"Give him the healing potion."

"Will."

"Stay safe."

"You too."

"Oh, I'm gonna be safe once I put this bastard in the dirt." The tentacles darted at her, and Diana summoned a blast of force. She sent it out in a wave from her position, cleared the debris around her, and shoved the grasping arms away. "Hey, scumbag. You're gonna pay for that."

His face twisted and he circled, which forced her to do

the same. He thought he was being crafty and graceful, but he merely looked like a child playing pretend. *Too used to being the top dog and not having to fight for scraps.*

He sneered, "Awww, did your boyfriend get hurt?"

"First, my relationship status is none of your concern. Second, bite me. Third…" She finished the sentence by summoning her flame fans again and thrusting into a sprint directly at the wizard. His eyes widened, and he released shadow bolts at her, but she deflected some with the weapons and dodged the rest. *I have to remember that I can't take any more hits since my deflectors are gone.*

She missed a block and a tentacle latched onto her ankle and yanked her upward with a swift, sickening tug. The thick material of her boot protected her from a cut, and she wrenched herself up in a stomach crunch to slice it away as more reached for her. She dropped, landed hard, and lost her breath but managed to roll out of the way of the continuing attacks. Her weapons vanished, and she covered herself in a force shield scant seconds before the tentacles wrapped around her and started to squeeze.

It was her nightmare yet again. Fortunately, repetition had decreased her panic. *I'm not sure why these assholes all have tentacles, but so be it.* Shadow blasts struck her cocoon as well, and Vincente cackled as he forced her to drain her energy to protect herself. She tried for another force blast to free herself, but the power was elusive and she couldn't get enough. For the first moment since she'd entered the Cube, she felt real fear that they might not win.

A furious troll raced into the room and made a beeline for the wizard. Vincente had no time to react when he finally noticed his new adversary and absorbed a series of six sharp blows from his batons to his knees, arms, and chest. The batons sparked as Rath shoved them into the mage, but incredibly, the enemy laughed. The shadow attacks on Diana failed as the man swatted his diminutive assailant away with his magic. The burned fabric of his clothes revealed some sort of chest piece underneath, and she realized it must be nonconductive and so dissipated the stun before it could damage him.

Bullets drilled into the wizard's chest, halted his laughter, and drove him back even though they didn't penetrate. Bryant slumped against the door. He looked whole but exhausted and his carbine drooped to point downward, but it was enough. Diana emerged from her protective shield and charged Vincente with a shout, leapt into a kick, and delivered the heel of her foot into his collarbone. She felt it break, and his head thunked back against the floor as she landed on top of him. Blood pooled from beneath his skull, and his eyes flickered closed.

She sighed and rolled off to lay beside him, avoided the spreading crimson, and stared at the ceiling that was scorched and pitted from the day's events. *I'm remarkably undamaged, despite being totally exhausted. Maybe I'm getting better at this stuff.* She pushed herself up on her elbows and looked at Rath and Bryant, who were together at the far wall. The man reached down a hand that the troll used to climb to his feet.

They both wore defeated looks on their faces, which didn't make any sense at all. She searched her mind for something clever to say to buoy their spirits when the catalyst for those expressions made itself known in a deep, gravelly Kilomean voice she had truly hoped never to have to hear again.

"Hello, Sheen. How about that round three?"

CHAPTER THIRTY-THREE

Diana rolled over with a groan, away from Cresnan, and snagged the energy potion from her belt. She drank it in fast gulps, then let the vial fall with a wink at Rath and Bryant. They both nodded almost imperceptibly and she pushed up smoothly as the draught's potent contents surged through her to eliminate her exhaustion and banish the aches and pains of the moment before.

Her movements were deliberately slow so her opponent wouldn't realize how good she felt. She wanted to dance, she had so much power flowing through her. *Jeez. It would be really easy to get addicted to this stuff.* She nodded her head. "Cresnan. Imagine meeting you here." He seemed larger and hairier than before and resembled a fairy tale giant even more than he had previously. She estimated he was a little shorter than Rath at his biggest.

He grinned, and so did the six Kilomea behind him. "We've come for the witch and the wizard."

She shook her head. "Nope, that won't happen. Do you really want all your people to die? I warn you, I've become much, much stronger since the last time we met, and that one didn't go all that well for you."

The ones on either side of him growled and stepped forward, but he stopped them with a laugh. "I warned you she has a sharp tongue, did I not?" The rest of the crowd joined in his laughter. *Apparently, being imprisoned gave the big chucklehead some sort of status with them.* "I have a counteroffer I think you might like."

Diana nodded. "Let's hear it."

He shrugged. "You and I. Hand to hand. No weapons. You win, we go without killing your friends over there. I win, you die, but your friends get to live."

Bryant whispered over the comms, "I can shoot them."

"Can't," Rath interjected immediately after. "Already exhausted. Will miss."

The man sighed. "I can probably shoot them."

"Rath fighting mode available." The troll snickered.

Diana considered the odds but concluded Bryant was too squishy right now to risk it. "Okay, big C, you have a deal. However, I need your word and those of your people that these terms stand regardless of the outcome. There's no going back on the deal if I beat you, and no using our fight as cover to attack them."

"You would trust my word?"

"I'm aware of your species' history as noble hunters. Despite choosing the wrong team, I hope that you retain some of that honor. Also, if you break the rules, I'll turn every last one of you into a pile of ash before you know what hit you." The only reason she wasn't doing that already was the fear that someone would get in a lucky shot on Bryant or Rath. Her inner voice, which had left her mostly alone during the fun at the Cube, chimed in. *Plus, you're an arrogant idiot who simply wants to kick his ass.*

Okay, sure, plus that.

He nodded. "You have it. And theirs as well." The others gave various signals of assent. Diana was confident that one of them was also a Kilomean obscene gesture, but it was close enough.

She made a show of removing her carbine, arm plates, jacket, and shock gloves, then of detaching and removing her vest. The tunic showed her muscles. Several trembled with the energy imparted by the potion. She looked at Bryant and noticed the appreciation in his eyes. When he saw her looking, he merely gave her a small smile and a shrug. She grinned and turned to Cresnan.

"Tell your people to get over there." She pointed at the furthest spot in the room away from her teammates. "If I see them take a single step, the deal's off and you're all dead."

One of them, gruffer-voiced than Cresnan, replied "And if you cheat, nothing will stop us from hunting and killing your friends. Even if we die, the rest of the pack will avenge us."

She nodded. "We're clear."

Her foe stepped away from the others and waved them toward the designated location. "We are. You and I, no tricks, as it should be."

She circled, and he matched her on the opposite side. A slow spiral brought them closer together with each step. Each feinted, but at this distance, the result was nothing more than a laugh from their opponent. He looked happy for some reason. She frowned. "Why so giddy, gigantor?"

He laughed. "Either way, I win. Our objective is achieved and I defeat you once and for all, or you defeat me and I no longer have to live with the knowledge that I've been bested, only that I've given my life in service of something bigger."

She snorted. "You think busting that idiot out of jail is something bigger? Please. Plus, it doesn't look like he'll make it, anyway."

He charged and delivered a two-fisted punch directly at her forehead. She bent backward and turned it into a flip kick to bring her boots up at his chin. He shifted his head barely enough to avoid the blow, and she pushed off her hands to finish the move and land facing him. He was there already, too close, and swung an elbow at her face. She dropped, and it deflected off her head. She fired a weak jab at his groin only to discover that he wore protection under the ragged torn-off bottoms of his prison jumpsuit.

Diana dove to her right to avoid the knee he threw at her and came up bouncing. "Hey, no fair."

He shrugged. "You still have your leg armor and boots. If you prefer to do this naked instead, I'm game."

She shuddered and raised a hand to point at Bryant without taking her eyes off her opponent. "Shut up, you." To the Kilomea, she replied, "Uh, no thanks, I've seen all of you that I want to. Ever."

He let his fists do the talking in reply and waded in like a boxer. She circled out of his path and snapped a roundhouse kick at his ribs, but he brought down an elbow to block it. As soon as she set the foot down, she pivoted and swung it back at his solar plexus in a sidekick, but he twisted away and blocked with the other elbow. He swiped a hook at her head and she ducked, but he delivered a jab to her chest that felt as if he'd punched her in the heart.

She staggered back in shock, and he lurched forward. Her instincts warned her that he would pick her up and smash her on the ground in a primal dominance display rather than simply hitting her again. *Literally adding insult to injury. Scumbag.* She remembered being in a similar situation before, and even though he was bigger, she'd gotten far stronger since her time in DC.

Cresnan grasped her tunic and she fell backward, put both feet on his hips, and levered him up over her head in a flawless Tomoe-nage. His fists tore her shirt across the chest as he tried to control his trajectory, and she slid her own hands up to grip his wrists and shorten his flight.

He landed hard and exhaled loudly as his breath slammed from his lungs. Diana rolled and brought his wrists with her to twist his elbows. The move put one of them against the other, and she threw herself forward and shoved the joint in a direction it shouldn't go to break the nearer elbow against the other. He howled in agony, and she rose to her feet and massaged the huge area of pain in her chest. She looked down, noticed her shirt was ripped, and said a small silly prayer of thanks that she'd worn a sports bra that day.

"Stay down, Sasquatch. This is your only warning."

He struggled to stand but swayed on his feet. "No. Death in battle for one of us is the only acceptable outcome."

"How about we change the deal? Your friends leave, you go back to prison, no one dies, and we keep the witch and the wizard."

The Kilomea charged with a roar, and she dodged and tripped him with a sharp kick to the shins. He went down in a bundle of arms and legs and screamed again as his shattered elbow met the floor. She looked at him sadly. "You lose again." A strange hum began and a grin spread on his face. "Only because you think you know what game I was playing."

A whooshing sound caught her attention as a portal opened in the corner of the room. A blast of force erupted from it at chest level to hurl both Diana and Bryant into the wall beside one another. She managed to prevent damage to both of them by using her telekinesis to mitigate the impact. A tall figure stepped through, clad in what appeared to be medieval armor including an ornate helmet that covered the top half of his face. She recognized it immediately and looked at Bryant. "Uh-oh."

He replied, "Is that the stuff? From the train?" She nodded.

The six Kilomea ran to the opening and jumped through, and the figure raised a hand and floated the witch after them. He laughed deeply at the remaining figures in the room. Diana sent fireballs at him, and he batted them aside negligently with shadow tentacles faster than any she'd seen. He raised a palm to her. "Out of respect for the Kilomea's promise, you live to see another day. A stupid strategy, but he served his purpose."

He lifted the wounded giant and Diana growled at the thought that Cresnan would get away again. But instead of a rescue, the man threw the Kilomea against the wall, the sharp crash a clear sign that there would be no round four. "And so he is punished for creating a situation where I cannot end you." He shook his head at the other body on the floor. "Vincente, too, has earned his fate."

He backed into the portal with a wave. "See you soon, Agent Diana Sheen."

Diana slumped against the wall and slid down next to Bryant. Rath came over and sat beside her. She sighed. "I'm not sure whether that was a win or a loss."

Rath answered. "If alive, definitely a win. For them?" He gestured at the bodies around them. "Definitely a loss."

She nodded. "You're right. Now, help me up and let's get the hell out of here. No doubt there's more work to be done."

CHAPTER THIRTY-FOUR

The week after the incident at the Cube passed by in a blur. Diana spent the first day asleep, as did Bryant, recovering from the stress the potions put on their systems. The rest of the team had received treatment for scrapes and bruises, and Cara for her broken nose and cracked ribs. Tony texted her hourly to tease her and Anik sent an edible fruit arrangement.

Diana sensed that there was something between him and Cara but was not inclined to press for details. She wished happiness for all her people in whatever way they could find it. As long as it didn't impede their ability to work, of course. His gift-giving inspired her, though, and she paid a Willen a necklace she rather liked to take one of the fruit baskets to Nylotte.

The fallout from the battle was beyond disappointing, and the only positive was the capture of some low-level thugs and the dispatching of Cresnan and Vincente. The guards at the far side of the tunnel were unable to prevent the escape, as they were ambushed upon arrival—which pointed to another serious information leak. Sloan had managed to call immediately after to let them know he'd been there but avoided most of the combat by volunteering to be transport. He'd only arrived after they'd already eliminated the defenders. They had all agreed that as much as everyone involved hated the idea, he should stay undercover with the group.

She and Bryant had headed to DC the first day they were physically able to do so. The discovery that Taggart had been attacked and was in a coma came to them in the same hour they learned that Bryant's apartment had been blown up in Hartford, both attacks timed with Lisa's kidnapping.

He stayed at a hotel and spent his days making sure ARES continued running seamlessly. She worked with the oversight committee and shared her evenings with Lisa at the house. Her friend claimed to be okay, but several times, Diana heard her moan and wake in her bedroom in the middle of the night. She was worried but didn't want to push. Instead, she simply tried to make it clear that she was completely available to talk about it.

She'd entrusted Rath with a vital mission before leaving. After Vincente died, a twitching snake had emerged from his stomach and transformed to merely metal and gems, a beautiful item. She knew it was one of the prized Rhazdon artifacts the instant it appeared, and its presence explained a number of things and the tentacles, in particular. Her initial desire was to burn it immediately, but Bryant had cautioned her against it, as neither of them had any idea how to deal with it safely.

As it turned out, Rath did. He'd discussed it with

someone named Emanuel, who had one in his possession already and considered it his calling to keep artifacts hidden and safe. The troll agreed to deliver it to the man. Diana's first reaction was to think it would be better off in an ARES vault, but given the inside information that must have provoked Lisa's kidnapping, she was unwilling to trust the organization any more than necessary. All the people on the ground were great, but the oversight committee? Well, there were some significant questions that would soon require honest answers if ARES was to continue.

The Cube was now officially a thing of the past and the senators had written it off as a failed experiment. All the prisoners would be transferred to Ultramaxes and the building itself would be imploded and buried. Anik, naturally, had volunteered to assist.

She knew there was sure to be another uprising, another fight, or another challenge down the line. But for tonight, Diana had put all that on hold. It had taken her an hour to get ready, which was at least thirty minutes longer than usual. Her hair fell in waves, her makeup was noticeable, and in place of jeans and a t-shirt, she wore high black boots that rose to below her knees and a tight black dress that stopped just above them. It gathered with a string around her neck and left her shoulders and arms bare. She'd applied coverup over the remaining scratches and bruises to avoid ruining the effect and finished her preparations with a light spray of Fracas perfume. *So appropriate.*

She steered the rented Dodge Charger in front of the doors to the ARES DC headquarters and leaned over to open the door for Bryant. He was in his work uniform, a navy suit that looked perfect on him, a pure white shirt, and a dark scarlet tie. *My, patriotism can indeed be sexy.* He slid in and gave her a smile. "This is all very mysterious. Calling out of nowhere and telling me to be outside at a certain time. Are you a spy or something?"

She lowered her sunglasses and batted her eyelashes. "FBI Agent Diana Sheen, sir. We need to ask you some questions."

He laughed, and they sang along to the classic rock station as she drove to their destination, a fancy restaurant off the lobby of a fancier hotel. She'd called ahead and ordered for them both—shared charcuterie as an appetizer followed by salads, steaks, and a shared dessert, each course paired with the perfect wine and topped off with an espresso to finish. They kept their conversation personal and avoided work topics by mutual agreement, simply two normal people celebrating the pleasures of being alive.

As they sauntered out to the lobby, Diana stopped Bryant before he headed to the exit. "I decided that since I'd be drinking, I'd stay here tonight. Walk me to the elevator?"

He gave her a quizzical look but shrugged and walked beside her to the lifts. Diana swallowed against the sudden dryness in her throat. *Idiot. You've got this.* She coughed slightly as she pressed the call button. She turned to face him. "I have a secret to share from the last battle."

He laughed and teased her. "I thought work was off limits. Way to screw up a lovely evening, Sheen. Okay, you might as well tell me."

"During the fight, Vincente was mocking me. He said something about you being my boyfriend." The elevator dinged, and the doors opened on an empty car. *Perfect timing.* She turned and walked inside, putting an extra sway in her hips, knowing the heels on her high boots would do good things for her figure.

He followed her and stood in the doorway, one hand up to prevent the door from shutting. He still looked confused. The voice of the Oracle from *The Matrix* came to mind. *Not too bright, though.* "And?"

She smiled. "Well, I thought maybe I'd like to try that out." She reached forward and pressed the button for her floor. He blinked, and she rolled her eyes. "Get your ass in the elevator and kiss me like you mean it, Bates." His laugh was deep and throaty as he stepped inside and obeyed her order to the letter.

The story doesn't end here. Follow Diana, Rath and FAM's adventures in <u>COVERT OPS</u>.

CONNECT WITH TR CAMERON

Stay up to date on new releases and fan pricing by signing up for my newsletter. CLICK HERE TO JOIN.

Or visit: www.trcameron.com/Oriceran to sign up.

If you enjoyed this book, please consider leaving a review. Thanks!

Seriously now, thank you.

Thank you for reading the *fourth* book in the Federal Agents of Magic series, and for continuing on to the author notes! I've been blown away by the reviews and comments about the first trio of books. I'm honored to be able to continue to share this story with you.

I had the distinct pleasure of finally meeting Martha Carr in the real world rather than the virtual one in May, and it was big fun. The author community that she and Michael Anderle have created around the Oriceran Universe is amazing to be a part of.

This book was a bear to write, for some reason. It might be because there were stories that needed closing, and others that needed opening, more than usual of both. It might be because I feel an increasing obligation to *you* to get these characters right. In any case, there was much more tinkering and editing this time around than in previous books. I hope the version that finally made it to you lived up to your expectations!

The next set of four books are going to be intense. More action, more tech, a couple more characters, big changes in the world. I can't wait to share them with you.

We appear to have a family of bunnies living under one of the many shrubs and/or weeds that the previous owners of our house planted. It's a joy to walk outside in the morning to take the kiddo to school and see one hanging out, or better, see two of the young ones chasing each other around. When I was in Chicago in May, I got an idea of what city living would be like, and while there's certainly an appeal, I would definitely miss the wildlife.

This month includes a visit to my longest-tenured friend's house with my daughter, which should be full of hiking, VR video gaming, and board games galore. It's also our first multi-day road trip together in a while. I'm glee-fully looking forward to it. I hope you have fun plans set for the upcoming season wherever you live!

Today I'm getting the broad strokes of books 5-8 down, and finalizing the plot moments for Book 5. Tomorrow (or maybe today) I start writing on that one. I'm pumped.

Kudos as always to Martha and the Oriceran team. Their work is phenomenal. When I saw the cover for this book, I was blown away by how gorgeous it is. Their passion for the process is phenomenal.

So, I *did* mention previously that plans and reality often fail to meet, and that was the case in this book. It was so packed with events that the Agents didn't have time to add the support they desperately need. It's my plan that they will in the next book, at least one agent and a tech. But, you know what they say about plans, they rarely survive enemy contact. So, we'll see.

Quick media notes: I was not happy with the quick wrap-up of *Game of Thrones*. The writers let a lot of things they'd set up fall by the wayside without resolution, which frustrated everyone. I read the books before the show, and I'm looking forward to the *official* ending whenever GRRM gets around to it. Finished Brownstone (awesome!), caught up on CJ Cherryh's *Foreigner* series (awesome!), and I have the latest Expanse book in my hands. I'm portioning it out slowly, chapter by chapter, to avoid doing no work while I binge the whole thing. I'm still looking forward to *Watchmen* on HBO, *American Gods, Deadwood,* and *Good Omens.* John Wick 3 was a lovely ballet of violence, but had substantially less plot than the two previous ones, which I didn't really dig as an artistic choice. And *Detective Pikachu* was surprisingly fantastic. I only saw it for the kid. Really. Stop looking at me like that.

If you want to chat media, the books, or whatever else, I check in pretty often on Facebook. Just search TR Cameron Author to find me. Or, less reliably, thom@trcameron.com.

Until next time, Joys upon joys to you and yours – so may it be.

AUTHOR NOTES - MARTHA CARR

MAY 30, 2019

Lately, even bigger opportunities have been coming my way. (More on that later – we're still building it) But growth – giant leaps of growth – can be scary and the past we thought we dealt with swings back by for another chat. The 'what ifs' pop up – I call those magical questions. There's no possible answer to them.

When faced with opportunity, I've learned the best answer is a simple yes, and to keep going. But I was wondering if it could be possible to remove the anxiety so I could enjoy the ride more. Maybe even see more opportunities because I wasn't so busy staring at the worries.

Time to be a little proactive. I've been checking out eye movement desensitization and reprocessing or EMDR for the past few months and the best way to describe it is personal growth on steroids. EMDR is a therapeutic device using sounds, light or tapping in a steady pulse while the person talks about a negative or traumatic event.

Normally, the brain doesn't know if that horror movie

you're seeing is really happening or not, same with memories. Therefore, talking about a traumatic event can retraumatize the brain and lead nowhere. But for some reason, with EMDR, brain knows the difference and it's possible to look at the same events from different angles, process it all and integrate it.

In other words, scale it back into proper perspective and put it away. We can stop filtering new decisions or opportunities through old events that aren't actually happening now. I wanted to explore my ability to see myself as prosperous and as part of a team – but leading the charge instead of waiting for directions – and at ease with it all. I'm just about there but I know that being all the way there can make a difference in how things go for everyone.

If I'm in a good place then I don't translate fear or misgivings and I look at setbacks as data and make adjustments and in general, just keep going. A lot of success in my life has been from just saying yes, doing the work, being open to change and that last part – I kept going. It's gotten me into my dream house and living rather nicely, surrounded by great friends and family.

Why stop now? I'm headed into the last section of life – I turn 60 in September – and I want to keep creating and wondering what's possible. Using EMDR as another tool to hack life, I've managed to grow calmer about just about everything. For me, it's been replaced with a general sense of well being that everything is going to work out okay, and if it doesn't, we'll all face that together too.

My goal is for my 60's to be the best years yet with a lot

of getting to see fans in person and wait till you see what we've got in mind. It's gonna be a lot of fun and I'm going to make sure I'm ready for all of it. More adventures to follow.

THANK YOU for not only reading this story but these *Author Notes* **as well.**

(I think I've been good with always opening with "thank you." If not, I need to edit the other *Author Notes!*)

RANDOM (*sometimes*) THOUGHTS?

I'm going to riff off of something TR spoke about in his Author Notes.

I have never watched the *Game of Thrones* (or read the books) so I don't have a lot of emotional investment in whether they got the ending right or not. However, I watched a lot of people who WERE invested and by and large, they weren't happy.

I decided to query my wife (who was a fan) about it, and weeks later she still had some heat in her voice about the lack of a good resolution.

(For the record, she didn't find that the sister seceding and it becoming the 6 Kingdoms was very true to the world experience. Further, she thought having the climax war resolve so early in the last season made it hard to gain the same energy as before the war when 'Winter Is Coming.')

The only thing that I've had happen for me personally was the Avengers: Endgame movie. I personally hated the cliffhanger and left that movie pretty annoyed.

Now, I've admitted that I did go see the resolution (Endgame) on the first weekend when the movie opened here in America, BUT - I think I did it more from wanting a night out and the movie looked pretty cool. (Plus, my annoyance was softened with time. If that movie had been out a month after Avengers 3 I would have probably skipped it.)

I think I have the same opinion for both Marvel and the team who did Game Of Thrones. Until both teams did what they accomplished, (one for the big screen, the other for television) I don't believe we had seen the sheer scope and audacity to put down the money bets HBO and Marvel (Disney) did with those projects.

My hats off to both of them for trying something completely different.

Except, I think Marvel got it 'more' right if you look at the fan comments post last movie / show.

AROUND THE WORLD IN 80 DAYS

One of the interesting (at least to me) aspects of my life is the ability to work from anywhere and at any time. In the future, I hope to re-read my own *Author Notes* and remember my life as a diary entry.

Hwy 287 - Driving through Claude, TX on way to Amarillo. *(Yes, I do plan on going to the restaurant with the 72 oz steak challenge. No, I don't plan on even trying to finish a 18 oz steak with the fixings.)*

The sun is burning my stomach up as it heats the black shirt I have on (admittedly not a great choice). I believe my stomach is probably burnt red right now - I'm scared to look.

There are hundreds of tall electrical windmills up here in the Texas Panhandle and I personally think it looks cool. My author mind is looking at the massive posts with wicked sharp looking blades imagining what it might look like if it was post apocalyptic 100 years from now?

Would the dust and dirt lock them in place? Would some storms possibly break them, their parts laying against the bent over polls?

Or, would we hear the screetch screetch screetch as the large blades turn round and round in the wind, powering nothing as they continue to work as designed…

With no houses around that need the power.

FAN PRICING

$0.99 Saturdays (new LMBPN stuff) and $0.99 Wednesday (both LMBPN books and friends of LMBPN books.) Get great stuff from us and others at tantalizing prices.

Go ahead, I bet you can't read just one.

Sign up here: http://lmbpn.com/email/.

HOW TO MARKET FOR BOOKS YOU LOVE

Review them so others have your thoughts, tell friends and the dogs of your enemies (because who wants to talk with enemies?)... *Enough said ;-)*

Ad Aeternitatem,

Michael Anderle

JOIN THE ORICERAN UNIVERSE FAN GROUP ON FACEBOOK!